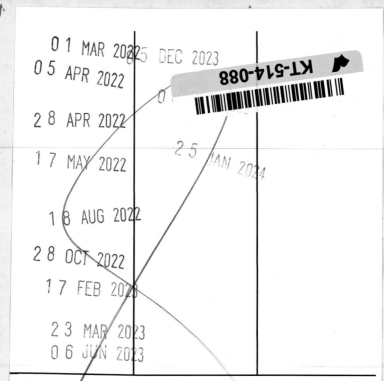

the critically acclaimed *Fall*, *Crimson Lake*, *Redemption*, *Gone by Midnight* and *Gathering Dark*. Candice's first collaboration with James Patterson, *Never Never*, was a *Sunday Times* and *New York Times* No. 1 bestseller. They have co-authored three further n̲_____ r Liar and *Hush Hu*

C334652202

A list of titles by James Patterson appears
at the back of this book

2 SISTERS DETECTIVE AGENCY

JAMES PATTERSON

AND CANDICE FOX

PENGUIN BOOKS

PENGUIN BOOKS

UK | USA | Canada | Ireland | Australia
India | New Zealand | South Africa

Penguin Books is part of the Penguin Random House group of companies
whose addresses can be found at global.penguinrandomhouse.com

Penguin
Random House
UK

First published by Penguin Books in 2021
001

Printed and bound in Great Britain by Clays Ltd, Elcograf S.p.A.

The authorised representative in the EEA is Penguin Random House Ireland,
Morrison Chambers, 32 Nassau Street, Dublin D02 YH68

A CIP catalogue record for this book is available from the British Library

ISBN: 978–1–787–46550–3

www.greenpenguin.co.uk

MIX
Paper from
responsible sources
FSC
www.fsc.org   FSC® C018179

Penguin Random House is committed to a
sustainable future for our business, our readers
and our planet. This book is made from Forest
Stewardship Council® certified paper.

2 SISTERS
DETECTIVE
AGENCY

PROLOGUE

SHE WAS A KILLER.

Jacob Kanular knew it, as soon as the girl put the gun to his head. It was the way she angled the barrel of the revolver: straight down from forehead to neck so that when she pulled the trigger, the bullet would pass cleanly through his brain to his spinal column. She wasn't trying to scare him. Wasn't messing around by putting the gun against his temple or his mouth. Whoever she was, she knew how to kill.

This was the only rational thought Jacob could manage. Everything else was just desperate internal screams. For himself. For his wife. For his baby.

There were five of them—three males, two females—and they were young and angry. They wanted to hurt, to destroy. There was at least one phone filming, a bright light too painful to look right at but illuminating snippets of what was happening next to him. Jacob was glad at least that they were binding his daughter, Beatrice, and wife, Neina, to chairs and not to the bed. Someone hacked Neina's ponytail off with a pair of scissors. A Taser zapped, threateningly, in Beaty's face.

Jacob looked at the girl with the gun on him, and his thoughts focused on what he'd do to these people if he survived. But the duct tape across his mouth prevented him from speaking.

"I could kill you," the girl said, as though she could read his thoughts. She seemed to really be weighing it up, tapping on the trigger so he could feel the vibration through the metal, through his electrified skin. An eighth of an inch from death. "But I'm a nice girl. So I'll teach you a lesson instead."

The others heard what she said and came for him. They pushed Jacob's chair over, and he lay strapped to it in his boxer shorts, trying to fold himself in two to defend against the blows. The girl took a golf club from the bag in the hall and came back, showed it to him before she raised it over her shoulder with professional ease and smashed it into his ribs. He tried to focus on something, another cold, emotionless thought to get him through. He saw a single curl of blond hair poking out from beneath her hood. He squeezed his eyes shut and thought about that curl, that golden spiral, as they kicked him half to death.

Beyond the huge glass windows, the ocean off Palos Verdes was calm and gray and flat, sparkling with moonlight.

The girl with the curl grabbed a hank of his hair and lifted his head.

"You learned any manners yet?" she asked.

"Hey, Ash. Look," someone said.

Ash, Jacob thought.

"Oh, man." A boy's voice. "She's not breathing right."

"Chill. She's faking it."

Through the pounding in his head Jacob strained to listen, and in the hot bedroom air he could pick out Beaty's wheezes and coughs and groans. She hadn't had an asthma attack since she was four years old. Six years since he'd heard that hellish noise. They didn't even keep an inhaler in the house anymore.

The girl leader stepped on Jacob's face. He felt the rubber grip of her boot tug down the corner of his eye.

"If she dies, it's on you."

Then they were gone, the sound of their running footsteps echoing off the high ceilings.

In the darkness of the car, Neina spoke for the first time, sitting in the back seat with their daughter in her lap. Jacob could hardly hear his wife's voice over Beaty's distraught, struggling breaths. The garage door seemed to take a year to slide up and let them free. There was still tape hanging from his left wrist as he gripped the wheel and floored it for the nearest hospital.

"Who the hell were they?" Neina cried.

"I don't know," he said honestly.

CHAPTER 1

"YOUR HONOR," I SAID. "My client is an artist."

The courtroom had been rippling gently with the sounds of conversations between the clients waiting in the stalls and their defenders, and of family members moving in and out of the wide double doors. At my words, the room fell silent. Judge Mackavin rested his chin on his palm, a single bushy eyebrow raised.

"Get on with it, Rhonda," the judge said as I soaked in the dramatic silence I'd created. Everyone was looking at me— for once a spectacle based on my words rather than my appearance.

As big as I am—260 pounds, some of it well-earned muscle and some of it long-maintained fat—there's no point trying to fit in with the crowd. The pink hair was just the latest shade in a rotating kaleidoscope of colors I applied to my half shaved, wavy quiff, and I always wore rock band shirts in the courtroom under my blazer.

"Mr. Reece Donovan comes from a long line of artists," I said, gesturing to my client, who slumped meekly in his chair. "His mother, Veronica, is a talented glass blower. His father sold portrait sketches on Main Street in Littleton as a youth. For the entirety of his sixteen years on Earth, this young man has been lectured by his parents on the importance of art as a commentary on the folly of humankind, and—"

"Counselor." Judge Mackavin leaned forward in his big leather chair. "You're not about to tell me that what young Mr. Donovan did was performance art, are you?"

There was a cough at the back of the crowded room. The only sound. Young Reece Donovan chewed his fingernails and looked like he wanted the ground to open up and swallow him.

"Hear me out," I said. "I'm just getting momentum."

"From the brief of evidence I have here," the judge said, lifting a page from those spread before him, "I'm to understand that Mr. Donovan was so upset by his mom's plan to marry her boyfriend that he filled the sprinkler system at the Colorado National Golf Club with red paint and rigged it to go off in the middle of their ceremony on the ninth green. Is that right?"

"That's correct, Your Honor," I said.

"I see." He nodded. "And his ingenious plan worked, it says here. He bathed the entire wedding party in paint, turning the ceremony into what visually resembled a violent bloodbath."

The judge held a picture of the dripping, mortified wedding party, snapped by the photographer moments after the sprinkler system launched. It looked like a scene from a horror film.

"It's a striking image, Judge," I said. "Some would say *bold*. Some would say *inspired*."

"He also managed to douse seventeen golfers standing at various stations on the course."

"Mr. Donovan didn't realize the whole sprinkler system was connected," I said. "He thought he'd isolated the ninth green and the wedding party."

The entire courtroom looked at my young client, who was wringing his long, slender fingers. In the front row of the audience, his mother and new stepfather looked exhausted. They'd forgiven him, but it had been hard work. I'd seen that expression on countless sets of parents over the course of my career.

"You know I support artistic expression in all its forms, Rhonda." Mackavin looked pointedly at my flamingo-pink hair and Metallica shirt. "But you're right out on the ledge here."

"The kid was angry," I said. "He wanted to make a statement. Yes, a lot of people got painted, but they were painted *red*, Your Honor. The color of passion. Of love! Of lifeblood, desire, longevity. An informed choice, I'm sure you'll agree, and a visually spectacular execution. And, Judge, where would modern expressionism be without Jackson Pollock's reckless determination to splash everything within ten feet of him with paint?"

The judge stifled a laugh, shook his head.

"Damages to the golf course, the sprinkler system, and the other golfers in attendance are into the tens of thousands of dollars," the judge said, regaining his frown.

"We're aware, Your Honor, and my client is very remorseful."

The judge looked at me, thought for a moment. A small smile played about his lips.

"I'm willing to reward your creativity, Rhonda, in trying to pass Mr. Donovan's actions off as anything more than pure idiocy here today," Mackavin said, writing up his decision in the big book before him. "You've amused me, which is not an easy feat. Four hundred hours of community service." The judge waved me away. "And tell the artist to keep it in the studio next time."

I turned and smiled at my client, but like the judge's, my humor was short-lived. Across the room I spied my next client, a handsome young man in an expensive blue suit, being led out from the holding rooms. Unlike the slouching, fidgeting juvenile offenders lined up on the bench behind the rail, Thad Forrester was cuffed. The bailiff escorted Thad Forrester to the end of the row and uncuffed him, and I felt the dread manifest at the center of my stomach as I headed over to greet the most dangerous kid on my list.

CHAPTER 2

THAD LOOKED ME OVER from head to foot as I approached, obviously skeptical, on the edge of disbelieving laughter. I get that look a lot, and not only from entitled frat boys up on rape charges. Thad would be just one in a crowd of people who'd underestimated me based on my appearance that morning.

"Mr. Forrester." I offered my hand, injected as little warmth into my words as possible. "I'm Rhonda Bird, your public defender."

"You can't be serious." He snorted. "Is this what passes for legal aid these days?"

"This is exactly what passes for legal aid these days," I said. "Passes with summa cum laude and a fifty-thousand-dollar research grant."

I hadn't actually taken the research grant, or the PhD offer. I'd wanted to get out there, into the courtroom, among the young and vulnerable people who I felt so deserved my service. People like Reece Donovan. Not people like Thad Forrester.

He smirked. "You should have spent the grant money on a personal trainer. And what the hell are you wearing? You look like you just stepped out of some lame-ass rock concert."

"You shouldn't judge people by their appearance, Mr. Forrester," I said. "The Metallica shirt doesn't make me any less of a lawyer, just like your Hugo Boss one doesn't make you any less of a rapist." Thad shook his head ruefully. I checked off his attendance on my clipboard. "I assume, because you're on my list, your expensive lawyer from New York hasn't arrived yet."

"That's right," he said. "So you need to get this thing canceled."

"It's an advisement hearing," I said. "The judge is just going to tell you what you're charged with."

Thad's charges were laid out vaguely on my list, but I'd heard the story from other lawyers in the courthouse halls. Thad's arrest related to an incident six months earlier, in which a local college sophomore had been found lying half-naked in bushes outside a frat-house party in the early hours of the morning. The girl hadn't reported a sexual assault, probably because she couldn't remember it, but pictures of her involved in sexual activity while obviously unconscious had circulated on the phones of some young men on campus in the following weeks. The girl had made an attempt on her own life, which had brought the whole tragedy to the attention of the police. The police had acquired the photographs and identified a scar on the wrist of her assailant as identical to that on Thad Forrester.

"You don't need a pricey lawyer for this stage of the legal

process," I told Thad. "No rulings will be made on your case today."

"How about you let *me* decide what I need," the kid snapped, with the practiced tone of someone used to giving commands. "I've had friends wrapped up in this kind of bullshit before. Every second I'm in the courtroom is being analyzed, and the last thing I want is to be associated with some freaky fat clown for my very first hearing."

I smiled and leaned in. "Mr. Forrester, from the brief of evidence attached to your file, these charges don't look like bullshit at all. That's your wrist in those pictures. Even this 'fat clown' can see that."

"It won't matter," he said with a smile. "We have a plan."

I backed up. I could see the rest of the case playing out as others had so many times before. There would be a large financial offer from the Forrester family to the girl's in exchange for a withdrawal of the charges. If her family didn't bite, Thad's expensive legal team would invade the girl's life like a disease, going after her sexual history, her grades, her family life, and her friends. Every slipup she'd had since she was in grade school would be exposed and examined under hot lights.

I'd dealt with scumbags like Thad a hundred times across my career as a juvenile public defender. I had to defend them, but that didn't mean I had to stop them from digging their own graves. I matched Thad's smile with my own.

Because I also had a plan. I would have the advisement hearing postponed, as he'd demanded, then I'd bring him to an interview room at the back of the courthouse under the guise of having him sign some release papers. There, while he relaxed, already mentally detached from the fat clown with the pink hair and the threat she posed to his courtroom reputation, I'd get Thad chatting about the night he assaulted the girl at the frat party, challenge his manhood, poke and prod him until he snapped. Little boys with big mouths like Thad didn't want to listen—especially to women. They wanted to talk. They wanted to be listened to. Obeyed. That's why witnesses had heard him bragging, why he'd taken and shared the pictures of the girl's assault. Boys like Thad couldn't keep quiet, and I knew the recording light on the front of the camera in interview room 3 wasn't working.

"Wait here while I go get a coffee, little boy," I said as the next client and her defender shuffled their way up to the tables before the judge. I gave Thad one last look as I turned to walk out of the courtroom.

That's when I saw his attacker approaching.

CHAPTER 3

I'D SEEN THE BRIEF of evidence against Thad Forrester, including the photographs of his victim he'd taken with his phone. Constance Jones's wide mouth and heart-shaped face were obviously a product of her father, a man I recognized now striding toward me up the courtroom's center aisle. At first I thought that, like the parents of so many victims over the years, he was coming for me. It's not uncommon for me to get berated for providing assistance of counsel to the young killers, rapists, thugs, and creeps of the Watkins region outside Denver. But one look in Mr. Jones's cold, hard eyes told me exactly where he was going. Constance's father was heading for Thad, and as I let my eyes fall from his face, I noticed a bulge at his hip.

Most people think you can't get a gun into a courtroom in the US unless you're a cop, a bailiff, or a US Marshal. Anyone who's spent enough time in courthouses, however, knows there are a thousand ways to do it if you're determined enough, if something has inspired you with enough icy fury to get the job done. You could sneak the gun in through the air-conditioning vents on the rooftop or mix it with equipment used by the thousands of workers who service the building throughout the year—plumbers, electricians, cleaners, painters, audio technicians, and repair crews. Hell, you could send it in on a coffee-and-sandwich cart while the vendor is out taking a leak. However Mr. Jones had done it, I realized I was the only thing standing between him and his vengeance. He was about to barge past me, his shoulder connecting with mine, when—

Freeze-frame.

Time locked in place.

It was only a fragment of a second, yet I spent incalculable moments suspended between two places. Was it ever all right to let violence go on unchecked, no matter who was committing the act or why? I knew Thad was guilty of inhumane acts. It hadn't been art. It hadn't been a protest. It hadn't been youthful foolishness. In some ways there was only one true punishment for it, and if I just let events proceed, I would be allowing that punishment to take place.

I made my decision. I spun as Mr. Jones shoved past me and launched myself toward him, barreling into his back. He was a big man, but I was bigger. We slammed onto the courtroom carpet together. I heard a wave of gasps and yowls of surprise all around us. Mr. Jones reached for his gun, and I grabbed the hand that was reaching as he squeezed off a bullet, our fingers mutually scrabbling for the weapon, the shot smacking harmlessly into the ceiling above us.

I ripped the gun from his hand and threw it aside, then sucker punched him as he tried to roll underneath me. When he doubled over, I grabbed his arm and twisted it behind his back.

"Bailiff!" I cried, looking up. Everyone in the big room had frozen, including a group of bailiffs near the row of defendants. "Little help here?"

They rushed to my assistance. I handed off to them a sweating, swearing Mr. Jones, protesting, "He raped my daughter! That boy raped my daughter!"

I stood watching as the courtroom guards dragged the furious father away. Someone handed me the gun I had gotten away from him, as though in confiscating it I had claimed responsibility for it.

Thad Forrester was laughing his head off. I realized my finger was resting gently on the weapon's trigger. All I had to do to stop that evil laughter was point, aim, and shoot.

Instead I handed the gun to one of the bailiffs.

My phone rang in my pocket. I walked out, ignoring the uncomfortable congratulations I caught on my way. I waited until I was outside the courtroom to pull the device from the pocket of my torn blazer.

"Hello?"

"Uh, is this Rhonda Bird?"

"It is. What do you want?" I said more sharply than intended. I realized the hand holding my phone was shaking.

"I'm calling about your father, Ms. Bird," the voice said, obviously cowed by my tone. "I'm sorry to have to tell you this over the phone, but he's dead."

CHAPTER 4

HE COULDN'T LOOK AT her. That's what scared him.

Jacob stood at the windows of his daughter's hospital room and gazed out at the parking lot, watching nurses arriving for the morning shift, toting coffees and chattering happily as they exited their vehicles. He saw a man in a blue sedan skid to a halt in the emergency parking bay, leap out of the vehicle, and run to the passenger-side door to help his heavily pregnant wife waddle in to triage. Jacob tried to focus on the activity outside because he couldn't look at his daughter, Beatrice, lying stiff in the bed behind him.

All her life, he'd spent every possible minute watching her. Those early days when she would sleep on his chest, her full lips moving in dream, her tiny hand gripping his shirt. Watching her had always been his greatest joy, but now he feared what he saw would be the last memory of her burned into his brain.

And it was all his fault.

The doctor and Neina were sitting on the edge of Beaty's

bed. *They always sit with you when it's bad news,* Jacob thought. It was as if by sitting they were telling you they had an extra moment just for you, before some other crisis drew them away, because *this* patient was special. As though doctors didn't deal in death the way garbage collectors deal with used kitty litter and bags of diapers.

"The severe asthma attack caused respiratory failure that starved Beatrice's brain completely of oxygen for a very dangerous period," the doctor was saying now behind Jacob. "Essentially, to protect itself, the organ shut down. We're not getting any brain activity showing up on our scans. But that doesn't mean—"

"She's brain dead?" Neina's voice was quivering. "Is that what you're saying? How do you know that?"

"She's not brain dead. We can't rule that out, but we're not ruling it in either. Not enough time has passed for us to...Look, Mr. and Mrs. Kanular, you need to maintain hope. The best think you can do for your daughter is to be here with her, talking to her, letting her know you are a united front."

Jacob turned away from the window. He went and gathered his wife into his arms. He said words he didn't believe. "We're gonna get through this, Neina. All three of us. We're going to be fine. She'll come back to us, I promise."

When Jacob had found Neina, when he'd decided to marry her and have a child, he'd wanted only the best for her and the baby. The big house. The fancy cars. Vacations in the Bahamas. It had all been for them. For years he'd traveled the world with only what he could carry in a bag. He'd done bad things in those years. Caused a lot of pain. A thought pushed at him, that the things he had done during those years had caused this. That this was his punishment.

But no. He gripped his wife tightly. Punishment was something you submitted to. He finally looked at Beaty in the bed. She was fighting her way back from the darkness. He knew it. He'd fight too.

When the doctor left, Jacob put the first step of his plan into action.

"Neinie," he said. "We're not going to report the break-in to the police."

She stared up at him, her mouth falling open. "What?"

"We're going to tell them Beaty had a nightmare, that she woke and the asthma attack was already upon her. It worsened as we drove to the hospital. We won't mention the home invasion."

"How can you…" Neina was lost for words. "Are you insane? These monsters attacked us! They nearly killed our child, Jake!"

"Listen to me," he said. "These attackers were highly sophisticated. They knew what they were doing. They cut the power, bypassed security. This wasn't their first time. If we bring in the police now, we might be inviting more trouble."

"Jake, are you kidding me?"

"Neina, there were five of them. The cops aren't going to catch them all at once. If we leave even one of them out there, running loose, they'll come for us."

"Jake—"

"Just stay here with Beaty. I'll handle it."

He tightened his grip on her arms. Not painfully. Just enough to let her feel his certainty, his determination. She could trust him to make them safe. She'd always been able to do that.

Neina nodded, and Jacob held her to him again.

At the house, he stood in his kitchen, looking at the big black streak the fire had left on the wall behind the four-burner stove. They'd tossed an aerosol can of something in there while they trashed the place. The sprinkler system had kicked in, dousing everything. His boots crunched over broken glass and ceramics as he made his way to the stairs and down to the ground floor. He crossed the lavish game room, skirting around the full-size pool table, and took the stairs by the bar down to the basement. The wide space was home to a few boxes, Beaty's bike, a treadmill Neina never used. There was a large desk, where he had drawn up the plans for the ornate jewelry box he was making for Beaty's birthday. The box was half assembled at the community-college woodshop, where he spent his days as a volunteer teacher. He'd hoped it would be a much-loved item, something she could hand down to her children. He didn't know if that was going to be possible now. He went to a large wine rack on the east wall and flipped a hidden switch, and the rack slid sideways to reveal a narrow alcove.

The smell hit him first. Gun oil, and the weird musty scent of used bank notes. In the alcove, stacks of unmarked bills bound in elastic bands reached knee height, consuming the floor space beneath the lowest of several wall shelves. On the shelf above the hoard of cash lay his passports and personal papers, and a battered old laptop that contained information to make the FBI's counterterrorism squad believe all their Christmases had come at once. Beside the laptop was a torn and dusty backpack. That tattered black backpack had accompanied him to Madrid, Belfast, Sydney, Honolulu.

Jacob reached for the second shelf, where, along with a few other weapons, the Barrett M82 sniper rifle he had used on his last job lay patiently waiting, as though it had known all this time that he wasn't done with his old life. He hadn't lined a man up in the crosshairs in twenty years, hadn't taken a job to kill business or political rivals, ex-lovers or friends, despised public figures or criminal adversaries, in every corner of the globe. In all that time, he hadn't watched a placid, unassuming face in the sunlight become red mist spraying all over the steps of some church or the front windows of a café. But the time had come to kill again.

Jacob picked up the gun and loaded it.

CHAPTER 5

TWENTY-FIVE YEARS. THAT was how long it had been since I'd seen or spoken to my father. I walked away from the courtroom in a daze, through the bustling courthouse halls and to the parking lot. I forgot all about Thad Forrester and Constance Jones's father, and the murder attempt I'd just thwarted. In a space toward the back of the lot, my lovingly restored 1972 Buick Skylark with a realistic hand-painted leopard-print paint job bulged from the tiny space allotted for it, its big square bumper hanging well out over the adjacent sidewalk. I unlocked and climbed into the car, making the suspension sing.

"Are you still there?" the voice asked.

"I'm here. This is…" I fumbled for words, gripped the steering wheel with one hand, phone still pressed to my ear. "Wow. *Wow*. What happened?"

"Heart attack in his office. His health was not at premium levels."

An image of my father from two and a half decades earlier flashed. The fixed chandelier of blue-gray cigar smoke hanging from his office ceiling, ash on every surface. The bottle of whiskey and chipped crystal glass on the edge of the table, take-out wrappers crunched down in the trash can under pill containers and bottles of Pepto Bismol. The place had always looked like a tornado had swept through it, depositing betting slips for horse or greyhound races everywhere.

"Sorry," I said. "I didn't catch your name. Or who the hell you are."

"I'm Ira Abelman, your father's attorney." I heard papers being shuffled. "Ms. Bird, I'm going to have to ask you to come to Los Angeles to see about Earl's estate."

"Oh, believe me, you can wrap it up without me being there," I said, suddenly and undeniably grounded in the situation. "I'd be absolutely stunned if he's left me anything. But if he has, just donate it to a charity of your choice."

I took the phone away from my ear, made a move to hang up, strangely angry with the lawyer for delivering the message. His voice stopped me.

"Ms. Bird, you are absolutely *required* here in Los Angeles."

"What do you mean?"

"It's essential that you attend a meeting at my office at your earliest convenience."

"I know what 'required' means, you jackass," I said. "Why am I required there?"

There was a silence. My stomach sank.

"Oh, Jesus," I said. "Let me guess. He's riddled with debt, and I'll have to be there because it has all fallen to me. I'm his only living relative so I'll have to assume the liability. How much is it?"

Still no answer.

"Are we talking tens of thousands?" My mouth was bone dry. "*Hundreds* of thousands of dollars?"

"Ms. Bird, I've been instructed to explain everything only once you arrive here in person," Abelman said.

I covered my eyes, felt suddenly crushingly exhausted, the last time I had seen my father turning over in my mind. I'd been thirteen, sitting in a big car like the one I now owned, squashed against the door by his bulk. I'd been excited. My parents' divorce had been rough. My father had packed his bags and walked out one cold, snowy night and left my mother to explain to me that Earl had picked up a girlfriend in California on his latest business trip and he was leaving us for her. When my father called and asked me to go out for coffee with him two weeks later, I'd been buzzed. It seemed wonderfully adult to be going out for coffee alone with my father. In my mind, we were going to bond, to drill down and discuss it all, to look each other in the eye across the table in a diner and negotiate our new, exciting future together as Daughter and Divorced Dad. He was going to give me the *real* story about this supposed girlfriend. He was going to tell me he was renting a cool new apartment in downtown Denver and I could come hang out with him there whenever I wanted. I would wave good-bye to my mother, climb into the car, and smile broadly at my unusually tanned father as we headed for town.

We hadn't gone for coffee. He'd driven me to the town courthouse, where he'd had a notary witness me signing over some stocks he had held in my name. After he'd reclaimed the stocks, he'd dropped me back home, and I never saw or heard from him again.

Something was pressing at me now, an instinct I couldn't deny.

"Something's wrong here," I said. "This feels like a trap."

There was a small sigh on the line, like the lawyer had been caught out. When he spoke again, his tone was sympathetic. It was the voice of a man who had dealt with my father for a long time and was as worn down by the experience as I was.

"You'll understand everything when you get here," Abelman said.

"I'm coming," I told him.

CHAPTER 6

IT DIDN'T TAKE LONG for Jacob to figure out who his attackers were once he had locked back into hunter mode.

As a young man, he'd wandered from job to job, his senses ticking all the time as he moved, feeling his way forward. Every interaction was a puzzle to be picked over, every face a mask of clues. Did the woman at the hotel counter recognize him from an Interpol alert? Was the man across the café an FBI agent surveilling him while fellow agents assembled? Every time he got off a plane, he'd wondered if officers were about to pounce. Every time he accepted a job, he'd considered the possibility that it had come from an undercover operative trying to set him up. It had been a long time since Jacob had employed such heightened awareness of himself and his movements, but it was easy to resume the behavior. Being a killer and fugitive was like riding a bike. The muscles remembered.

He walked now through the bustling shopping mall toward the security office, past brightly lit stores pumping out techno music. He was sure he was on the right track as he followed the signs overhead to a narrow hall between a juice bar and a sushi place. A group of elderly mall walkers passed him, with heavy tans and wearing bright athletic suits, little dumbbells gripped in withered fists. The mezzanine café was crowded with daytime shoppers taking a break between stores, piles of shopping bags at their feet. Jacob clocked every face, noted when his glance was returned. He felt like a fox creeping through night fields, into the henhouses where dozy chickens slumbered.

In his retirement, Jacob lived a quiet life. Too quiet, to the trained eye. He had the volunteer job at the local community college, teaching trade skills and joinery to young people. He'd learned carpentry while stalking a target for six months in Alaska on a rare long-term job. He didn't stop to chat with the other fathers when he dropped Beaty at school, making like he was shy. People probably figured he was self-conscious about being one of the older dads. He passed politely on dinner-party invitations, didn't return friendly calls or texts. He didn't borrow tools from his neighbors, didn't stop to chat at the grocery store, didn't have golfing buddies, fishing buddies, or buddies of any kind. He let Neina attend functions alone, making excuses for him, and while she had complained in the early years, his persistence had paid off. After a while she had stopped trying to push him. He went through life offending no one and befriending no one, someone purposefully difficult to remember, a smudge at the edge of a picture.

Which made it easy to remember the last time he'd offended someone. The girl who had attacked them in his house had accused him of needing to learn manners. There was only one thing remotely rude he'd done recently. A mistake caused by the pressures of time.

At the security office, a lone man in a black-and-white uniform lounged behind the counter, one hand hidden in a bag of Cheetos, the other tapping away on the PC on the desk.

"Excuse me," Jacob said, his eyes on his shoes, affecting uncertainty. "I don't mean to bother you. I know you're probably busy."

"What's up, pal?"

"I was just in TJ Maxx on the first floor, and there are a bunch of kids in there. I saw one of them slip a pair of sunglasses into his backpack. I tried to alert staff at the store, but they were all busy."

"Oh, man." The mall cop shot upward in his seat like a dog spying the park from the back seat of a car. "Thanks for telling me. I'm on it. I'm on it!"

Jacob stood back as the mall cop thrust open the barn door of the security office and bounded away. When the man had disappeared, Jacob reached over the counter and flipped the lock, walked to the desk, and settled into the still-warm chair. He knew the exact time and date he was looking for. He clicked through the security cameras on the PC until he found the northeast corner of the mall parking lot at 9:47 a.m. two Tuesdays earlier.

There he was on the screen, pulling his Tesla quickly into an empty space against the concrete wall and jumping out, totally ignoring the little red convertible Mustang that had been waiting patiently for the spot to be vacated. He'd been in a mad hurry to get into the mall. Beaty had called him from school in tears—she'd forgotten to bring a roll of blue craft board needed for a group project that day. Jacob watched a petite girl with blond ringlet curls stand up in the passenger seat of the convertible.

The footage had no sound, but Jacob could see her yelling after him as he jogged toward the mall entrance. Jacob remembered the moment distinctly, could hear her voice in his mind.

Hey, asshole! That was our spot!

He didn't typically do something like that—take people's parking spots or cut in line. People remembered that kind of thing, and he avoided being remembered.

In the video footage, Jacob watched the girl jabbering excitedly to the teenage boy in the driver's seat and pointing angrily at Jacob's car. He watched as she took out her phone and tapped something into the device as the driver pulled away.

He knew what she was doing. She was writing down his license plate number.

Jacob smiled. He paused the footage, zoomed in, and took out his own phone. He snapped a photo of the computer screen and noted down the license plate of the red convertible.

"See you soon," he said.

CHAPTER 7

NOT QUITE HALFWAY TO Los Angeles, I decided to stop for the night in Hanksville, Utah. I'd known some nice guys named Hank in my life, and I liked the look of the town on the bright phone screen. I never flew anymore. Like my father, I'd bought a car with a wide bench seat and lots of elbow room on the sill, something slightly worn but kept with love that I could sling my fluffy, lime-green court bag into or spill milkshakes in without much drama. I liked the way the Buick's suspension groaned when I got in, like climbing on an old familiar spring mattress on a weary night.

Hanksville was tiny. As far as I could see, all it had was a pizza place, a pharmacy, a motel, and a bar and grill. I chose the bar first. It was full of big hairy bikers bad-mouthing one another and playing pool at large tables under low gold lights. A smattering of biker chicks was among them, hanging around the edges of the pool game or sitting at a round table near the door, playing poker.

I sat at the bar and ordered a rare steak with onion rings and a side of mac and cheese, then slowly devoured it with a glass of red wine. The steak came covered in a thick, creamy gravy, and the mac sauce was orange, stretchy, and liquid hot. The bikers who came to the bar eyed the wine suspiciously but, unlike most people, didn't let their eyes travel down my body, assessing how big I was and in which ways my fat assembled itself. There were no glances to the barstool to measure how the unlucky piece of furniture was coping with my bulk. I'd received the Fat Person Look-Over a million times in my adult life, so often that I noted when it didn't happen. Bikers were rarely judgy. I got a couple of appreciative nods at the tattoos on my forearms: a big yellow lion on the right and a couple of pinup girls on the left.

"How was it?" the bartender asked as he retrieved my empty plate. His mustache was so heavy and thick it completely covered his mouth and stayed in place as he spoke, so at first I wasn't sure he had spoken.

"Great," I said eventually. "Really, really great. In fact, I'll go for round two."

He shrugged and smiled, punched my order into the register again. The cook in the kitchen gave me a thumbs-up through the window behind the bar as he started my second steak.

The Chalet Inn, what appeared to be the only motel in town, was within walking distance of the bar, but I was exhausted from the drive so I drove there. Regret over the second dinner hung like a coat on my shoulders, so I told myself I'd get up early and walk it off before I continued my drive tomorrow.

The sky was huge and crowded with stars. I hadn't been able to settle on how I felt about my father's loss, but as I walked from my car toward the motel entrance I got a small, wistful rush of sadness. It wasn't that I missed him, but I realized suddenly that any chance we had of reconnecting was now gone. I'd always known it was ludicrous to imagine that Earl Bird would ever have swept back into my life and become the dad I'd always wanted him to be—gentle, loving, supportive, interested—but now it wasn't just ludicrous. It was impossible.

The old guy who shuffled out of the motel owner's room to the reception desk was small and stern faced. I stood before him and received my first Fat Person Look-Over since I'd arrived in Hanksville.

"What do you want?" the owner asked.

"A room," I said. "One night."

"Nope," the man said. I waited for more, but there was none. As though to illustrate his point, the man flipped closed the heavy ledger lying open on the counter between us. The book was so unused to being closed that its cover came unstuck from the counter with a *clack* sound.

"What do you mean, 'nope'?" I asked. "The motel is full?"

"Nope to that too," the man said. "I got one room left, but it's right there."

He pointed to room 8.

"It's right next to mine." He pointed to the owner's room visible behind the counter. "And you look like you snore. So while there is a room available, I ain't renting it to you, lady."

I took a deep breath and let it out slowly.

"I do snore," I said. "You're right. But the nearest hotel from here is fifty miles away, and I've been driving for seven hours already. Being someone who purveys temporary sleeping environments for a living, I imagine you've got some earplugs back there behind the counter?"

"Sure do," he said.

"Why don't you rent me the room and use those for the night? Between the brick walls and the earplugs, I'm sure you won't have any trouble."

"Nope."

"Why the hell not?"

"Because this motel is old," he said. "We got old furniture here." His eyes wandered over me. "It's wood. It won't take your heft."

I grabbed the counter and held on, giving my hands something to do other than twitch with the desire to throttle this guy. I swallowed a swell of fury that leaped into my throat.

"I didn't catch your name," I said.

"It's Amos."

"Listen, Amos," I said. "You obviously have a problem with me. And I think I know exactly what that problem is."

"It's that I don't like fat people," he said.

"I thought so." I nodded.

"I don't think it's a problem so much as an opinion," he continued. "Everybody's got an opinion. Some people don't like cats. Some people don't like going to the beach. Some people don't like the Jews. I don't like fat people. They're selfish and they break things. They either break them by sitting or lying on them or they knock them over 'cause they're just plain clumsy."

"Well, Amos," I said, "I don't like assholes. So I guess we were never going to be best friends."

I walked to the door.

"And you're right," I added. "Fat people are clumsy."

I nudged the vending machine as I went by, a slight sideways bump. The vending machine tilted to the side, then smashed back down onto the tiles with a noise so colossal it made my heart sing. I turned and tipped an imaginary hat at Amos and then went on my way.

CHAPTER 8

ASHTON WILLISEE LET THE back door of the Beverly Hills Playhouse swing closed behind him. The parking lot was almost empty. He'd sat for ten minutes on the edge of the stage in theater room 6 after class had finished, staring at the empty seats before him, visualizing.

Ashton's mother had been reading books on psychic energy and the power of mindfulness, and she'd told him that as important as the acting classes was a ritual of creatively visualizing what he wanted, closing his eyes and really *feeling* himself succeed. Ashton thought the creative visualization stuff was probably bullshit, but he'd been taking classes for a year and only had one unsuccessful audition for a toilet paper commercial to show for it, so he figured he'd give it a whirl.

As he walked to his car at the far edge of the lot, a light distracted him. Two spots from his red Mustang convertible, a battered white Econoline van sat idling, the cabin light glowing brightly. Silhouetted against the light, a man in a ball cap stood, poring over a map.

"Hey, mate," the man said as Ashton moved toward his car. Heavy Australian accent. "Could I borrow you for a sec?"

"Yeah, sure." Ashton started walking over.

"Is that Gregory Way over there?" the man asked. "I'm looking for a place on the corner of Gregory and Arnaz."

"That's Robertson," Ashton said, taking out his phone and nodding to the road that accessed the parking lot. He hadn't seen anyone use a paper map in years. He pulled up Google Maps as he walked. "Gregory Way is—"

He was interrupted by a hiss sound, and the sharp, shocking sensation of a fine mist of liquid hitting his face. At first he thought the man had sneezed. Then Ashton saw a hand emerge whip fast from beneath the map, and the unlabeled aerosol can.

Then he saw nothing.

CHAPTER 9

ASHTON WOKE TO THE sensation of the van thumping over a pothole in the road. There was no telling how long he had been lying there, facedown on the rough carpet, swaying gently with the motion of the vehicle. His mind whizzed backward in terror, like a spring recoiling. He remembered the van. The nondescript Econoline—anonymous serial killer van of the ages. He remembered the silhouette of the man against the cabin light, the ball cap pulled low, obscuring his face. He remembered the Australian accent that had lured him in, made him think he was talking to a tourist. The hiss of whatever paralyzing chemical he'd been sprayed with, which had shunted through his system, switching out the lights.

Ashton understood the situation immediately. He was being driven to his death.

He curled now into a ball, eyes wide in the dim light, his heart hammering. His wrists were bound with something thin, like wire. There was tape on his mouth. He shifted, looked around him. Nothing he saw brought his terror into check. A case lay beside him, hard and black, three-quarters the length of his body. An unzipped duffel bag, which he could see held pliers, drills, clamps. A folding chair and sheets of plastic.

Ashton told himself that he could talk his way out of this. The guy probably wasn't a serial killer. Why pick off a rich kid from Beverly Hills and cause a media sensation when you could grab a dozen homeless kids from Culver City without anyone batting an eye? So if he knew Ashton's family had money, that meant the guy was a businessman. This was a kidnapping.

He'd heard tales from other kids at school about this sort of thing. A guy in economics class had a cousin who'd been abducted in Tapachula for ransom while his father was working down there on trade deals. The cartels could smell money and had clocked the family as soon as they arrived in town. Ashton shook in the dark, staring up at the motionless silhouette of the man in the ball cap in the driver's seat, as he remembered the guy in school saying the family had paid the ransom but never got their son back. A few months later a shriveled hand had arrived in the mail at the family's mansion in Brentwood.

The van stopped, and Ashton lay panting in the dark. He squeezed his eyes shut and swallowed down sobs as the man crunched through what sounded like gravel outside the van.

The van doors opened. Ashton was dragged and dropped onto the ground. His ribs crunched. He spotted dark mountains. A distant road, the red and yellow lights of passing motorists. Too far to hear his scream. He still couldn't see the guy's face.

The man caught Ashton's wrists, cut the tie. Ashton ripped the tape off his mouth and scrabbled away on the ground, almost crawling right over the edge of a gaping ravine lit by silvery moonlight.

He thought of running, but the van blocked both him and the man on an outcrop of rock with only a narrow escape route on either side. Ashton let a few sobs escape as the man went back to the van and returned with a huge black rifle.

"Oh, Jesus." Ashton's voice was high, thin. "Oh, please. God. Please no. Listen! Listen! Listen! I know what this is."

"You do, huh?"

Ashton didn't recognize the voice. He cowered on the edge of the cliff, blinking at the silhouette against the van's headlights.

"I-I-If you look in the contacts list on my phone," Ashton stammered, "you'll get my parents. They can have the money here in-in-in—"

"Do you recognize me yet?" the man asked.

Ashton's stomach sank. A person didn't kidnap someone who knew them. "This is a mistake!" he cried.

The man shifted the rifle in his grip. Ashton scrambled back as far as he could, sending rocks and dirt crumbling into the ravine.

"There's no mistake, Ashton," the guy said.

"I don't know you, man!" Ashton pleaded. He glanced over the rocky edge into the blackness. "Jesus! I don't—I've never seen you before in my life! I—Please, man, please! I'm sorry. I'm sorry! Don't hurt me. I'm just a kid!"

A *thunk* sound. A spray of dirt. Ashton realized with sickening clarity that the guy had shot into the ground at his feet, an inch or two away from the toe of his right sneaker. The rifle had a suppressor on it the thickness of a Coke can. Ashton backed onto the last few inches on the edge of the cliff. There was no-where to go. *Thunk, thunk.* He screamed and curled into a ball on the ground, his feet hanging in the dark air over the edge.

"Just a kid, Ashton?" the guy said. "Just a child? An innocent child? Tell me, what do children deserve, Ashton?"

Another spray of dirt. The guy had shot into the ground near his face. Ashton drew his arms up over his head and face, too terrified to move. It was the sound that drew him out of it. He expected another *thunk* from the suppressor, or a grinding sound as the mere inches of dirt and rock on which he perched over the deadly drop gave way. But instead there was a *blip*. A short, high-pitched wail. Ashton blinked through tears. Down on the distant road, new lights had joined the snail trail of yellow and red. They were blue and red.

Ashton looked up. The guy's silhouette was watching the distant lights too. Paused, calculating. Ashton gripped the ground for life, hanging on to dry shreds of grass and sharp rock, his teeth clenched and toes curled, his clothes soaked through with sweat and piss.

"Go," the guy told him.

Ashton didn't have to hear the word twice. He fast-crawled toward the van, squeezed past it, then bolted down a slope beside the cliff. He ran blindly downward, no idea if there were sharp falls or loose embankments ahead, thinking only of getting away from the van on the cliff above him.

Another *thunk* behind him. Another into the boulders of granite on either side of him. He followed the narrow natural trail, stumbling over cactus and rocks, falling and getting up and pulling himself onward as the shots followed him into the night.

CHAPTER 10

THERE WAS A BEAUTIFUL young Black woman sitting in the waiting room of Ira Abelman's office on Wilshire Boulevard in Central Los Angeles. I guessed her to be around twenty-five. She was the first Angeleno I'd seen up close. True to the city of beautiful people, she was tall and rake thin, and I'd bet she paid her hairdresser more than I paid my mechanic. She gave me the Fat Person Look-Over and turned back to her phone, clicking a moody selfie of herself in the plush leather chair.

The morning had begun with the broken promise of a walk to burn off the second dinner, feeling too stiff from sleeping in my car to push myself physically. Vegas had whizzed by my car windows, a searing, glaring kingdom surrounded by sand. I sunk into a chair two down from the beauty in Abelman's waiting room. I felt only a mild sense of annoyance as she took a *Diet Right* magazine from the coffee table before us and slapped it suggestively on the chair between us.

I'd set my expectations of my father's debt at a hundred grand. If I sold my condo in Watkins, that might give me enough to stave off debt collectors for a while. Then I'd probably have to make some unwelcome business decisions. Being a public defender paid my bills, but it wouldn't pay my father's. I'd never been in it for the money. I liked helping young people who were stuck in a criminal jam. I felt like those early offenses—usually fueled by plain stupidity, emotional overreaction, or the spirit of adventure—could make or break a kid and determine whether they became a lifelong criminal. When I helped a kid who was on a dark path, when I spared them jail time and got them a second chance, I felt like I was actually doing that corny thing all lawyers profess to want to do at some point in their career: making a difference in people's lives.

But shouldering my father's mistakes might mean giving that up for steadier, higher-paying legal work. I sat staring at my feet as the minutes ticked by, trying to remind myself that it wasn't good practice to hate someone who was dead.

Abelman, a small man in a suit with terrible hair plugs, emerged as the young woman was taking her sixth or seventh selfie and I was sucking on an over-chewed fingernail.

"Ladies," he said gravely, gesturing to his inner office.

"Huh?" the girl said. She looked at me.

I shrugged. Abelman had already disappeared back into his office.

"This is *my* appointment," she said, giving me another completely uninhibited dressing down with her big Bambi eyes. "You can wait. I was here first."

"Ladies!" Abelman called. "I haven't got all day!"

The beauty huffed as she entered Abelman's office ahead of me. The hot, heavy trepidation that had followed me all the way from Colorado was thumping in my temples now, alarm bells ringing, and they were focused on the self-obsessed young woman. She was almost glowing in my vision, a beacon of danger. I lowered myself cautiously into a chair in front of Abelman's cluttered desk, next to the one where the pissed-off beauty slumped.

"I've been trying to figure out a way to do this properly for the past three days," Abelman said. He raised his hands, held them wide, helpless. "I can't do it. There's no gentle way to go about it. So I've decided, now that you're both here, I'm just going to say it straight up."

I gripped the arms of my chair. When I looked over, I saw the young woman was gripping hers too.

"You two are sisters," Abelman announced.

CHAPTER 11

I RELEASED MY GRIP on the arms of my chair. A strange, unfamiliar sensation rushed through me, and it wasn't the boiling horror I'd expected to feel at this moment as I sat there before the lawyer. It was a strange, giddy relief. I found myself looking over at the young woman with an astonishment so heavy I was able to completely ignore the twisted expression she had on her face as she looked back at me.

"Whoa" was all I could say.

"Wait." The girl swallowed hard, pointed at my face. "You're my dad's... My dad..."

"This is Rhonda Bird," Abelman told her, gesturing to me. "Early's daughter with his first wife, Liz Savva."

Abelman gestured to the girl. "This is Baby—uh..."

"Baby?" I scoffed.

The girl glared at me.

"Barbara Ann Bird." Abelman rolled his eyes. "Everyone calls her Baby. I've dealt with the family since she was born, fifteen years ago."

"You must mean twenty, twenty-five years," I said.

"No," Abelman said knowingly, with the gravity of someone who was very tired. "I don't."

"She's..." I felt my mouth was gaping open, but I didn't seem able to close it. I turned to the girl. "You're *fifteen*?"

"Not only is she fifteen, Ms. Bird," Abelman said, "but she's also now your legal charge."

"What?" Baby and I said together.

Abelman picked up a manila file sitting at his elbow, flipped it open, and extracted a single sheet of paper from the top of the pile, holding it up as he read. "'I instruct my lawyer, Mr. Ira Abelman, to inform my daughter Rhonda Mavis Bird of the existence of my second child, Barbara Ann Bird, on the occasion of my death. Should Barbara be under the age of eighteen, it is my wish that Rhonda assume full custody and legal responsibility for Barbara from that point onward.'" He put the paper down. "Early told me it would be best to inform you of this decision in person, Ms. Bird, which is why I was so reluctant to share this information over the phone. He was concerned that if I explained the entire situation to you from afar, there was a chance you would not come to Los Angeles to assume care of Baby."

"This is not happening," Baby said. She was sitting bolt upright in her chair now, as white as lightning, like someone on a plane listening as the captain patches through the Brace for Impact call. "This is *not happening.*"

"I can't be someone's mom," I said. I couldn't believe the words that were coming out of my mouth. I got up and grabbed the manila folder from under Abelman's hands and started shuffling through it. "There should be a letter to me, telling me why—"

43

"There isn't one," Abelman said.

"This is a joke. Dad is . . . He's joking. Is he here?"

"I assure you, Ms. Bird, Early is deceased."

"Where's your real mom?" I asked Baby, who was staring out the window, mouth hanging open, crashing toward the earth on her imaginary plane.

"She is also deceased," Abelman answered for the girl. "Ms. Bird, as of now, this young woman is officially in your care. You're her guardian. There's no way around it."

CHAPTER 12

BABY GOT UP AND ran out of the room. I stared after her in disbelief, waiting for a reality show camera crew to leap through the doorway after her and reveal to me that I had been punked. They did not. I felt a strange panicky sense of horror as I heard the outer door slam after her.

My child is running away, I thought.

"She's not my child," I said aloud.

"Well, if I know one thing it's that she's not *my* child," Abelman said. "This is why I don't do family law. I made an exception for Early. He said everything would be fine. That you'd take care of it."

"The guy didn't even know me." I turned and headed for the door. "He wouldn't have recognized me if he ran into me on the street."

"I'm sure he would have. You look just like him."

"Thanks."

"Here's Earl's wallet. Inside is Baby's credit card," Abelman said, pushing a fat leather wallet toward me. "I wouldn't give that to her if I were you."

I took the wallet and turned again to leave.

"Before you go!" Abelman shouted. He tossed me a key. "You better go secure your father's office. It's in Koreatown. Baby knows the address."

"Secure it?"

"Yeah." He looked at me meaningfully. "I'd suggest you do that as soon as possible."

CHAPTER 13

I HEARD THE GIRL before I saw her. She was talking in a high, wailing tone, making strange sucking, gulping sounds between strings of frantic words. The street was blazing hot and so bright I had to stop under the awning of the office building and rub my eyes. A group of actors carrying manuscripts, rehearsing while they walked, ebbed and swirled around me for a moment as they walked down the street quoting lines from *Pulp Fiction*.

Baby was tucked into an alcove, holding her phone aloft and rambling to it. The sucking sound was her dragging deeply on a vape pen at the end of every sentence like she needed the candy-flavored nicotine to fuel her words.

"I don't know what I'm gonna do." Baby sucked on the vape so hard her cheeks drew inward. "I don't know what full custody means. I still don't have access to my credit card. We've got eight hours to go. Stay tuned and I'll get you all updated as soon as I can."

"Who the hell are you talking to?" I asked.

"My followers." She used the phone's camera to fix her hair. "Oh, God. This is the worst day of my entire life. This is the worst day in the history of humankind."

"That's..." I shook my head. "That's a big statement. Not the least because your dad died three days ago. Our dad."

"He had it coming." Baby continued to inhale deeply in between sentences.

I scoffed.

"The guy had a twelve-pack of doughnuts for breakfast every day," she said. "What did he think was going to happen?"

I'd seen some tough-talking teenagers in my time, but Baby's performance now was very convincing. I could almost believe she wasn't hurting at all over the loss of our father. I realized I was looking at a girl who had been raised by a hard, hard man. She spoke and stood and smoked the way I remembered he used to do, two and a half decades earlier, and she was looking at my eyes the same way, begging me to challenge her, just itching for an argument. Baby had her defenses up, her hackles raised. It was the same feeling I got when I stepped into a police holding pen to get my client and the bailiff pointed out the kid in the corner with the mean eyes and the scars and the broken teeth. I knew I had a wild child on my hands here.

"Give me my credit card," Baby demanded. "I know you have it."

"Let's just talk for a second first, okay? What happened to your mom?"

"It doesn't matter," Baby said. She put her hands up. "I'm only gonna say this once, lady. You're not my mom. You're not my real sister. You're nothing to me. I don't care what Ira says about custody or . . . legal charges . . . or whatever-whatever. I'm going to Milan."

"You're . . . going to Milan?"

"In eight hours." She glanced at her expensive-looking smartwatch. "Seven hours fifty-five minutes, actually. I've had tickets to the Spellbex Music Festival there for months. My followers are expecting me to go. I'm going. You're not stopping me."

"Barbara—"

"It's Baby. Baby Bird."

"Baby," I said carefully. "Your father just died. There's a woman here you've never met who's supposed to take care of you. Everything is upside down. I understand that you're scared—"

"I'm not scared."

"And upset. But let's just slow down. I'm also kind of freaked, just in case you were wondering. In eight hours, we're still going to be working this out, and that's going to be kind of difficult if you're on a plane to Milan with . . . Who were you going with?"

"I'm going by myself."

"Wow," I said, incredulous.

"There's nothing *wow* about it. I go everywhere by myself. I just got back from Puerto Rico and the Fixy Life Festival. This is what I *do*. This is my *job*."

I held my head. "Your job? Baby, I can't even begin to explain what I think about a fifteen-year-old traveling the world by herself just to tell hundreds of strangers on the internet what she thinks of the live music scene."

"Hundreds? Excuse me?"

"Let's get in my car and—"

"Yeah. Okay. Fine. Show me to your car." She flicked her hand at me. "I'll explain it all to you while you drive me home so I can pack."

She stormed off importantly. I had to laugh, to stave off the urge to cry.

CHAPTER 14

JACOB KANULAR SAT BESIDE the bed, listening to the soft clicking and bleeping of the machines monitoring his daughter in the cool dimness of the room. Outside the small space, the hospital thrummed with life, nurses chattering as they walked, soft bells calling for assistance to different rooms. Jacob had sat in rooms like this before, looking over strangers in beds, a night shadow slipping in while family members took breaks in the cafeteria or outside the hospital doors. Clients had hired Jacob to speed up the inheritance process, or to finish the job some two-bit amateur hit man had botched. Often all that was required was the simple blockage of a tube, the flipping of a switch, the gentle press of a pillow over a placid face. At least, that's how it had been back then. But now his ability to do the job again remained in question.

He'd been ready to kill Ashton Willisee. He'd told himself that, as he'd loaded the unconscious boy into his van, as he'd dragged him out of it, moaning and crying. But his first attempt at justice for Beaty had been a failure, which wasn't something Jacob had ever experienced on the job. He just didn't *do* failure. He didn't choose stupid locations. He wasn't caught out, as he had been the night before, by the strange coincidence of a police squad car pulling over a vehicle within distant eyesight of where he had planned to torture and kill his mark. Jacob was never interrupted. He was never seen. He never left evidence. And yet there he'd been, watching his mark run off into the ravine, the rabbit bolting from the wolf's jaws.

Had he wanted to fail? Could he really kill again? Or had time, love, and family done away with the monster inside him, the man who had been capable of taking the lives of others with such ease?

Even as he wondered these things, holding his daughter's cold, limp hand, his other hand held Ashton Willisee's phone, flipping through folders of videos. He found one entitled "Midnight Crew" and opened it.

Ten videos. He clicked the one at the top of the screen, the newest, dated a few days earlier. He recognized the range hood in his own kitchen. The camera swept to the dining room, where the big kid with the golf club was lining up Neina's sculptures on the table. He saw his own figure slumped in a chair, unconscious, Neina bound beside him. He watched as the girl in the black catsuit with the single blond curl hanging from her hood forced a screaming and crying Beaty into another chair, winding tape around her chest.

"Please, please don't," Beaty cried on the video. "Mom! Mom! Mom!"

Jacob felt his lip twitch. It was the only outward sign of the boiling, searing rise of fury inside him, the stirring of old reserves of killer rage. He rolled the video back. Ashton's main focus had been on his own activities in the kitchen. He'd only filmed a snippet of the girl tying his daughter to the chair. Jacob isolated the clip and played it again.

Please, please don't. Please don't. Please.

The phone screen went blank. An error message told him the phone had been remotely disabled.

Jacob let the phone fall from his fingers into a nearby trash can.

He had what he needed.

CHAPTER 15

I HAD TO GET the address for my father's office on South Alexandria Avenue in Koreatown from Abelman because Baby wanted to go home and would only give me her own address. The girl hunkered down in the passenger seat of my Buick, her long insectile legs crammed against her chest, eyes behind huge round sunglasses level with the door of the car, and a scarf she'd extracted from her tiny handbag pulled over her head.

"This is so embarrassing. This is. Urgh. Urgh. This car. This paint job. Worst day of anyone's life. Ever," she muttered to herself.

"This paint job was done by a very talented kid about your age," I said, "as payment for me fronting his bail money on a public exposure charge. I'm pretty fond of it."

"Why would you front some kid's bail money?"

"I'm a youth public defender back in Colorado."

"Oh, great. You're the law? That's just great."

I got the impression that Baby's reaction would have been the same even if I'd told her I was chief selfie appreciator at

Instagram headquarters. She had recovered quickly from the horror of our meeting in Abelman's office and was now settling comfortably into angry denial, huffing and sighing, shaking her head disgustedly at the situation. We stopped at a set of traffic lights beside a huge homeless encampment. Tarps had been strung between haphazard structures made from wood and rusted metal. Panhandlers flooded the cars around us. I waved off an old man wearing a huge pink sun hat. Above us, a billboard towered: Jennifer Lopez looking strangely miffed about her diamond bracelet.

"Help me out here," I said. "Where did my—our—father die?"

"In his office," Baby said. "He was probably taking a phone call. He was always screaming down the phone."

"Who informed you of his death?"

"Ira."

"And who's been staying with you for the past three days?"

"Some kids from the beach."

"Which kids?"

"Oh, my God. It's started already. *Who were you with? Which kids? Give me their names! Where were you?*" Baby rummaged in her purse for her Juul. "Listen, lady, all this interrogation stuff is *not* gonna fly with me."

"Interrogation!" I laughed. "Baby, if I was interrogating you, you'd know it, because you'd be sweating like an orchid in a greenhouse. Are you telling me that after you were informed of your father's death you were allowed to go home alone to hang out with a bunch of other fifteen-year-olds? That can't be right. Who's been taking care of you? Who's had custody of you until now?"

"No one."

"This is insane! You're a minor! Why didn't Abelman take charge of you himself?"

"Ira knows not to mess with me." She gave a mean smile as she put the vape pen to her lips.

I reached over and flicked it out of her mouth. It sailed out the window into the wind. I had been flicking cigarettes, joints, and vapes out of kids' mouths for years and was right on target.

"Goddamnit!" she screeched.

"No vaping in the car," I said. "No vaping ever, in fact. You're *fifteen*. By the time you're twenty-five you'll sound like Marlon Brando."

"Who?"

"Oh, God," I said.

"Look." She turned toward me. "Dad brought a hundred girlfriends around, and all of them tried to take a swing at being my new mommy. So I'm gonna tell you what I always told them."

"Okay," I said.

"I haven't had a mother since I was two, because that's the last time I needed one. I don't need anyone to *care* for me. I take care of myself. I'm fully autominous."

"Autonomous?"

"That's what I said."

"Baby, you're a child. You're grieving."

"That's where you're wrong. I'm *not* a child. I have a job. I travel. My dad always gave me the credit card when I was going away or when he traveled and I stayed at the house by myself. We had a system, and it worked," she said. "If you've got, like, maternal instincts or whatever-whatever, you can take them elsewhere." She flicked her hand at me again, like she was dismissing an incompetent servant.

"Man." I shook my head. "When they were handing out sass in heaven, you loaded up a truck."

"Damn right." She extracted another vape pen from her purse.

"So what happened to your mom?" I asked. "Did she leave him?"

"They were never together. Their thing was a one-night stand."

"What? Are you kidding?"

"I'm dead serious. He couldn't even remember who she was at first. He was hanging out with a lot of lady folk at the time if you catch my drift."

I sighed.

"She dumped me on his doorstep with a letter and a picture of the two of us."

Baby pulled out her phone and tapped to a grainy photo of a tall, attractive Black woman with curly dark hair and brown eyes, holding a baby.

"How old were you?" I gaped.

"Two." She exhaled a cloud of smoke. "I'm definitely Dad's, though. He got a DNA test."

"Oh, I bet it's the first thing he did," I said. "I bet he grabbed your little hand and the car keys and went and got it immediately."

"I don't remember." She rolled her eyes. "You got water in your ears? I told you. I was two."

"So what happened to your mom exactly?"

"She washed up on a beach in Papanoa, like, three weeks later." The girl shrugged. "Somebody tied her to a cinder block."

"Oh, Baby. I'm sorry."

"I don't care." Baby snorted in the feigned nonchalant way I'd seen a thousand teenagers do before her. "I didn't know her."

"But—"

"He tried to find out who killed her, but he couldn't." Baby exhaled more smoke at the dashboard. "He found out everything about her, found some family and all, but he couldn't solve the crime. He had fun trying, though. It was like a mystery, I guess. He liked mysteries. It's why he started doing this job."

"What job?" I flicked the vape pen, sending it sailing out the window.

"*Goddamn*it, bitch! You do that again and I'm gonna smack you, I swear to God."

"Dad gave up being an accountant?"

"An *accountant*?" Baby burst out laughing. I pulled into a parking lot in front of a strip mall and found a space. "He was an accountant?"

"Last time I saw him he was," I said.

"Well, when he got landed with me, he had a shop on Sunset that sold taxidermy."

"Oh, sure." I rolled my eyes. "Because that makes complete sense. So what was he doing lately?"

Baby gestured through the windshield. We were parked outside a small office door wedged between a busy nail salon and a crab boil restaurant covered in nautical paraphernalia. The stenciling on the door read EARLY BIRD PRIVATE INVESTIGATION— WE'LL GET THE WORM!

CHAPTER 16

" 'WE'LL GET THE WORM' was my idea." Baby jutted her chin proudly. "When he started out he was mainly just catching cheating husbands and bail jumpers. You know. Worms."

"Genius," I said.

I opened the office door, which led to a stairwell, and was hit with a wall of cigar stink mingled with the smell of crabs from the restaurant next door. There was something else there too: my father's cologne. Trumper's West Indian Extract of Limes. I'd smelled it now and then on my clients' fathers over the years, and it always struck pain into my heart. I walked up the rickety stairs as Baby reassured herself behind me.

"Seven hours and four minutes," she said. "That's still plenty of time to get home, pack, get to the airport. Settle into the lounge nice and early. Nab a spot by the window."

"You're not going to Milan, Baby. Not this time."

"It's hilarious that you think you can stop me," she said. "You're gonna give me my credit card, and I'm gonna go."

In a tiny office above the crab restaurant, my father's desk sagged under a three-foot-high pile of papers, books, take-out containers, and unopened UPS packages as well as scrunched gambling tickets and receipts, all sprinkled with cigar butts and ash. Just as I had anticipated. The only difference from the office I remembered in Watkins two and a half decades earlier was the weapons. From the doorway I could see four knives—two big hunting knives lying in the pile on the desk, a penknife on a windowsill crowded with used Starbucks cups, and a kitchen knife stabbed into the wall by the window—plus a huge Magnum revolver lying on the seat of his battered leather chair.

I sighed and moved the gun, then sank into the chair. My dad's groove in the chair fit my butt exactly. Baby shoved a pile of debris off an old sofa onto the floor with the familiarity of someone who had done it many times, then she reclined dramatically with an arm up over her head, holding her phone aloft.

"The woman is trying to take over everything," Baby narrated to her followers. "She's ransacking my father's office now. I can tell she's going to try to dominate my entire life. She thinks she's my mom already. She says I'm not going to Milan, and she still hasn't given me my credit card. This is going to be a battle, people."

"Are you out of your mind?" I said. "Ransacking? I've touched one thing since I walked in!"

"The woman is trying to lecture me now," Baby narrated.

"I have a name. It's Rhonda."

Baby ignored me. I tried to shake off the hot, heavy annoyance creeping up between my shoulder blades, a sensation that had begun in the car and was peaking now. Baby had clearly hung out in this office a lot. My dad had brought her around his work. He'd let her brand the business with a slogan. He'd spent enough time with her that she'd picked up some of his mannerisms—that aggressive hand flick, and the jut of her chin at her own cleverness like a happy cat looking for a scratch. She'd been dumped in his lap as a tiny toddler, and instead of foisting her off on her mother's relatives, he'd chosen to raise her himself. There was no mistaking it.

I was deeply jealous of this girl.

My entire life, my dad had been aloof, stern, or completely absent. When I reached age thirteen, he'd had enough of me. What did Baby have that I didn't? What was wrong with me? I strummed my purple-painted fingernails on a small bare spot on the desk.

"What was the lawyer getting at when he said I needed to secure this place?" I asked. "Both doors were locked."

Baby said nothing and tapped furiously on her phone. I was starting to shift the stuff on the desk into piles when Baby finished her post or whatever it was and popped up again.

"I'm gonna go get a crab stick," she said. "I assume you want one. Maybe more than one."

"You assume right," I said, refusing to take offense. "Get me three. And if you try to run off to Milan, I will find you so fast it'll make Liam Neeson look like an amateur."

"Who's Liam Neeson?"

"What? Liam Neeson isn't even Marlon Brando old. He's current!"

"If you say so."

Baby didn't get far in the hall, it seemed. I heard her bump into someone, and racked with guilt, I went to the door to listen in.

"I don't have time for this," I heard Baby say to them. "I'm trying to make a run for it."

CHAPTER 17

I PUT MY HAND on the knob but paused when I saw Baby's reflection in the mirrored surface of another door in the hall. She was standing with a teenage boy who looked so tired and terrified, I forgot all about Baby's escape attempt and froze where I stood, observing them.

"I need help." The boy swiped back his long, ragged hair. "Is your dad here?"

"He's dead."

"What?"

"What the hell do you need him for?" Baby cocked her hip and folded her arms. "Jeez, man, what's it been? Two years? I haven't seen you since..."

"The thing."

"Yeah." Baby stared at her feet. "The thing."

Both kids stood in the awkwardness, fidgeting with their clothes. It was Baby who came out of it first.

"You got tall," she said.

"You too." The boy wrung his hands. "Look, I'm in trouble

and I can't go to the cops. I need your dad. What happened to him?"

"What happened to you?"

"I . . . I was abducted last night."

"What? What the hell does that even mean?"

"It means someone abducted me." The boy smoothed down his shirt. It was dirty and wrinkled. "Like, for real. Like, the guy knocked me out and tied me up and put me in a white van. He had a gun."

Even as the boy spoke, I could see him mentally backtracking. He swiped at his face, and I could see his hands were shaking.

"Are you high right now?" Baby asked.

"No, I'm not high." The boy's voice dropped so low I could barely hear it. He took a step closer to Baby. "Look, your dad was always a cool dude, and he came through for us that time. I just thought maybe . . . maybe, like . . . Okay, look. It doesn't matter. I shouldn't have come here. This was a stupid idea."

The boy turned.

I pulled open the door of the office and pointed at him. "Not one more step," I said.

CHAPTER 18

BABY'S EYES WERE FULL of terror. Not the physical kind. The social kind. Just opening the door and showing myself in all my aesthetic horror to someone she knew was clearly terrifying enough, but as I spoke, her eyes somehow got bigger. She was horrified that I might reveal who I was and make some kind of scene, which is exactly what I did.

"You two, get your butts in here." I pointed to the office.

Baby and the boy walked into my father's office. Baby's expression slowly turned into a furious, threatening glare as she moved to the couch.

"What's your name, kid?" I asked the boy.

"Ashton Willisee."

"Ashton, is it true what you were saying?" I asked. "Were you abducted?"

"Whoa!" Baby put her hands up. "Rhonda, what…we… You-you don't get to listen in on people's private conversations!" she blurted.

"Yeah, I do." I shrugged. "When they involve crimes and the possible endangerment of the people around me, I do."

"I'm out of here." Ashton tried to get up.

"Sit down and tell me what happened to you," I said.

"Nothing happened." Ashton slithered down in his seat. Ultra casual. He actually yawned, let his eyes drift half closed. I knew from my years of watching tapes of kids in police interrogations that adopting an overly casual or relaxed stance was often a coping mechanism for kids in danger. I'd spent much of my professional life advocating for kids who appeared callous or indifferent during false confessions when really they were terrified.

"Nothing happened?" I pressed.

"Look, I just—" He gave a humorless laugh and gestured at Baby. "I know Baby from school. I was just in the area, and I thought I'd see if she was here and...uh...pull a prank. Make up a story. I'm sorry, okay?"

"Look at me," I said.

Ashton stared at the floor.

"Ashton, look at my eyes."

The boy glanced at me for a fragment of a second before straightening back up in the chair.

"I can help you," I said. "We can go to the police together. If there's some reason that you—"

"I've gotta go." The boy leaped to his feet. "I don't need any help, lady. It was just a prank, okay? That's all."

He was out the door before I could get across the room to him.

"That was *so* uncool. I just..." Baby was shaking her head disgustedly at me. "I've got nothing. I'm, like, speechless."

I ignored her and went to the window, where I watched Ashton fast-walk to a Mercedes parked at the end of the lot. There was a bumper sticker on the back of the car, which was unusual given the expense of the vehicle. I had to squint to read it. PROUD PARENT OF A STANFORD-WEST ACADEMY STUDENT.

"Hey, Baby," I said, keeping my eyes on the Mercedes. "What's the name of your high school?"

She snorted. "I'm too busy to go to school. I've been homeschooling myself since I was thirteen."

"Dad let you do that?" I sighed. "Jesus."

"People don't *let* me do things, Rhonda," Baby said. "I just do them."

I found a set of car keys on the windowsill. My father's car had to be out there in the lot somewhere. "So do you think Ashton was abducted?"

"Probably," she said. "But that's not the point. You can't eavesdrop on me and my friends."

"Baby, the abduction *is* the point," I said. "I know you're mortified to be around me. I get that. You've made it perfectly clear. But you saw how obvious his body language was, didn't you? I mean, he was clearly telling the truth to you out there in the hall but lying when he was in here."

"I guess," she said as she took out her phone and lay back down on the couch with a huff. "I don't know about body language. But he had drag marks on the backs of his shoes. Fresh ones. There was still dirt on them. So I guess he *was* probably abducted."

"Really?" I was genuinely impressed. "You saw drag marks?"

"Yeah, right here." She lifted a foot and touched the back of her heel without taking her eyes off her phone. "I saw that once on one of Dad's cases. I was looking at the crime-scene photos of some chick who got raped and killed in the woods up at Big Bear. Dad showed me the drag marks on her shoes like someone had dragged her unconscious body across gravel or concrete. You don't get marks like that if you're fighting and kicking."

"I can't believe Dad let you look at crime-scene photos," I said, fiddling with the car keys.

"You are so not listening to me." Baby turned her body to face the back of the couch. "I don't need anyone to *let* me do things."

I pointed the key fob at the window and clicked it. None of the cars in the lot flashed their lights. I hit the button again, looked around. Nothing. I clicked and clicked, until something behind me clicked in response under the desk. I turned and knelt, pressing the button on the key fob and listening for the responding click beneath the worn blue carpet.

I pulled up a corner of carpet that was curled against the bottom of the desk. Beneath it was a badly fitted wooden hatch set into the floor. The key fob disguised as a car key was clicking the lock on the hatch open and shut.

"Like Milan," Baby was saying from the couch, out of sight. "I'm going. You can tell yourself whatever you want about *letting* me. But I'm getting on that plane."

I opened the floor hatch to reveal a space filled almost entirely with a black duffel bag. I unzipped the bag.

Cash. Stacks of cash, in mixed denominations, bound with elastic bands. I pushed experimentally against the stacks of money, feeling for depth and density. A quick estimation told me there were millions of dollars here. It was more money than I'd ever seen anywhere in my entire life.

It was bad news. The mere sight raised the hairs on the back of my neck.

"In fact, we should go," Baby said. I heard her roll off the couch. "I've got to pack."

"Yeah," I said, zipping the bag closed. "Let's go. I'll meet you at the car."

CHAPTER 19

VERA ARRIVED LATE. SHE always did. She liked to keep them waiting, give them an opportunity to talk about her. The more people talked about you while you weren't around, the more mythical you became. The more powerful.

She threw the keys to her convertible at the Soho House valet and wore her sunglasses all the way up the elegant white stairs to the restaurant, right to the table, so they wouldn't be able to tell whether or not she was pissed off at having been called to a meeting. Her crew were all watching her as she sat down. The tension was so palpable, a group of people at the next table—which included Jennifer Aniston and her manager—looked over too.

The twins, Sean and Penny, were slumped in their chairs, looking bored as usual. Ashton looked puny, dwarfed by Benzo beside him, whose sinewy muscles were barely contained in Hugo Boss. The waitress saw Vera and turned midstride so abruptly she almost tripped. Vera had once scalded a waiter here with her bowl of soup for ignoring her, so now the staff always attended to her promptly.

No one spoke. The waitress came, and Vera said, "Coffee, black," without looking up. She pushed her sunglasses up into her blond ringlets.

"You can explain," she finally said to Ashton.

Ashton sagged with relief. "There's not much more to add about what happened other than what I said in my text," Ashton began. "Guy grabbed me right outside the Playhouse. He let me go in some shithole off the 405 near Mulholland. I wouldn't have escaped if it hadn't been for the cops driving by. He was gonna kill me."

"And why do you think this has something to do with our game?" Penny asked, idly perusing the menu.

"He knew who I was," Ashton said. "He knew my name. He was, like, angry. Really pissed. He was talking about what children deserve..."

"What do you mean, what children deserve?" Benzo snorted.

"I don't know! He was, like, 'Don't you know who I am? Don't you know what children deserve?' Something like that. I can't remember exactly. I was freaking out."

"Children." Penny rolled her eyes. She looked over at Jennifer Aniston's table, where a pair of publicists, or whoever the hell they were, were still ogling them. "What are you assholes staring at?"

The publicists snapped to attention, turning away.

"Ashton, if this guy knows who we are, we're in deep shit," Sean said. "I can't believe you could let this happen. Did you disable your phone?"

"Yeah," Ashton said. "It's dead."

"How long after he took you did you disable it? Could he have gotten all your contacts? Your videos?"

Ashton didn't answer.

"The guy doesn't know who *we* are," Vera said. Her voice sliced through the growing tension like a knife through butter. She hung an arm over the back of Ashton's chair—let them see she thought it was no big deal. "He knows who *Ashton* is."

The crew considered this.

"He grabbed you outside the Playhouse, right? You said he was waiting for you there," Vera said.

"Yeah." Ashton nodded.

"So he's been watching you onstage," Vera reasoned. "He sounds like some creep kiddy fiddler looking for a fresh young boy to play around with. He probably came snooping around a few months back, saw you doing the Romeo soliloquy or whatever the hell, and got a boner, thought he'd wait for you after class. Give you what children deserve."

"That makes sense," Benzo said.

"I don't know," Ashton said. "I feel like it was connected to the game. Like someone figured it out."

"That's because you've been thinking we'll be found out since we started the Midnight Crew." Vera shook her head. "You feel guilty and you want to get caught. Funny, you weren't feeling so guilty when we hit your drunk uncle's house to teach him a lesson about smacking your aunt around. I seem to remember you enjoying that one very much. You were guilt-free."

Vera's coffee came. Penny shut the menu in disgust and flung it on the floor. The waitress darted back and scooped it up.

"Completely pedestrian," she snapped at the waitress. "Ginger granola? Who designed this menu? Are you serious? Is Raoul back there?"

"Raoul's off today," the waitress said. "Our resident chef this morning is—"

"Let's go." Penny stood. "We might as well go to Burger King at this rate."

"Please don't go." The waitress fluttered about the table. "Take a moment to decide what you'd like, and I'm sure we can accommodate your preferences."

Penny smiled as the waitress scrambled away. Penny had been a waitress for a week once. Her mother had wanted her to experience a "real job" as punishment for Penny ramming her birthday Mercedes into a tree because she'd wanted a Jaguar instead. Penny had hated waitresses ever since.

"This guy, whoever he is, he isn't the threat," Vera said. "Ashton is. It's what Ash did that could get us all killed."

CHAPTER 20

"WHAT ARE YOU TALKING about?" Benzo leaned in.

"Ashton blabbed to a private investigator that he was abducted. He went crying to some—"

"I took it back," Ashton blurted. "I told them I was lying. They're not gonna—"

"Never interrupt me," Vera snapped. She felt the gaze of nearby diners on her. "Never. Ever. Interrupt me."

The crew turned to Ashton. He hunkered down, sulking.

"What did you say to these people?" Penny asked.

"I didn't tell them about the Midnight Crew," Ashton said.

"You better not have," Benzo snarled, his nostrils flaring.

"It was stupid," Vera said. "I'm not even sure 'stupid' cuts it. It was moronic. It was dangerous."

"I made like it was a prank. It's not going to go any further."

"Do you understand?" Vera said. "If the cops find out about what we've been doing with the Midnight Crew game, we're all doing time. People like that hate rich kids from the hills. They'll make a circus of the whole thing. They'll put us in jail.

Real jail. With actual criminals. How long do you think you'd survive in prison, Ash?"

"I know I'd be fine." Benzo flexed his pecs.

"Whoever the guy who grabbed you was, he wasn't one of our victims," Vera continued. "We've never hit anyone who wasn't a coward or a loser, and we've never really done anything bad enough to make people want to find us. We give them a scare, that's all. Make them realize the kind of pathetic, mindless, *blessed* lives they're living. We do them a favor. Because we're nice people."

Sean snickered. He was watching the waitress pour his water. A drip splashed on the tablecloth. He leaned over to Benzo and murmured, "If my entire working life revolved around serving people and I couldn't figure out how to pour a fucking glass of water properly, I'd hurl myself out a window."

Benzo gave a heavy chuckle.

Sean continued watching the waitress for a moment, calculating, measuring. "Can I make you a deal?" he asked her eventually.

"Excuse me, sir?" The waitress looked around the table as if for help.

"What's your name, honey?" Sean asked.

"Janice."

"Janice, I want to get you out of here," he said.

Vera smiled despite herself. She liked Sean's little amusements.

"You can't do this job. It's not for you," he continued.

"Leave her alone." Ashton rolled his eyes.

"The deal is this," Sean said, taking the waitress's wrist. "Get under the table right now and blow me. Right now. In front of everyone. Do that, and I'll give you a million dollars."

"Sir, I can't do that." The waitress laughed uncomfortably.

"He's serious," Penny said. "You know who my brother is, right? We're Michael Jay Hanley's kids. Our dad is the most powerful guy in this city. Sean's good for it."

"He's doesn't mean it," Ashton told Janice. "He's just messing with you. Sean's gay."

"I gave the same deal to a bartender at Freeze last week. She quit her job right that minute." Sean pulled out his phone, tapped through to his bank account. "Here. See? That's my transaction right there to her account. Give me your details, and I'll transfer it the moment you're done."

He unzipped his fly under the table. Janice looked around at the dozens of patrons all around them, her manager at the end of the room, checking in new guests. Vera watched the waitress's mind ticking over. Calculating. The job. Her dignity. The money. The life-changing, destiny-altering money. A few seconds of humiliation for all that cash.

The waitress sunk down uncertainly. Everyone at the table except Ashton erupted into laughter when her knees hit the carpet. The waitress got back up and rushed away. The manager of the restaurant looked over at them but didn't respond to the incident. In a few moments, they had all forgotten about it.

"What about that kid last time?" Penny yawned. "She got pretty sick."

"She shouldn't have been there," Vera said. "She was supposed to be at a sleepover."

"Is she okay?" Ashton asked. "Did you che—"

75

"She's fine," Vera said. "I checked."

"But maybe—"

"It's not the sniveling old guy," Vera insisted. "No one could have found us that fast. It's not anyone we've ever hit. We're fine."

She took a notebook out of her bag and set it on the table.

"Now pay attention," she said. "Because we're hitting our next target tonight."

CHAPTER 21

THE HOUSE IN MANHATTAN Beach sat on the esplanade, a towering four-story white mass that blazed proudly in the sun. The single strip of concrete separating it from the scorching beach, called the Strand, was toured by Rollerbladers and dog walkers and looky-loos peering into the luxurious homes, while narrow streets between the lines of grand houses funneled families with towels down toward the glittering water.

"This is not Earl's house," I said as we idled on the street.

"It isn't?" Baby raised her eyebrows at me.

"No," I said. "This is not the house of a former accountant, former taxidermy salesman, now-deceased gumshoe with an office above a crab shack."

"Well, I think I'd know where I live." Baby snorted. "Turn here. Park in the garage."

Baby had a small device in hand that was opening the double garage door, and I parked beside a black Maserati.

I wanted to scream at Baby that everything I'd seen that day was telling me Earl Bird had been a bad, bad man. Not only bad but also likely a dangerous, corrupt criminal. But I reminded myself that she was a kid who'd only just lost her father and who was now trying desperately to stop me from changing anything else about her existence. Trying to radically adjust her perception of our father probably wasn't a good idea at the moment.

We passed through a door in the back of the garage and walked into the first floor of the house. It looked like there'd been a massive party held here last night: beer bottles and red plastic cups on every surface, overflowing ashtrays on the arm of every sofa. Greasy pizza boxes were stacked on the landing of the stairs, and discarded clothes were piled in the corners of the rooms or hung off pieces of furniture. But the layer of dust over everything told me this hadn't happened overnight—this kind of filth was the result of months of neglect.

A teenage girl in a bikini lay sleeping on a couch in the first room we entered, the coffee table in front of her dominated by a huge glass bong.

"Who is that?" I asked, pointing.

"Some girl," Baby said.

"You don't know her?"

"I told you, I invited a bunch of kids from the beach over when Dad died," Baby said. "Some of them are still here."

"I thought you meant friends, not random kids from the beach," I said. I went and roused the girl. "Hey. Hey. Excuse me? Honey, you've got to go."

"You can't kick her out," Baby snapped at me. "This is my house. My guests can stay as long as they like."

"You don't know these people."

"So?" Baby said. A boy with black dreadlocks wandered into the room from what looked like the kitchen. He let his bloodshot eyes drift over us and kept walking without a word.

"I'm going to go pack for Milan," Baby said, turning to go.

"Baby." I grabbed her wrist. "You are not going to Milan."

"It's so funny that—"

"I'm serious," I said. "Listen, I get it. I totally get where you're coming from here, okay? Your dad is gone, and some woman who's only been in your life for five minutes starts bossing you around. You've had all the independence you've ever wanted, and now a stranger thinks she can walk in and change that instead of trusting you, like your father trusted you, to take care of yourself."

Baby glared at me.

"But you have to see where I'm coming from too," I said. "Dad created this situation, and it doesn't matter how stupid or selfish it is—this is the situation we're in and we've got to deal with it. And it's going to take more than a few hours to do that. You can't run off to Milan before we've straightened all this out."

Baby grabbed a beer bottle from a table nearby and flung it at the wall beside us. It shattered, startling the girl on the couch and two other girls I hadn't noticed earlier, sleeping on blankets by the windows.

She pointed at the wall now dripping with beer. "Give me my credit card and get out of my face or next time that'll be your head."

"Baby, I've been visiting teenagers in juvenile detention since before you were born," I said. "If you think having a beer bottle thrown at me is the worst threat I've ever faced, you're dreaming. You're not getting the card. You're not going to Milan. End. Of. Discussion."

She stormed off. I did the same, internally raging at my father for having done this to us, and at myself for doing a terrible job of handling Baby so far. I didn't get her. She wasn't responding to sympathy, humor, or stern directives. I worried that eventually I would run out of my usual grab bag of strategies for dealing with teenagers in peril. It didn't make sense to me that I couldn't level with or relate to my own sister.

I reminded myself that now wasn't the time to panic or decide I'd failed. After all, I'd known her only a couple of hours. Baby and I would grow to understand each other eventually.

I went back into the garage and popped the trunk of my car, then hefted the duffel bag of cash out. I carried it upstairs and found my father's bedroom on the second floor. I could tell it was his room from all the cigar stink. In the en suite bathroom, I knelt and gave the block of wood under the cabinet doors an experimental push. It tilted out from its housing and toppled over.

Creature of habit, my father, just like me.

When I was a little kid, maybe six, I discovered my father's hidey-hole in our home in Watkins. I walked in on him grunting and sweating, his body bent and his arm shoved deep into the small space under the vanity in my parents' bathroom. I thought for a moment he was fixing a plumbing problem, as I had seen workmen do around the house, but catching my father doing manual labor was as bewildering as if he had been in there training a monkey to do backflips. Then I saw him pull out a small jewelry case from the hidden space and place it on the floor by his knees. That's when he noticed me standing there and snapped with sudden, shocked rage. "What the hell are you doing?"

"Nothing!" I cowered. "What are you doing?"

"None of your business, kid." He grabbed his knees, his face reddened and puffy. "What in the world has your mother been teaching you that you think it's okay to go creeping around people's personal business? You're so nosy! God*damn*it!"

He shoved the case into his back pocket, and I hung around guiltily in the bedroom while he recovered.

"You still here? What are you, my supervisor? You gotta watch everything I do around here?"

"Is that a present for Mommy?"

"Is what a present for Mommy?"

"The box." I pointed at his pocket.

"Listen, kid." He bent and pointed a finger in my face. "You tell your mommy about that box, or that little hole under the sink, and I'll gut every toy you own and stuff a nice big pillow for myself with their insides. You understand?"

I'd waited for the little jewelry case to turn up at my mother's birthday dinner or at Christmas. Month after month I'd waited, but it never showed up.

Now I bent all the way down and looked into the dusty darkness. It was clear items had been hidden in the space over time, but there was nothing there now. I could see shapes outlined in the dirt and grit but couldn't tell what they had been.

I unzipped the bag and took one last look at the money. A few stacks of bills had slid around, revealing a key on a yellow plastic tag near the top of the pile. The label on the tag was for a storage facility in Torrance. Trepidation washed over me. Whatever Dad was keeping out in Torrance must be as secret and full of malignant potential as the hidden cash itself. I took the key, secured the money in the hidden compartment under the vanity, then walked into the hall and saw Baby on a balcony overlooking the beach.

"We've got to go," I said.

"Where?" she asked. She swiped quickly at her face to hide her tears.

"Torrance," I said. "I have a feeling Dad's got more surprises in store for us."

CHAPTER 22

JACOB MOVED LIKE SMOKE. It was a skill he'd learned early in his time as a killer, when he'd been too raw and inexperienced to kill up close. He'd ventured silently into hotel rooms in Paris and London to replace pills in bathrooms with lethal capsules full of ricin powder or arsenic, leaving no trace of himself.

Feather-footed despite his size, he now wandered the second floor of Derek "Benzo" Benstein's house in the dark, overhearing the young man's voice echoing off the high ceilings as he talked loudly on the phone to a yacht broker in San Francisco.

"Well, that's just too bad. I need it sooner than that," he heard Benzo snarl. "I told you I wanted the forty footer with the double rain shower in the main bathroom. I'm throwing a party on Sunday, Doug, and I need the yacht in the marina by that morning for the caterers."

Jacob wandered out onto the upstairs deck and stood in the shadows, looking over Benzo's property. Two high-class escorts were sitting in the Jacuzzi, one playing with her phone,

one yawning and braiding her wet hair. When Benzo returned from the phone call, the girls would be back "on," would fawn and giggle over the eighteen-year-old homeowner, but for now they looked as bored and tired as if they were waiting for a late bus.

"*L.A. Style* starts shooting me at nine," Benzo shouted down the phone. "So if the cover of next month's issue has me standing on the pier with a captain's hat on my head and my dick in my hand, I will personally come up there and kick your ass." Jacob went to the second-floor railing and looked down into the foyer in time to see Benzo smash the phone, scattering the fragments on the marble tiles.

Roid rage, Jacob guessed. His workup of Benzo had revealed just how much maintenance the son of Los Angeles's most successful film agent put into his appearance. Benzo's calves, pecs, and six-pack were implants, and the young man had a standing appointment for flanks, belly, and buttocks liposuction twice a year to counteract the fat gained during his notorious weekend yacht parties. His lips and cheekbones were filled, and he was recovering from a recent brow shave. Jacob had crept through Benzo's online bank accounts the way he was wandering through the boy's house now, noting his purchases of creatine, beta-alanine, and conjugated lino-leic acid to build muscle paired with Prozac and duloxetine to combat the effects of a mind filled with self-loathing. Benzo was a walking concoction of chemicals, bioplastics, and silicone.

Jacob snuck down the stairs and followed Benzo into the huge living room, standing just out of sight while Benzo flopped onto the big couch and flicked the huge television screen over to a paused point-of-view shooter game. The assassin watching from the doorway wasn't surprised that Benzo had seemingly forgotten all about the hookers waiting for him in the hot tub. The girls were just another example of the toys available to Benzo wherever he went, machines in standby mode, waiting to be taken up again.

But, Jacob understood, there was no toy quite so entertaining as a real-life victim tied to a chair and twisting away from Benzo's Taser. Unlike the screams of his video-game victims, the prostitutes' false squeaks of pleasure, or the admiration of those who crowded his yachts each weekend, Neina's fear had been real, and Benzo was always chasing the real. Jacob smiled. It felt good to understand his target. It made the takedown all the more satisfying.

CHAPTER 23

JACOB LIFTED HIS GUN and fired a bullet into the television screen. The suppressor's *thunk* was overshadowed by the thunderous blast and crack of the screen, the dramatic sparks and white flash of light that heralded its end. For a moment Benzo sat stunned on the couch, staring at the smoking hole in the screen before him—convinced perhaps that the machine had simply exploded on its own—before some extrasensory awareness alerted him to Jacob's presence behind him. He leaped off the couch and stared wide-eyed at the intruder.

No recognition. Jacob shook his head in disgust. Sure, he probably looked different, alert, dressed, and ready for the hunt as he was now, unlike how Benzo had last seen him— gagged, bound, and helpless in his Dodgers T-shirt and boxer shorts, covered in his own blood and sweat. But more likely, Benzo didn't recognize him because his life was a constant parade of people who didn't matter—salespeople, bartenders, gardeners, cleaners, chauffeurs, and masseurs. Benzo looked at the gun, and all his muscles tensed, a whole-body reflex that in anyone else would have been terror but in Benzo was chemical rage.

"Dude, what the fu—?"

Jacob lifted the gun and fired at the wall beside Benzo's head. It had been years since he'd done any marksman's training, but his old self was returning. The bullet whizzed past the boy's ear, close enough for him to hear it. He cowered but recovered quickly.

"Okay, okay, okay!" Benzo said, hands up, his posture bending to Jacob's will but his eyes speaking of a mind that was boiling with anger. "Who are you? What do you want? Is this about my dad?"

"Look closely at me," Jacob said. "Think hard."

Benzo's breath quickened. "Oh, dude... Oh, shit. You're that Palos Verdes guy. The guy with the family."

"That's me." Jacob's fury almost choked off his words.

"Look." Benzo gave a short laugh to try to soften the seriousness of the situation. He swallowed hard. "There's no need to go all John Wick on our asses."

Jacob held his pistol in one hand and used the other to pull a long, thin black rod from its holster on the back of his belt. He gave the cattle prod trigger a demonstrative pull and watched Benzo's eyes twitch as the end of the device sizzled and snapped with light. Jacob could almost feel Benzo's heart sink.

"Man, it was nothing personal," Benzo said. "At least not for me. I didn't pick you. Someone else did. I don't even know what it was about. For me it was all just a game, okay? Just a bit of fun. No one got hurt, right?"

Jacob fired a bullet into Benzo's thigh. The boy was tough.

He screamed but didn't fall. Jacob watched the boy clutching his limb with a detached sense of admiration.

The pain seemed to give him courage. Benzo grabbed a lamp from the table by the couch and flung it in Jacob's direction, using the distraction to make a limping run for the glass doors that looked out onto the yard. Jacob followed at a walk, stepping around the blood trail Benzo was leaving on the marble tiles. He fired again and hit Benzo in the calf just as the boy reached the glass doors, which Jacob had jammed shut with a stone from the garden. Benzo beat on the glass with his fist, but the doors and windows to the garden were triple-paned, installed after neighbors had complained about Benzo's late-night guitar sessions in the huge, empty house. Beyond, in the dimly lit garden, one of the escorts was resting with her head hanging back over the hot-tub rim as the other chatted on her phone, staring into her champagne glass.

Benzo sank by the doors, his legs useless. "There's fifty thousand dollars in a safe upstairs," he said.

Jacob zapped the cattle prod trigger again and smiled. "You like electricity, huh, Benzo?" he asked.

Benzo's lip twisted in a sneer. "You come over here, old man, and I'm going to snap you in half like a twig."

Jacob walked forward, gripping the cattle prod hard in his hand.

CHAPTER 24

BABY DIDN'T SPEAK TO me the whole way to Torrance. I tried to explain my perspective a couple more times, but she just sat there with her bony arms folded, staring straight ahead, her mouth locked in a pout. Her phone was bleeping incessantly in her handbag—her followers, I assumed, wanting to know whether she'd made it onto the plane. This was just a challenge, I assured myself. Baby wasn't distinctly different from any troubled teenager I'd dealt with before. She had the same wants, needs, fears. I just had to find a way in. I tried a different approach as we pulled into the all-hours storage yard emblazoned with a big green giraffe.

"Why would a kid lie about being abducted?" I wondered aloud, inviting anyone who might be within earshot to chip in.

"He said it was a prank."

"Weird prank," I said.

"I know Ash from school. He and I had like a…" She shrugged. "I don't know. Somebody told me that he liked me, but I wasn't interested at the time. He was really short."

"That doesn't sound shallow at all, Baby."

"I'm talking epic short. Like Tom Cruise short."

"Ah, you know who Tom Cruise is." I breathed a sigh of relief. "So you're not irredeemable. Ashton said Dad came through for you two? What was that about?"

"Oh, man, it was so stupid." Baby snorted. "We were all partying down on the beach, and Dad came down to hang out with us for a while. Me and some of the kids had blow. The cops showed up and wanted to frisk us, but Dad slipped them a couple of bucks and told them to hit the road."

"How old were you then?"

"Like, thirteen maybe?"

"So our dad bribed some cops to help you get away with snorting cocaine at age thirteen." I glanced over at her. "Am I hearing you correctly?"

"He was doing it too." She shrugged. "This is Los Angeles, okay? You're not in Chicago anymore."

"I'm from Colorado."

"I don't know why Ash lied about not being abducted or whatever-whatever," Baby grumbled. "Seems to me like he was scared out of his mind. If I had to put money on it, I'd say he *was* abducted but he didn't want you to know."

"Why not?"

"You're not trustworthy."

"What? How could he tell that just by looking at me?"

"You send mixed messages." She gestured to me. "The hair and the rock band T-shirt and the tattoos say *Look at me*, but everything else says you hate yourself and don't want to be looked at."

"What's everything else?"

Baby didn't answer.

"My weight?" I laughed. "You think I hate myself because I'm fat? Is that what you're saying?"

Baby shrugged again. "I don't know why you care about Ash anyway." She huffed. "You're not taking the case. You're here to mother me to death, not solve mysteries. Maybe Ash didn't really want anyone to go looking for the guy. Not the cops. Not you and me."

"Why not?" I asked, feeling tired.

"Maybe he was looking for Dad because sometimes Dad would smack a guy around if you asked him to. You know. Like sometimes people would come hire Dad not just to find a guy but to find a guy and break his nose," she said.

I massaged my brow, tired and torn between the desire to know more about my dad's life as a thug for hire and the instinct that the less I knew the better.

"Or maybe the guy's got something on Ash that Ash doesn't want the cops to know," Baby said.

"Like what?"

"I don't know—what do I look like? A psychic?" She rolled her eyes.

"Well, you were doing all right on some things. You're a terrible psychologist, but you noticed the drag marks on Ashton's shoes," I said. "You've got instincts. Observational skills. I like bouncing ideas off you. You're smart."

"Stop buttering me up," she snapped. "I'm not a piece of toast."

I laughed. My dad had always said that when I was a kid, whenever he caught me sucking up to him for treats, attention, money. Hearing the big man's words coming out of Baby's mouth tickled me.

My father's storage unit was number 66. I unlocked the door, bracing for more mysterious bags of cash or a bigger cache of weapons than the one I'd found at his office—perhaps racks of neatly arranged knives and swords, big guns in cases stacked against the walls. I was ready for a host of other surprises—illegal exotic animals, stolen gold bars, bomb-making materials.

Instead, the storage unit seemed completely empty. I switched on the light. In the center of the ceiling was a hook, and from the hook hung a thin chain. On the chain was another key. I pulled it down. There was no label, no tag.

"Goddamnit," I said.

"Chill." Baby yawned. "It's just a key. We can go now."

"This isn't good," I said.

"Why not?"

"Because the key to this unit was hidden," I said. "I found it tucked away among Dad's stuff in his office."

"So?"

"So Dad didn't want anyone to find *that* key. But on the off chance that someone did, he's got another unmarked key waiting here. Whatever he's hiding, in order to find it you'd have to find the first key to get all the way here, then figure out what this key is for to get all the way *there*. It's like a puzzle."

Baby yawned again. "Pretty stupid puzzle."

"Whatever this key unlocks, it can't be good," I said.

"Can we stop and get nuggets on the way there?" she whined.

"We don't even know where 'there' is," I said.

"Well, obviously it's in the desert. Just go back and check out the navigation system to Dad's car, see where he's been lately. Try to find something, like, desert-y, I guess."

"How do you know it's in the desert?" I asked.

She pointed to the floor, shuffled her sneakers on the concrete. There was a fine layer of orange sand scattered in a path from the door of the unit to the light, leading to the key in the center of the room. Baby let out a resigned sigh.

"He brought it in on his shoes," she said.

"Oh," I said. "Right."

"It's all about the shoes, this stuff," she said.

"Spoken like someone who's been running a successful detective agency for a decade, not a fifteen-year-old kid whose dad let her hang out with him on the job a couple of times."

"Yeah, well, maybe I'm just quick," Baby said as she walked back out of the unit. "If you're gonna keep hanging out with me, you better keep up, lady."

CHAPTER 25

THE DESERT WAS ALIVE at night. Our headlights picked up a dozen creeping, crawling, and slithering things as we rolled down a long dirt track between low mountains, an hour and a half out of San Bernardino. A rattlesnake crossed our path, skimming over the sand to the side of the road. I was drowsy and filled with dread at the idea of more surprises from my father's ghost but spurred on by a desire to see all the demons exorcised before I slept. Baby was wide-awake in the passenger seat, her face lit by her phone screen as her thumbs danced over the glass.

In a shallow valley ringed by Joshua trees, a rusty shipping container sat lit by moonlight. I checked the navigation system we'd taken from my father's car and saw that the last route visited led directly to where we now sat.

I reached over and opened the glove box in front of Baby, taking out the Magnum revolver I'd confiscated from my father's office.

"Look," I said. "Technically I'm wading into hazy legal territory here. This is not my gun. It's not registered to me.

Given the circumstances, I'm not even sure it's Dad's gun, but I—"

As I was speaking, Baby pulled a .25 Baby Browning pistol with a pink pearl-lite grip out of her handbag.

"This isn't registered to me either," she said.

I just sat there with my mouth open. She flicked the safety off the gun with an expert motion of her hand. I took the weapon from her carefully, flicked the safety back on, and unloaded it, popping the round from the chamber. I slipped the magazine into my pocket and the gun into the glove box.

"Hey, I—"

"Just don't," I said.

She threw her hands up and huffed a huge sigh.

We both exited the car. The desert air was warm and heavy. Baby might have been one of the toughest kids I had ever met, but as we neared the storage container, she closed the gap between us until she was right on my tail, her eyes big and round in the night. She grabbed my arm as I fit Dad's key into a giant padlock on the front of the container.

"What's that?"

"What?"

"Listen!"

From inside the container came a long, regular grinding noise.

The sound of snoring.

CHAPTER 26

I UNLOCKED THE CONTAINER and threw open the door. A thin man on a narrow bunk snapped awake, sat upright. The movement rattled a long chain that ran from his ankle to a D ring bolted to the floor of the container. He mussed his shaggy brown hair and shook himself into consciousness.

"What? What? What is it? What time is it?" he stammered.

"Oh, my God," I said. I walked into the container, completely forgetting Baby or the possible presence of hidden dangers as the situation unfolded in front of me. Along the side of the container opposite the man and his bunk, a long row of tables had been assembled behind transparent sheeting attached to the ceiling and floor. The tables were littered with huge steel canisters, glass flasks, beakers, tubes, and a series of machines I didn't recognize, which squatted under the tables among a mess of cords and wires.

Everything not in that section of the container was devoted to the man on the bunk: his pile of soiled clothes, his miniature refrigerator, a thrumming portable air conditioner with a tube running out of a small hole in the wall, a small lamp by the bed casting everything in shadow. I looked up and saw a camera haphazardly bolted to the ceiling just inside the door, its red light blaring in the dimness.

"What is this, Rhonda?" Baby asked. "Is this like...a sex dungeon?"

"It's a meth lab," I said. "Although a sex dungeon might have actually been preferable." I went to the man on the bunk. "Sir? I'm sorry. I'm so, so sorry. Are you okay?"

"What's happening?" His bloodshot eyes followed me as I came to unlock his chain. "Are we moving?"

"You're moving the hell out of here," I said. I prayed silently that the key that unlocked the padlock on the door fit the one on his ankle chain. It did.

"Who are you ladies?" the man said. I was surprised when he didn't bolt from the container as soon as the chain hit the floor.

"I'm..." I paused, thought about giving a fake name, but realized there would be no point after I revealed the whole situation to the police. "I'm Rhonda Bird. My father—"

"Is Earl." The man nodded. "You look just like him."

He stood and started gathering his dirty clothes into a backpack. I looked at Baby, who shrugged. The man wasn't acting like someone who'd been held prisoner and forced to cook meth for an unknown period of time in a stinky shipping container in the middle of the desert. He stuffed a stack of paperbacks into the bag, then glanced around, hands on hips, to make sure he hadn't forgotten anything important, like he was leaving a hotel room after a comfortable stay. "Can you tell me the date?" he asked.

"Ah, sure, it's…" I looked at my watch. "It's the fifteenth?"

"Oh, yes!" He laughed, pumping a fist. "Excellent. Excellent. Excellent. Five days to go."

"Until what?"

"Until the Miffy's Tornado Tower of Doom chocolate shake promotion is over," he said. "They only do it once a year. Could I trouble you to drop me at the Miffy's in San Bernardino? They'll still be open. They're twenty-four hours."

He strolled out of the container, leaving Baby and me staring after him in bewilderment.

CHAPTER 27

THE MAN WAS SITTING in the back seat of my car, staring straight ahead, when I emerged from the container. Baby was sitting in the front seat, playing with her phone. I stood on the dirt road and watched them, trying to decide if all this was some kind of dream. I had switched off all the electricity to the meth lab to ensure nothing exploded before the police could process the whole thing as a crime scene. Under the table in the lab section I'd found about six kilos of crystal meth, which I'd wrapped in a sheet and bundled into the back of the car while Baby was clicking away on Instagram. I'd add it to Dad's bathroom hidey-hole later.

"He's delirious," Baby told me as I slid into the driver's seat. "The guy says he's been in the container for about three weeks. But he hasn't stopped talking about that stupid chocolate shake the whole time we've been sitting here."

"What's your name, sir?" I asked, starting the car. "Can you tell me how you got into that container?"

"I'm Dr. Perry Tuddy," he said, watching the container disappear out the back window of the car. "Your father put me there."

"Bullshit!" Baby held up a hand. "Dad isn't a goddamn meth dealer who locks people up in the desert. This guy is crazy. Let's just dump him outside a hospital and go home. A new show I want to watch just dropped on Netflix."

"The Miffy's in San Bernardino would be much appreciated," Dr. Tuddy reminded me.

"Look, Dr. Tuddy, if I'm honest, you're not acting like someone who's just been freed from a pretty hellish situation," I ventured. "Should you lie down maybe? Baby, there's a water bottle on the floor at your feet."

"I'm fine," the doctor said. "The situation you just relieved me of hasn't been that 'hellish,' at least not in my experience."

Baby and I looked at each other.

"This isn't my first incarceration," he said finally.

"Excuse me?"

"The first time I was abducted, a cartel in Mexico City put me in a basement under a steelworks factory. It was hot, loud, damp. They kept me in the dark, like a mushroom. I caught a foot fungus down there that took me three months to get rid of after I was released," he said.

"How long were you down there?" Baby asked.

"Five months," he said. "It was my own fault. I kept resisting cooking the meth for them. Trying to escape every chance I got. Attacking the men who were guarding me. Now I just do what I'm told. I usually get let out or sold to another cartel after a couple of weeks when I've made more meth than the gang can sell. So when I get an opportunity to leave, I try to make myself difficult to find."

The car filled with silence.

Baby adjusted the rearview mirror so she could see his

face better, then took out her phone and started tapping. I drove on through the dark, trying to process all this, trying to envision my father as a cartel man. I *had* just come from his inexplicably lavish dwelling on the sand in Manhattan Beach. My heart sank in my chest.

"He's telling the truth," Baby said, flashing her phone screen at me. "There are tons of missing persons alerts on this guy. Look. 'Dr. Perry Tuddy, last seen at Walmart in Studio City, missing two weeks.' 'Dr. Perry Tuddy missing three weeks, feared dead.'"

"What makes you such hot cartel property, Dr. Tuddy?"

"Perry is fine." He was watching the desert roll by the windows, the distant highway a string of gold lights. "They want me because while I was studying for my PhD at Claremont I developed an alternative to methylamine, which is essential in the production of crystal meth. The cartels were having trouble getting hold of pseudoephedrine, so they started using methylamine because it's cheaper and easier to get. My alternative is even cheaper and easier than that. Things are getting competitive for meth dealers with fentanyl use on the rise."

"Fentanyl is stronger and cheaper than meth," Baby said, pulling a vape from her purse. "I saw that on *Dateline*."

"I was studying the effects of methylamine and some other chemicals on the brain in pursuit of a cure for Alzheimer's, not illicit drug production," Perry said. "But my discovery was culture changing. The *LA Times* ran a story about my work and how pharmaceutical companies were bidding for the patent. I was abducted for the first time a week later."

"Why the hell don't you just leave the country?" I asked, reaching over and flicking Baby's vape from her hand. She squealed and punched the dashboard. "Why stay here and keep getting abducted over and over?"

"Because Los Angeles is my home." He snorted as though the suggestion was preposterous. "I won't be driven out of my own city."

"Well, if you're so desperate to stay here, why don't you hire a team of bodyguards with all the money you made selling your recipe for metha...meffle..." Baby looked at me for help.

"Methylamine," I said.

"Meth..." She thought for a moment. "Metha-lama-lama-whatever-whatever."

"Because this is my life," Perry said. "I'm not going to go into hiding like a criminal just because I'm a genius. I'm not going to have goons shoving people out of my way everywhere I go."

I opened my mouth to reply, but I couldn't decide what to think of his comment about criminals and his own genius, and his apparently casual acceptance of regularly being abducted because of it.

A purple chrome Subaru WRX roared past us on the highway, heading in the opposite direction, green lights under the rims making it look like a spacecraft hovering just above the surface of the road. Cartel men? I quickly took the next exit before they could realize they'd just passed the women they saw on the shipping container camera liberating their captive genius.

CHAPTER 28

AT THE MIFFY'S IN San Bernardino, Dr. Perry Tuddy wrangled his tall, gangly body from the back seat of my car and walked off toward the brightly lit restaurant without saying good-bye or thanking us for releasing him. Baby hung an elbow out the window and watched him go, shaking her head in disbelief.

"Maybe he just likes being abducted," she said.

"You think so?"

"Could be kind of exciting." She shrugged. "Not knowing when you're going to get grabbed next. Always looking over your shoulder. I can see how it would make life interesting."

"Your life is pretty interesting already, Baby, from what I can tell."

"Wrong."

"You might be right about Tuddy, but those cartel guys don't mess around," I continued. "It's only a matter of time before they stop playing catch and release with the good doctor. You know what they say. It's all fun and games until someone winds up in a mass grave outside Tijuana," I said.

"They say that? Who says that?" Baby said. "Anyway, he's wrong about Dad. He was a genuine asshole, but he wasn't a crook."

I didn't have the heart to break it to Baby that clearly our father was as much a stranger to her as he was to me, even if she had spent the last thirteen years living with him. Instead, I rolled out of the parking lot and switched on the radio. A news broadcast was just beginning.

"...*of the eighteen-year-old has not yet been ruled a homicide, but LAPD officers have issued an urgent call for witnesses who might have seen a white van in the area of Trousdale Estates.*"

"Trousdale Estates," Baby said. "That's in Beverly Hills."

"White van," I said, turning up the radio.

CHAPTER 29

IT WAS THE MOMENTS before the raids that Vera liked the most. When all the preparation had been done, when she had run the choreography through in her mind a hundred times and had nothing more to do than enjoy the beautiful dance as it began on the stage.

Vera had recognized the same electric excitement in her father and his friends on the nights he held meetings beside the pool at their lavish home. Vera wasn't stupid. She'd known from age thirteen that her father was in the Russian mob and those meetings were probably about killing someone. Those were the only times when a bunch of guys ever got together so quietly, without drinks, without food, without women. She'd watch from her bedroom on the second floor, but never heard anything. She just knew. It was the whites of their eyes, their heads bent close together, mouths working fast as a plan was formed. A week later, there was always a funeral. Big floral wreaths and lots of serious handshakes.

The whites of their eyes. Ashton's were big and almost blue against his dark pupils in the night. They were gathered at the back of Vera's car in the dark beneath a huge oak tree as she handed out the voice-distorting mouthpieces, which they pulled over their heads and tightened with straps behind their ears like gas masks. They always distorted their voices when they hit the house of someone they knew.

"Where's Benzo?" Vera asked, switching on her headpiece. Her voice came out deep and robotic. "Did anyone get an answer yet?"

"He probably just forgot," Penny said. "Benzo's been sweating over some stupid yacht he's trying to buy from up in San Fran. I told him two yachts is enough for anybody, but he wouldn't listen. Nobody ever listens to me."

"What?" Sean nudged her. Penny slapped at him.

"He's never missed a Crew meeting before," Ashton said. "And he always answers. I think we should abort. This isn't right. And hitting one of our teachers? It's too risky right now. It's too close to home, and with everything that's been—"

"We're not aborting," Vera snapped. The other three watched her, eyes bugging. "I've been looking forward to this one. We've done all the research. If Benzo misses out, that's his fault. Bitch needs to learn how to set an alarm."

"Yeah, let's do this." Penny high-fived her twin brother. "I've been ready to hit that smart-ass prick Mr. Newcombe forever."

Vera pulled a skull mask over her mouthpiece and tightened the straps on the wrists of her gloves. The excitement was hammering in her now, a hot, heavy thumping of her heart behind her ribs. Her Midnight Crew had hit twelve homes, and the raids were always good—but they were even better when she picked the target.

Vera's science teacher, Mr. Newcombe, was constantly dropping hints that he knew about Vera's father. Asking if Vera's dad had any tattoos, if that old Viggo Mortensen movie *Eastern Promises* was accurate. A couple of months earlier, Mr. Newcombe had been reading a newspaper while the class worked through exercises from their textbooks. On the front page had been a story about a cocaine shipment arrest at LAX linked to the Russians.

"How are things at home, Vera?" he'd asked, grinning, flipping the page of the newspaper suggestively.

Vera didn't know if the teacher wanted to be a part of her father's world or if he was simply lording over her that he knew about her criminal family. Whatever the case, she didn't like it. She had the feeling Mr. Newcombe wanted her to feel small. She'd known teachers like him before, men who'd been picked on in school and who now spent their days punishing the popular and powerful kids in their classes as revenge. Vera was going to make him feel small that night. She was going to make him feel like the lowliest of creatures.

CHAPTER 30

THEY TURNED ONTO Mr. Newcombe's street and approached his home. Vera nodded to Sean as he clipped the wires on the neighbor's surveillance camera, so the device wouldn't catch them going in. Ashton and Penny were breathing hard, making their voice-distorting devices growl quietly. Vera led them down the side of the teacher's house to the back porch, where Ashton set up a mobile jammer on the railing to block the signals of any devices on both floors of the house. Vera took the key she had copied from Mr. Newcombe's set, which he regularly left on his desk in the classroom throughout lunch, and slipped it into the lock of the back door.

This wasn't like the jobs they'd done in rich suburbs like Palos Verdes or Brentwood, where they'd had to overcome security patrols, infrared cameras, guard dogs. Darrel Newcombe's teacher's salary provided locks on the doors and not much else. Their biggest obstacle had been ensuring Newcombe's neighbors on all sides would be out on the night of their entry, so no one would hear their activities and call the cops. Having each household coincidentally win tickets to a one-night-only performance by Neil Diamond at the Hollywood Pantages Theatre had taken care of that.

The house was dim and silent. Ambient light that would usually have been generated by electronics was gone, but Vera had cut school the day before and taken a tour of the man's house, memorizing the path to the stairs. She'd stopped to look at a framed photograph of Newcombe and his boyfriend on a skiing trip in Austria on the walk up the stairs. She tapped it gently as she passed now.

"I want this," she said. She glanced back. Ashton's silhouette nodded in the light from the porch window. The four of them slipped quietly into Newcombe's bedroom and stood around the bed where two sleeping men lay, one of them snoring raggedly. Vera inhaled. She smelled skin lotion and used sheets, air freshener from the adjoining bathroom. Intimate smells. She had invaded Newcombe's most private space and stood now relishing what was about to happen as something instinctual roused the teacher from his sleep and his figure twisted in the sheets.

"Wha—what?"

The crew pounced on the men in the bed.

CHAPTER 31

IN VERA'S EXPERIENCE, MOST people didn't try to flee or fight when presented with a situation as sudden and terrifying as a home invasion.

They froze.

Mr. Newcombe and his boyfriend did just that. Vera ripped the sheet from the bed, exposing their naked bodies, and after some initial surprised yelping and scrambling, the men went stiff and silent as Penny, Sean, and Ashton dragged them out of the room and down the stairs. They hardly resisted being cable-tied to the heavy dining room table. When the men were secured, Penny and Sean dashed away to indulge their violent fantasies—Penny grabbing objects off the shelves and smashing them on the tiles, pulling down curtains in the living room, while Sean crudely scrawled "FAGGOTS" on the wall with black spray paint. Sean probably thought he was being clever, seeing as he was gay himself, throwing the authorities off the trail by making it look like this was a hate crime. Vera decided any opportunity Sean got in his life to feel clever was a rare occurrence, so she let it go. Ashton smashed open the frame on the wall in the stairwell and ripped the picture out, stuffed it into his backpack.

The men were splayed across the tabletop, one at each end, their wrists bound to the upper joints of the table legs. Vera watched Mr. Newcombe struggle for a while. His body was smooth and hard, surprisingly beautiful, something that had always been a mystery to her in the classroom, underneath his boring plaid shirts and Walmart trousers.

"Darrel Newcombe," Vera said, leaning on the table. The two men looked at her, wide-eyed, and she smiled beneath the mask. "Yeah, this is about you, asshole. This is about you believing you're better than the people who have to obey you. We're here to teach you that you're a lowly little worm. At any minute one of us could decide to squash you."

Sean and Penny raced up the stairs, laughing. Vera heard the floorboards creak above her as they jumped from one piece of furniture to another like little children, springing onto the bed, playing games.

"See," Vera said, drawing a small silver revolver from the back pocket of her jeans, "there are people who have power, Darrel. And there are people who *think* they have power."

"Whoa," Ashton said. He was frozen midstride in the kitchen, the broom he had been using to knock items from shelves gripped in his hand like a club. "What the hell is that?"

Vera released and pushed open the revolver's cylinder. She drew a small handful of bullets from her front pocket, showed Mr. Newcombe the objects in her hand. She loaded one, two, three bullets into the six slots in the weapon and spun the barrel.

"Hey, hey, hey." Ashton rushed toward her. "Where did you get that?"

Vera held the gun to Darrel Newcombe's temple. Ashton stopped. The teacher was sweating and whimpering. Across the table, his boyfriend had burst into sobs behind his tape gag.

"We're not doing this." Ashton's robotic voice was deep and hard. "We never—"

Vera pulled the trigger.

CHAPTER 32

THE GUN CLICKED.

"Oh, my God!" Ashton dropped the broom.

Vera laughed. Her voice came out through the modifier in a terrifying cackle. "Ah, God! Did you feel that?"

Ashton watched in horror as Vera spun the chamber of the gun and snapped it shut again, held it to her own temple.

"We have the power, you understand?" she asked Mr. Newcombe. "We were born with it. It's real. You want to see it again? Watch this."

She pulled the trigger. The gun clicked. Her whole body twitched with excitement, terror, a relief that was almost sexual.

She spun the barrel again.

"Stop! Stop! Stop!" Ashton grabbed for the weapon as she put it back against the teacher's head. He managed to knock it away as she pulled the trigger, and a bullet smashed into a cabinet by the stairs. Ashton let Vera's arm go, and she pointed the gun at him, his black mask identical to the cardboard targets she was so used to obliterating at the firing range.

The room was swirling, dancing in her vision. It was joy. Pure joy, the unpredictability of it all, the clash of possibilities. Live. Die. Kill. Spare. Destroy. Consume. Burn. The wheel was going round and round. What would happen next? She was shivering with excitement, just trying to account for all the possibilities. *This* was what Vera had come here for. The punishment and the possibilities. The game of chance and will.

"What the hell is going on?" Penny asked from the stairs. She and her brother had barreled down at the sound of the shot.

Vera lowered the gun. A decision made. A path chosen. She was ready for her next ride.

"Let's go." She swung an arm and they followed, as she knew they would.

CHAPTER 33

MORNING CAME TOO SOON. At the Denny's on West El Segundo, I ordered the Grand Slam with extra pancakes and sat making phone calls, one after another, dealing with my suddenly abandoned life back in Colorado and the present situation in Los Angeles. Baby ordered black coffee. She sat sipping it while I smothered my pancakes with maple syrup.

"You eat this kind of thing every day?" she asked when I was off the phone, her eyes wandering over the spread in front of me.

"Only when I've just had a 120-pound orphan dumped on me."

"*Excuse* me?" She scoffed and looked around in case someone had heard my overestimation of her weight. Baby turned her phone camera toward her face and touched a hand to the fashionable headscarf that dangled over her shoulder.

"I'm adjusting to my life as a mother," I continued, ignoring her. "I need the energy."

"You're not my mother," Baby said.

"I've got a piece of paper that basically says otherwise."

"If you skipped breakfast a few days a week you'd lose weight," she said. "Intermittent fasting. Google it."

"Did you body-shame Dad too, or am I just lucky?" I asked.

"That's different," Baby said. "It's okay for guys to be fat."

"Excuse me," I said to the server as she topped up my coffee. "Could you please tell me what year it is? My daughter here thinks it's 1959."

The two of us shared an eye roll.

"I'm not your daughter," Baby said after the server left.

"Look at this," I said, pushing a newspaper toward her. The Los Angeles *Daily News* had a little more on the murder of Derek Benstein than we had heard on the radio the night before. The eighteen-year-old, pictured beside a huge yacht, had been shot dead in his home while two female "acquaintances" were outside. The women had discovered the body and raised the alarm with police. Witnesses mentioned seeing an out-of-place white van without plates parked two blocks from Benstein's house.

"Whoa." Baby sighed. "I knew that guy."

"Oh. I'm sorry."

"Not well. We were at school together. Never shared a class or anything."

"Could the 'acquaintances' have been people you knew?" I asked.

"No. Hookers," Baby said, perusing the article. "They always say 'acquaintances' when it's hookers."

"How do you know that?"

"One time Dad went night swimming down the beach after a big party at the house. He was really drunk. Five female *acquaintances* left over from the party had to go in and pull him out of the surf." Baby slid the paper back to me. "It made the news."

"What eighteen-year-old has hookers over to his mansion on a Thursday night?" I asked.

"Benstein and Miller are, like, the biggest film agents in LA," Baby said.

"When I was eighteen, I was going to slumber parties at my friends' houses and watching horror movies in my pajamas," I said.

"That one hundred percent doesn't surprise me," Baby said dismissively. "What were you doing at fifteen? Playing with dolls?"

I went quiet. At fifteen I'd been a huge professional wrestling fan and had used my birthday money to buy action figures of all my favorite wrestlers.

"Oh, my God," Baby yelped when I didn't answer.

"They weren't dolls, they were collectible figurines." I huffed. "Try to focus. We've got two eighteen-year-old rich kids targeted in the same week. White van at both incidents."

"Hmm."

"Do me a favor." I pointed to her phone on the edge of the table. "Find out if Derek Benstein and Ashton Willisee are friends on Facebook or Instagram or whatever the hell."

Baby fished around on her phone while I gripped the edge of the table, waiting for her answer. It was clear now that my curiosity was piqued over what had happened to the kid I had seen in my father's office. Why had he lied to protect someone who had apparently tried to abduct him? Was it the criminal investigator in me, my propensity to want to learn the truth and see justice done whenever I could manage it? Or was it just that I sensed this investigation was something Baby and I could do together, a project we could share that might bring us closer?

"Bingo," Baby said, showing me her phone screen.

I saw Ashton Willisee's picture beside an image of the brawny and taut-faced Derek Benstein.

In the parking lot, Baby stopped by my Buick, still playing on her phone.

"So thanks for the free breakfast and all, but I've got to roll," she said, tapping away. "Places to go, people to see— you know how it is."

"First of all, that wasn't breakfast," I said. "You consumed exactly zero calories in there. We've still got Dad's funeral to organize, and I need your help with—"

"Black carriage with horses," she said. A purple chrome Subaru WRX was pulling into a space behind her. "He always said he wanted a black carriage pulled by six black horses for his funeral. That's all I know."

Of course Dad had told Baby about his funeral plans. It was one of a million conversations he'd chosen to have with her and not with me over the last decade and a half. A spark of anger flared.

"Are you kidding me?" I sighed, snuffing it out. "A carriage and horses? This is present-day Los Angeles, not Victorian England."

"You'll figure it out." Baby sighed. "Call a movie set or something."

"I want to look into this Willisee and Benstein thing," I said. "There's something there."

"Not my problem," Baby said. "I gotta bounce."

I was about to tell her she wasn't going anywhere, but her retreat was halted by a force much more persuasive than mine. She turned and slammed into the chest of a big thick-necked guy in a black shirt covered with roses. Three more men emerged from the purple Subaru, which I recognized from last night. They were all around us before I could even begin to form a plan of escape.

"Rhonda, right?" the big guy said to me. "We want to talk to you."

CHAPTER 34

I TOOK BABY BY her impossibly small biceps and pulled her backward, away from the huge lug in the ugly shirt. The four guys seemed to be attendees of some kind of bad shirt convention. Embroidered roses, lilies, and hibiscus flowers adorned lapels and cuffs all around us. And the poor aesthetic choices didn't end with fabric and car paint. The guy closest to me had a gun tattooed on his right cheek, the barrel edging on the corner of his mouth.

"I'm Martin Vegas," the big one said. "We've got a problem."

"You bet we do," I agreed. "Baby, get in the car."

"No way." She stuck close to me, as she had in the desert, her hip and shoulder against mine as though my physical bulk could protect her. Her voice dropped to a murmur. "I'm not leaving you alone with these guys."

"What are you gonna do?" I murmured back. "Unfriend them to death? Get in the car." She didn't budge.

"We can probably skip right to it," Vegas said. "We're friends of Earl's. Or at least we were. I understand he passed away a couple of days ago. Sorry to hear it."

"Yeah, you guys look real torn up about it," I said.

"We are torn up. About losing not only Earl but our very talented cook too." Vegas was looking Baby over. "Tuddy was hard to obtain. He's very in demand. A real asset. Your dad played a big part in bringing him in, and now the two of you have undone that arrangement."

I tried to stifle the fear and dread running through me at the mention of *your dad*. I could imagine how these men pieced together that Baby and I were connected to Earl—we'd been seen on a camera likely monitored by the cartel at the shipping container, and freed their meth cook, after all. It was even reasonable that Vegas could know my name—Baby had probably mentioned it in the container. But if Vegas knew we were Earl's *daughters,* it meant he probably knew everything. He would know I was staying at my father's house. He would know about my job in Colorado. He would know I was the only adult in Baby's life. And those were very dangerous pieces of information for drug cartel guys to have in their pockets.

"Well, we won't waste your time," I said, pulling Baby toward the car. "You must be anxious to go find Tuddy again. Good luck. Last time I saw him he was on a Greyhound bus to Seattle."

I stepped back. The assembly of men moved around us. One of the guys leaned on the passenger-side door of my Buick, preventing me from shoving Baby in. I found myself wishing I had let her go to Milan after all.

"Tuddy will show up again," Vegas said. "What we're anxious about now is getting our money and product back."

"We don't have that stuff," Baby said. Her voice seemed impossibly small and squeaky in the circle of big men.

"Yeah, we do," I corrected her.

"What?"

"I took all the meth from the shipping container," I said. "And about three million bucks in cash from Dad's office in Koreatown."

"First, why the *hell* would you do that?" Baby slapped at me. "And second, why the hell would you admit all that *right now*?"

"They'll figure it out eventually. They're rubbing at least two brain cells together, although probably not much more." I glanced around the circle of guys. "And I took that stuff because I didn't have a full grip on the situation yet. That's what I do in my job. I gather all the pieces together and hold on to them until they make sense."

"Well, now you've got a grip," Baby said. "So give the guy what he wants before his goons kill us. My Wikipedia page can't say I died in a Denny's parking lot!"

"Goons?" the guy with the gun-mouth tattoo said.

"Sorry." Baby pulled her head in like a turtle. "I meant, like, helpers?"

Gunmouth glared at her.

"Henchmen?" she squeaked.

"I could probably accept henchmen," he grumbled.

"Look," Vegas said. "We're offering you an opportunity to put things right here. We're businessmen, okay? We don't like losses, either of assets or useful relationships. I don't know what you've seen on TV about the Mexican drug cartels. But we're not like that."

"You're not?" I glanced at the purple chrome car and the roses on his shirt.

"We're not," he confirmed, oblivious to my scrutiny. "We're practical people. So your father didn't brief you on what you were supposed to do when he died. That's okay." He waved a consoling hand. "Not your fault. No need for things to go sour between us. Just give us our stuff back, and we'll all move on from this."

"No," I said.

Vegas blinked in disbelief.

"You might have read *Business Ethics for Dummies* cover to cover, but that doesn't make you any less of a drug-peddling scumbag," I said. "I don't know what I'm going to do with the meth or the money. But I do know I'm not giving it to you."

All the air seemed to go out of Baby at once. She wavered a little by my side. I didn't. I held strong, because someone my size does that—stands steady and as immovable as a sea cliff, ready to take the brunt of a storm before it ravages the land.

Gunmouth moved first. But I wasn't far behind him.

CHAPTER 35

BABY'S HEADSCARF WAS THE perfect handle. Gunmouth went for it, grabbing it like the end of a rope. I covered his hand with mine. My hand was bigger; my fingers squeezed his like a mitt around a baseball. One of the most useful things you can have in life is good grip strength. You can punch, kick, and scratch at an adversary as much as you like, but if they latch on to you and you can't get them off, you might be in for some serious damage. I had learned that lesson the hard way, trying to intervene in a fight between two teenage girls in the courthouse waiting room one morning. One of the girls latched on to my arm like a cat on a tree, her nails digging in. It took three bailiffs to get her off. I still had scars from the claw marks.

Gunmouth's eyes widened as I increased the pressure on his hand. In less than a second, something in his hand made a dull pop sound. He screamed. I held on. Baby was wailing, bent double, her hair and scarf enclosed in our two fists.

I kicked out as another guy came for me, a sideways donkey-style kick to the side of his knee. Another crunch.

His leg bent at an unnatural angle, and he released a guttural scream. I squeezed Gunmouth's hand one last time, heard another pop, and let him go.

Two men on the ground, wailing, two standing looking very unsure of themselves—Vegas and his only remaining henchman, who looked less than enthused by the prospect of attacking someone who had broken three bones in three seconds. Vegas wasn't going to lower himself to a physical fracas. His *Business Ethics for Dummies* reading would have told him that physicality is power—he needed to stay high and proud, as reliably rigid as a skyscraper.

I knew they were thinking about drawing their guns, but the windows of the Denny's beside us were now crowded with people, some filming on their phones, others probably calling 911. We all knew the smartest thing for Vegas and his crew to do was make a hasty retreat.

"Get in the car, Baby," I said a final time. She slipped into the vehicle, and I got in after her, refusing to make eye contact with Vegas as he glared at us all the way out of the parking lot. I didn't need to see his hateful gaze to know what it communicated: that he would be back in my life sooner rather than later.

CHAPTER 36

JACOB SAW NEINA IN the hospital cafeteria. Hurt and confusion flashed over her face, because he hadn't come right to the room where Beaty lay slipping away, maybe dying. He had gone to the cafeteria instead.

He'd done it because the food fueled him, and he needed strength before facing his child. Killing Benzo had done to Jacob what he'd expected: both invigorated and drained him. His first life taken in twenty years. He'd watched the beat of Benzo's heart stop suddenly, a vital irrigation system shut off, the traffic of blood cells through the boy's body stilled. In that moment he'd felt the great relief of sating his rage for a moment—as well as the overwhelming terror that one of these days he might see the same switch flicked off in his daughter. There'd be no going back and punishing Benzo a second time.

He could kill them all, but he couldn't save Beaty. That fact had lit the fire of Jacob's rage again in seconds.

"How long have you been here?" Neina asked. She'd crossed the colorless space in front of the sandwich counter and stood with her head down, looking miserable. He reached for her, but she folded her arms across her chest.

"Ten minutes. I just needed a coffee."

"Where the hell were you all night?"

"I went home," he said. "Cleaned the house a little."

"We don't need a clean house. We need our daughter."

Jacob didn't know what to say to that, so he said nothing. Neina was used to it. Over the years, he'd always shut down if she asked about his past, about the scars all over his body, about the things he said in his sleep.

She wasn't stupid. He could have found a stupid wife in any city in the world, but he'd chosen Neina because of her lightning-fast wit and her strong, gifted hands. He'd seen her through the window of a pottery school in Studio City, teaching a bunch of retirees how to turn cereal bowls on a wheel. On their first date, she'd made him laugh, a rare and wonderful thing for him: the loss of control, the sound fluttering from between his lips.

Around them, the cafeteria bustled with families of the sick and injured wandering in, eating, wandering out. But they were still, the two of them standing there: Jacob determined to move ahead into the darkness, Neina determined to call him back into the light.

"Come up and see her," Neina said. "Hold her hand."

"I will," he said. "I'll just finish this."

He gestured to the half-drunk coffee on the table. But her eyes went to what was beside it. The newspaper showing the image of a dead teenager, squad cars outside a mansion nestled behind tall palm trees.

Neina was smart enough to know that Jacob had done bad

things in the past. And, very likely, that he had begun to do them again.

"Leave the coffee," she said. She put a hand out. "Come."

He didn't take it. He couldn't meet her eyes.

When he looked up again, she was gone.

CHAPTER 37

"YEAH, SOOOOO," BABY SAID in the car. "Can we, like, make a deal?"

"I'm listening," I said.

"Can you maybe tell me the next time you're going to break a guy's hand? Like, maybe give me some warning?"

"It's not something I usually spend a lot of time planning," I said.

"Where's the money?" she asked.

I laughed.

She folded her arms and huffed. "What, you think I'm going to take it all, drive to Vegas, and have a wild time?" she asked.

"That does sounds like something you would do." I shrugged. "That or spend it all on teeny-tiny handbags."

"Seriously, though, you bust into my life all, like, *Hey, Baby, guess what? You can't do this. You can't do that. You're too young. You're too irresponsible.* Then you go and steal from a Mexican drug cartel?" She threw her hands up.

"I wouldn't say *steal*. I prefer *confiscate*."

"Those guys chop people's feet off," Baby said. "I read the news. The police in Mexico City just found a big barrel full of feet last week on the side of the highway. Just feet! Nothing else."

"What do you want me to say here, Baby?"

She shook her head but didn't answer. Traffic was backed up on the 105 heading east toward the 110. Palm trees stuck up like ragged black fingers out of the sea of warehouses and car lots. The Hustler Casino was advertising unlimited garlic bread with dinner Friday through Sunday.

"If you're not going to give the cartel their stuff back, what *are* you going to do with it?" Baby asked, cleaning her huge sunglasses on the hem of her tank top.

"I don't know yet."

"Why don't you give it to the police?"

"Because the police will want to know where I got it," I said. "And the answer will implicate our father in a major criminal enterprise."

"So? What do you care?" she asked. "The guy's dead, and you hated him anyway."

"How do you like the idea of being homeless?" I said, gesturing to a homeless encampment on the strip of land alongside the freeway. Under a crumpled blue tarp strung between eucalyptus trees, a woman was giving a toddler a bath in a plastic tub. "If the police think Dad was a drug dealer, they can take the house. They can empty his bank accounts. They can take anything he owned."

Baby just stared at the homeless mother and her child.

"And I didn't *hate* him," I said, hearing the uncertainty in my tone. "He just...He abandoned me."

Baby snorted.

"What?" I felt anger rising in my throat.

"'He abandoned me,'" she repeated. "That's kind of dramatic, isn't it?"

"It's the truth," I said. "I haven't seen the guy since I was thirteen years old. That's twenty-five years. A quarter of a century. He had me cash in some stocks that were in my name, then he dropped me at my mom's house and disappeared. He didn't even tell me he was leaving. He didn't even say good-bye."

Baby shifted uncomfortably in her seat. The words were spilling out of me suddenly, my palms sweaty on the steering wheel.

"Twenty-five years," I said. "That's twenty-five Christmases that passed without him trying to reconnect with me. Twenty-five birthdays. He missed my high school graduation. He missed me learning to drive. He wasn't there when I got my first boyfriend."

"Okay." Baby held up a hand. "I get it. I get it."

We fell into a long, uncomfortable silence.

"If it makes you feel any better, he didn't come to any of my school functions either," Baby said eventually. "And a couple of boys from the beach taught me how to drive before I got my permit."

I strummed the steering wheel. Her words had actually made me feel a little better, but I didn't want to acknowledge that I was jealous of Baby. In my mind, her relationship with our father was just peachy, everything I'd always wanted to have with him. I imagined he'd been supportive of her. Encouraging. Loving. Interested. But the more time I hung around with Baby, the more I was learning that Earl had been a problematic father figure for her too. I felt her sharing my pain, even though I knew it was probably a complicated issue for us both.

I turned onto the 110, following the signs for Downtown LA.

"Where are we going?" she asked.

"Back to school," I said. "I think some kids are being hunted."

CHAPTER 38

BABY SAID NOTHING AS I punched into the GPS the address for Stanford-West Academy, which I remembered from the out-of-place bumper sticker on Ashton Willisee's Mercedes.

The huge wrought-iron front gates looked impressively secure as we drove up—but all it took was some vague mumbling about being a lawyer, here to see Ashton Willisee, before the bored guard rolled back the gates without question.

I drove through the immaculate campus grounds, past rolling sports fields, toward large cream buildings nestled among lush green trees. My lovingly restored 1972 Buick Skylark's leopard-print paint job stood out among all the high-end automobiles parked in the lot next to the school's administration building. I figured I'd have more trouble in the school office, but at the first mention of the word *attorney,* the receptionist simply pushed a button and asked someone on the other end of an intercom to track down Mr. Willisee. She let her eyes wander over me, but I couldn't tell if she was appreciating my System of a Down T-shirt or giving me the Fat Person Look-Over. Baby tugged at the bottom of her impossibly small denim shorts as though she could somehow extend them down toward her knees.

"A lot of lawyers come through here?" I asked the receptionist.

"Sure do," she said with a yawn. "About five a day. Lawsuits mostly. These kids are always suing someone, or someone is suing them." As she turned back to her computer, I could see a game of solitaire reflected in her glasses. "School hours are the best time to meet with child clients. Can't pay the maid to listen in here."

Baby and I exchanged a look at the receptionist's candor. Before long, Ashton came around the corner of a long hallway chewing his nails and watching the floor pass beneath his feet, his mind obviously elsewhere. Being called into the school office was obviously not a novel experience for him. But he stopped short at the sight of Baby and me.

"Oh, no." He shook his head. "Nope. No. We're not doing this."

"Five minutes." I held up my hand. "We're here to help you."

Ashton didn't even look at the receptionist as he gave the command, "Call security."

"You can give them five minutes," the receptionist shot back. "System of a Down fans are good people."

"Rock on." I flipped her the sign of the horns.

Ashton didn't put up much of a fight. He walked quickly to a cafélike area off the administration building that was enclosed by walls of bright pink bougainvillea. Students were sitting clustered in groups, ignoring one another as they tapped on phones or laptops, little white earbuds plugging their ears. The space was eerily quiet.

"I remember when a bunch of kids being together meant noise," I said, trying to lighten Ashton's mood. "All I hear now are computer keys."

"So you're old," the boy said, sliding onto a chair across from us. "Get over it."

"What happened to Derek Benstein?" I asked.

"Who?" Ashton folded his arms.

"Don't try to bullshit us." Baby rolled her eyes and huffed, teen code for the lameness of the situation. "The two of you are all over social media together. You guys posted about eating at Soho House, like, yesterday." Baby waved her phone.

I was silently thankful and awed at young people's propensity to let the internet know exactly what they were doing at all times.

"Okay, so?" Ashton snapped. "My friend was murdered. I don't know anything about it. I wasn't with him at the time, and I don't know who did it. What do you want from me?"

"Is that what you'll be telling the police when they eventually get around to you?" I asked.

"Sure is."

"So you're going to claim it had absolutely nothing to do with your abduction two nights ago?" I asked.

"I wasn't abducted!" Ashton gave an angry laugh. He took out his phone and fired off a text so fast I barely saw the movement. "God, you're, like, obsessed with me, lady. Don't you have anything better to do than try to get all up in my life?"

"Not right now," I admitted.

"Well, that sucks for you," he said.

"I don't think so. This is what I do." I could feel Baby's eyes on me. "Everything about you is screaming *I need help,* and it has been since the moment I laid eyes on you."

Both Ashton and Baby fell into stillness, silence. Ashton broke himself out of it by glancing at his Rolex.

"I don't have time for this," he said. "Look, Benzo was a friend of mine, and what happened to him is, like, really fucked up, but he was into a bunch of bad stuff, okay? He was using really rare black-market steroids and stuff to get big. The kind of stuff you can only get from criminals. He probably tried to rip off his dealer and got shot."

My phone rang. I glanced at it, planning to ignore it, but the call was coming from my legal office back in Colorado. I excused myself and walked a few feet away to take the call, knowing I had cases that needed reassigning. Baby and Ashton sat sullenly slumped in their chairs. When the call ended, I pretended to type out an email, my ears pricked for their conversation. I knew it was helpful to allow myself to be seen as the bad cop at times, to let them align with each other against me. I hoped they would get real with each other the way teenagers sometimes can without the presence of adults. I found myself smiling as Baby attempted to do just that.

"My life is crazy right now," Baby said. "I did *not* see it coming, Dad dying on me."

"Heart attack?"

"Yeah," Baby said. "Good guess."

"Wasn't hard. He was always yelling, those veins in his head popping out."

"I still pick up my phone and try to call him." Baby sounded sad. "I tried to call him just this morning, all like *Dude, you've got to help me. This crazy chick is trying to take over my life*. It's like he's still around."

"Are you trying to relate to me right now because Benzo's dead?" Ashton asked. "You think that's going to work? I don't even know you anymore. And I don't know that bitch at all."

"Rhonda's pushy," Baby said. "I get it. Try spending days with her. I'm about ready to blow my brains out."

"What is she, like, your mom or something?"

"No way." Baby sounded offended. "Umm, does she look like she could be my mom?"

"I don't know. Maybe."

"She's my sister," Baby conceded. "Kind of. Half sister. We have the same dad. She turned up when he died. She's here from, like, Chicago or something."

Or something, I thought, exhausted.

"Maybe she's exactly what you need right now, though," Baby said. "Someone you don't know."

"What?"

"If there's nobody in your life who can help, maybe it's going to take someone from outside to save you," Baby said.

"That is some Hallmark-level bullshit right there," a new voice said.

I turned and saw a girl with white-blond ringlets approaching the table. She was dressed neck-to-knees in expensive black silk, immaculate leather ankle boots, and a handbag that was three times the cost of my car. She let the bag fall on the stones beneath the table like it was a sack of trash.

It's not often that I feel the wave of dizzying heat and electricity that seems to come with purely bad people, but I felt it now as I stood before this nameless girl. Every animalistic sense in my body went on alert.

Big trouble had just arrived.

CHAPTER 39

SOMETHING CHANGED IN ASHTON. Though he maintained his slouch, his spine seemed to stiffen, drawing hard on the tendons in his neck.

"And what are you doing back here, Teacher's Pet?" the girl asked Baby.

"Don't." Baby turned and glanced at me, her eyes wild. "Just leave it, okay?"

"What's going on here?" I asked. I gestured to the new girl and Baby. "Do you guys know each other?"

"No," Baby said. "We don't. And I think we're done here, Rhonda."

"Are you sure?" the girl asked. "Because what you've been doing is harassing my friend here about his buddy, who was brutally murdered yesterday. He's traumatized and emotionally vulnerable, and you're questioning him without warning, consent, or police presence."

She waved a hand at the chair nearest to me.

"Please, take a seat," the girl said. "Stay longer. Minute by minute you're racking up millions in a civil lawsuit for emotional damage caused by you violently bursting in to interrogate him over his friend's murder."

"Fine," I said. "We're done here, Miss..."

"Miss Go Fuck Yourself." She smiled.

Baby and I left the blonde with Ashton and headed back to the car, Baby sticking so close behind me, she kept stepping on my heels.

"Baby, you need to give me some space," I said. "You're just about climbing into my back pocket."

"Don't stop," she said, glancing back like we were being chased.

"Jesus. If I'd known you were this twitchy I'd have come here alone."

"Yeah, well, I didn't think anyone except Ashton would recognize me." She smoothed back her hair. "I had braids then, and I'm about a foot and a half taller now, and my skin is so much clearer. Australian pink sand exfoliating scrub. You should get on that."

"Uh-huh."

"It's been two years. Things change so fast around here I figured everybody would have forgotten," she said.

"About what?"

"Just drop it, Rhonda."

"This is *the thing* you and Ash were talking about in the hallway outside Dad's office. You hadn't seen him since *the thing*. What happened?"

She didn't answer.

"I'll google it."

"Yeah, only if you're a nosy, invasive, obsessive bitch, you will," Baby snapped.

"I *am* a nosy, invasive, obsessive bitch." I shrugged.

Baby didn't respond. When we reached the car, I unlocked the doors, and she silently slipped into the passenger seat, her coldness telling me the discussion was over.

I got in and turned the key in the ignition.

Sparks zapped and zinged along the base of the bench seat beneath us.

"Oh, *shit!*" I said, as flames burst from the floor of the Skylark and began to coil around our ankles.

CHAPTER 40

"WE'RE DEAD," ASHTON SAID.

Vera yawned and took out her phone to text the twins. She and Ashton were the only Midnight Crew members who still attended high school. Penny and Sean had technically graduated, though their disregard for formal education had increased as the time until their trust funds kicked in dwindled. And Benzo had never been an academic. His parents had basically bribed his teachers to pass him every year since kindergarten, until they'd given up in embarrassment halfway through high school.

"We're not dead, Ashton. We're fine."

Vera needed to rally her people. A meeting would be required with the entire posse over Benzo's murder. Excitement was coursing through her, but she needed to maintain a nonchalant air with Ashton, the most panicky of their number. The coward might interpret the thrill Vera now felt as fear unless she presented herself calmly.

"I know a guy who lives across the street from Benzo."

Ashton leaned in, gripping the tabletop with white knuckles. "He said they brought him out on a stretcher, and he could see marks on one of Benzo's legs. Like, weird bruises."

"Maybe he was tortured." Vera shrugged. "Pay one of your therapists for double sessions for a while. You'll be over it in a couple of months."

"If I'm not dead by then!" Ashton said. "How are you not losing your mind over this?"

"Because whoever we're dealing with, they're stupid," she said. "He came after the weakest members of the group. First, he tried to pick off your pussy ass outside the theater. Somehow, incredibly, he fucked that up. Then he went for the second biggest loser, Benzo. If he really wanted to take us down, he should have gone right for the snake's head." She tapped her chest.

"So you're admitting you were wrong? That this is someone we've hit with the Midnight Crew and not just something random?" Ashton said. "It's someone who wants to take the whole crew down. Someone who wants revenge."

Vera gave him a dangerous look. He sunk back in his chair.

"Now that we know he's after us," she continued, "we'll be prepared."

"Right. So we'll get out of town." Ashton nodded. "We can go to my mom's place in Aruba, wait it out there. Penny and Sean's aunt is, like, in the FBI, I think. She can track this guy down, try to pin him with something that has nothing to do with us. She did it for that twenty-five-year-old guy Penny was seeing. Remember? She didn't ask any questions. She just zeroed in and nailed him with bank fraud. This shouldn't be hard for her. We can provide her with a list of everyone we've hit, and she can figure out which one of them is the goddamn psycho."

"You've been working on that little plan all morning, haven't you?" Vera reached over and gave Ashton a condescending stroke on the shoulder. "You must be tired."

"Come on, Vera."

"We're not running from this asshole," she said. "My people don't run."

"Your people?" Ashton asked, but even as the words left his mouth he seemed to want to snatch them back from the air. Vera's father, Evgeni Petrov, was thought to be somewhere in New Jersey, living under an assumed name, being protected by allied factions of the Russian and Armenian mobs. Vera wasn't stupid—she knew it looked to everyone else like he'd run away from bad debts and underhanded deals inside the mob. But her father had done this many times before over the span of her life. He went underground, dug in, raised his hard back against his pursuers, and took the worst against his unbreakable spine. Then when things settled, he rose and attacked. It wasn't cowardly. It was smart.

"We're going to find this guy ourselves." Vera lifted her bag and slung it over her shoulder. "We're not kids anymore. We deal with our own problems."

Ashton stepped in front of her as she turned to go, blocking her path. She was impressed with him for challenging her, holding her glare. Ashton had always been weak; Vera liked having weak people around her. They were malleable and predictable.

"This is getting out of control," Ashton said. "*You're* out of control. You brought a gun to the raid last night. That's against the rules—rules that *you* came up with. This thing that we do—it only works because we all know the boundaries."

Ashton poked her in the shoulder. Vera's eyes narrowed.

"You said from the beginning, 'No one gets hurt,'" Ashton continued, seemingly thriving on the terror and exhilaration of finally asserting a bit of power in his miserable little life. "You also said, 'If we ever get found out, we back away, go underground, come up with a smart plan.' This isn't smart, Vera. This is reckl—"

Vera grabbed Ashton's balls through his tight jeans and squeezed slowly. Ashton bent double as his mouth slammed shut.

"I'm saying something different now," Vera said. The people around them were all looking up from their screens, tugging earbuds from their ears. "And you better listen carefully, because I make the rules, and they've changed."

CHAPTER 41

I LUNGED SIDEWAYS AND grabbed the handle of Baby's door. In one movement I barreled us both out of the car in an awkward, painful roll just as the front of my car exploded.

The ball of flames quickly consumed the engine and led to a second explosion. I felt the sonic boom of the blast in the ground beneath me, as the cars all around us bounced on their suspensions, the windshields of two or three of them dissolving into showers of glass.

I knew Baby was screaming, but I couldn't hear it. For what felt like a long time there was only ringing in my ears as we crawled into the middle of the parking lot, out of the reach of the flames.

As I dragged myself to my feet, Baby hung off me by her fingernails with one leg wrapped around my waist and her armpit smooshed against my mouth. I had to peel her off and place her on her feet, where she stood trembling and watching the car burn.

"What happened?" she wailed as my hearing sucked

back into functionality. "What happened? What happened, Rhonda? What did you do?"

"What did I do?" I brushed singed pieces of fabric off my shoulders. I could feel the warm California breeze through the holes in the back of my clothing. "I pissed off a Mexican drug cartel, that's what."

People were rushing out of the administration building. Where once they might have run toward us to assist, the sight of the burning car had everyone bolting in the other direction, disappearing back into the building almost as fast as they had emerged. Unexpected and dangerous events on school grounds, explosions included, meant active shooters to these people. Baby and I stood alone, watching the flames, as sirens began to wail from the buildings around us.

"All right, listen up," I told Baby. "We've got to get our story straight."

CHAPTER 42

JACOB KANULAR PUT DOWN his sandpaper and blew the sawdust off the surface of the jewelry box. He had begun teaching woodworking at the community college five years earlier, when Beaty started kindergarten—his days had felt empty without her crashing and bashing playfully around the house. A lot of the young men and women he taught were underprivileged high school dropouts or juvie regulars, but he'd run a tight ship from day one. He'd refused to let anyone go at the end of class if the workshop wasn't up to scratch. For a couple of weeks, this had resulted in a lot of complaining. Slowly, however, it had made for disciplined and organized students who put tools on racks and brushed off machines, swept the floor until it was bare. He stood now in one of his immaculate classrooms, working at an otherwise spotless bench.

The box he was making for Beaty had a big knot right in the center of its lid. A lot of people who worked with wood would have called the placement unsightly. But Jacob liked knots. This one was a dark circle coiling in on itself, narrowing to an unseen eternity. His old teacher—a guy in Alaska whose body he had eventually fed into an industrial mulcher—had taught him that knots formed when the trunk of a tree thickened and enclosed the base of its branches, expanding over any lower branches that had dropped off, sometimes because they had been starved of sun. To Jacob, the scarred lumps inside the stretching, yawning, living tree were representations of the beauty in imperfect, lost, fallen, unrealized things. Many a branch that eventually formed a knot had begun to grow in a certain way and was interrupted, killed, banished to darkness. While others grew, these branches were sacrificed.

He knew Neina was there long before a less dangerous man would have. He'd heard her footsteps among the dozens of others moving about as classes broke for lunch outside his empty room. A lifetime of hunting men had given him that ability, and while the ability had lain dormant for many years, Derek Benstein's death had gotten the old machine running again. He smelled her too as she entered the doorway. The scent of hospital soap, trying to combat days spent at a darkened bedside.

She tried to sweep the box off the counter as she came in, but he slammed a hand down on its lid before she could. When her gesture failed, she took aim at his face, smacking Jacob hard. He bore the blow silently and stiffly, though the predator inside him ruffled like a disturbed bird of prey.

"She showed brain activity," Neina said. "And you weren't there."

Jacob smoothed the box with his hands. He took up the sandpaper and turned the object on its side, rubbing down the front of the lid.

"What was it?" he asked.

"A small electrical pulse in the amygdala," Neina said. "The...the primal control center of the brain. Less than a second. But they got it. It was there."

"If her amygdala's working and not much else, she'll wake up a vegetable," Jacob said.

That got to her. Neina threw herself at him, raged against his chest. He grabbed hold of her until she stopped.

"What the fuck is *wrong* with you?" she screamed.

He couldn't even begin to explain. Something had always been wrong, he supposed. There was a door in his mind, and behind it, nightmarish things lived. He'd discovered the door as a teenager, when his mother and brother were crushed between two semitrailers in a car accident. From then on, he'd begun opening the door and tossing hurtful and violent and disturbing things behind it, until he realized as an adult that those things hadn't disappeared. They had grown and twisted together and spawned new things.

Whenever he opened the door and let the things out, he could commit deadly acts, like pushing a man he respected and loved into a wood mulcher or ignoring his child in her hospital bed.

"I know what you're doing," Neina said.

"You couldn't possibly know," he said.

"Oh, you'd be surprised," she said. She was standing apart from him now, brushing off her bare arms as though his touch had made her dirty. She didn't say any more, but he could sense the rest of it. *You'd be surprised what a woman can tolerate, ignore, deny.* She straightened. "They asked me today if you're beating me."

He said nothing.

"One of the social worker types. She was very discreet," Neina said. "She gave me a card with a number to call. Told me to hide it. Other people can see it in you now. They can see that you're dangerous. You think perfect strangers can see it and I can't?"

"It's nothing for you to worry about," he said. "Go back and sit with Beaty. I'll be done soon."

"This isn't what I want," Neina said. "I want my family back together."

He knew she was crying, but he wouldn't look. Jacob began sanding the box again.

CHAPTER 43

BY THE TIME THE SWAT team had evacuated the school and handed the parking lot crime scene over to the local police, it was sunset outside the Stanford-West Academy. Baby sat on the curb with her chin in her hands, her phone for once forgotten in the handbag at her feet. Neither Ashton nor Miss Go Fuck Yourself had been among the crowds that eventually came around to gawk.

I'd offered a range of explanations about the Buick Skylark's explosion to the officers who'd approached me as the hours passed. I'd feigned flat-out confusion. I'd claimed the car was possessed by an angry demon, or by the ghost of my deranged father. My words initially managed to shut down further explorations by the authorities of what had happened. The men and women who dealt with the scene seemed simply relieved that there had been no one seriously injured.

While I waited for another round of questioning, I stood in the corner of the lot and watched a forensic photographer unload equipment from his car. Sometimes it's the people on the sidelines, those quiet, unobtrusive workers, who offer the most assistance when working an investigation—the photographers, crime-scene sketch artists, cleanup crews, and junior officers who work crowd control. I had learned from many years of experience looking for witnesses and new angles on my cases that these people were far more useful than the higher ranking, more "important" people involved in solving a crime.

I approached as the photographer was clipping a lens to the front of the camera hanging around his neck.

"Ma'am." He smiled, showing bright white teeth. "How many dead?"

"None," I said.

"Oh." He seemed a little disheartened.

"It's my car that exploded." I pointed. "So I'm having a terrible day. How do you like the idea of doing a favor for a woman who could use some cheering up?"

"Depends on what it is." The guy smirked.

"You must know some other crime-scene photographers in town, right?"

"Sure." He shrugged. "Couple of guys I know who work up north."

"Do you know who worked the shooting in Trousdale Estates last night? The teenager?"

"Maybe." He shrugged again. "Why?"

"I'm just interested in those pictures."

"You a journalist?" he asked.

"Maybe." I mimicked his shrug. I reached into my pocket and pulled out my wallet. I'd taken some cash from the three-million-dollar bundle of trouble now hidden in my father's bathroom. I fanned them discreetly for the photographer. "Does it matter?"

"Nope," the photographer said. He had the money and my business card smuggled inside his chest pocket in a flash. This was someone used to making the maneuver. "I'll get in touch."

I headed back to the smoking wreck of my car. I knew I was in trouble when a new officer approached. He strode toward me across the lot in what was the most formfitting police uniform of the day, a pitch-black outfit that hugged his enormous muscular frame. It was obvious that Los Angeles police officers had a thing about appearances. I'd seen a number of them check their reflections in the cars around me while they guarded the wreck of my vehicle.

Officer Summerly's name badge gleamed in the setting sun, making me squint as he stood squarely in front of me. This didn't seem like a man who was going to be as easy to manipulate as the crime-scene photographer. He was not going to be easily brushed off with strange tales about the explosion like his fellow officers had been.

"Okay." Summerly took off his cap and wiped sweat from his temples with a stark black handkerchief he had taken from his trouser pocket. "Let me hear it."

"Ejector seat," I said.

"Excuse me?"

"The car is a retired stunt car," I lied, looking at the smoking wreck. "Or it was. The car was mechanically altered in preparation for a small film that was supposed to be shot in Watkins, Colorado, in 1993. *The Adventures of Leopardo Smith.* You ever hear of it?"

"Wha—No." Summerly shook his head like he had water in his ears.

"Leopardo was a spy. The ejector seat was a security measure, for if he was ever cornered by villains in his car," I said. "There was a whole scene scheduled where a henchman would attack him from the back seat, and he'd shoot to safety. I bought the car off the lot when the film's funding was withdrawn. I guess after all these years the mechanism exploded. Maybe the heat here in Los Angeles set off the...the ignition plugs, or whatever." I shrugged helplessly.

Summerly scratched his blond, neatly shorn hair. He put his cap back on and breathed in deeply.

"Lady," he said. "That's the most incredible thing I've ever heard."

"I know, right?" I laughed. "Lucky no one was injured."

"No, I don't mean incredible like amazing." Summerly put a hand up. "I mean incredible like *in-credible*. You say that's a stunt car? It had an ejector seat that accidentally exploded? You expect me to believe that?"

Summerly waited. I didn't respond. He turned and pointed to the officers milling around behind him.

"See that officer over there? Name badge says Hammond?"

"I see her," I said.

"She says you told her you ran over a can of gasoline."

"It's possible I said that." I nodded.

"That officer over there by the tree says you told him your car was possessed by a malevolent spirit." Summerly pointed.

"Mmm-hmm." I nodded again. Baby was listening carefully from the curbside.

"That officer tells me you stated to him that you'd accidentally filled the steering fluid valve with plant fertilizer," Summerly said.

"Yes," I said.

"And for me"—he gave a frustrated laugh, tapped his chest—"you come up with this . . . this *ejector seat* tale?"

"I saved the best for last," I said.

"What really happened here, Miss . . ." He jutted his chin at me.

"Bird. Rhonda."

"Bird." He clicked the top of a shiny black pen, slipped a notebook from his chest pocket. He set the pen to the page. "From the beginning."

"No comment," I said.

Summerly lifted his eyes from the notebook. I noticed that they were the color of dark chocolate.

"Are you kidding me?"

"No," I said, putting my hands in the pockets of my tattered jeans. "I have no comment for you. I don't have to make a statement on what happened here today. I wasn't even legally obliged to give you my name. But I did, because I'm nice."

"Oh, God." Summerly sighed. His whole body deflated slightly. "A lawyer."

"That's right."

"Your car exploded in a school parking lot, Miss Bird," Summerly said. "You have to tell us what happened."

"No, I don't," I said.

"Yes, you—"

"Are you going to charge me with a crime?"

"Hell yeah, I am." He laughed again. He took a pair of gleaming handcuffs off his belt.

CHAPTER 44

SUMMERLY BRANDISHED THE CUFFS in one hand. "Unless you tell me who blew up your car, then, yes, I'll charge you. This is... uh. Well, it's public endangerment, at least. *Child* endangerment. It's probably a misuse of explosives. It's lying to police."

"I haven't lied to the police."

"All of your stories are conflicting!"

"Well, how do you know I don't believe they're all true at the same time?" I shrugged. "I might be crazy. Traumatized. Concussed. You would have to prove my intent to purposefully deceive you in a court of law to make that charge stick, Officer Summerly."

Summerly opened his mouth and closed it again, glancing around the parking lot as though looking for help. He shook his head and laughed again. I liked the sound of his laughter. It was heavy and husky and strong.

"You've caused a lot of damage here to other vehicles, to that building over there," he said.

"An accident on private property," I said. "Not a criminal

act. My compensation of the Stanford-West Academy for the damages I may've caused is between me and them."

"Miss Bird, when I examine this car—"

"You don't get to examine my car," I said.

"What?" Summerly squinted.

"I don't give you permission. And under the search and seizure laws of this state—"

"You can't be serious. It's a piece of evidence."

"Only if there's a crime," I said. "So I'll ask you again. Are you going to charge me with a crime?"

Officer Summerly's eyes wandered over my face. I could see his mind whirling, trying to find an out. I'd cornered him. He took a step closer and lowered his voice, beckoned me into a two-man huddle. I went willingly.

"You know what I think happened here?" he asked.

"Please tell me." I smiled.

"A couple of months ago," he murmured, "Danny Trejo and Benicio Del Toro, I think it was, were in this action movie where they played Mexican cartel guys. Their signature move was to rig explosives under the driver's seat in people's cars. I saw the movie. Good movie."

I waited, listening. I could smell Summerly's sweat after a long day spent rounding up the bad and the ugly in Los Angeles.

"Bombs in cars haven't ever been a cartel thing in real life," Summerly said. "The IRA used to do it, across the pond. And the Italian mob used to do it back in the sixties. But ever since that movie came out, there's been a rash of copycat car bombings all over the southwest, as far east as Arkansas."

"Okay." I shrugged. "So what's that got to do with me?"

"Are you tied up with a cartel, Miss Bird?"

"No comment." I smiled.

Summerly backed up. He took off his hat again and fanned his face.

"Look, Miss Bird, it has been a long, hot shift," he said. "My last stop was a dog stuck in a crawl space under an industrial oven in a bakery. I'm dirty, sweaty, hot, and tired. I just want to go home."

"So go home," I said. "There's no crime here. Your presence is no longer required."

Summerly gave up. He took a card from the back of the notebook and slapped it into my palm. DAVID SUMMERLY.

"When you're ready to talk, call that number."

Baby appeared beside me as Summerly departed. She caught me checking out the officer's ass as he walked away.

CHAPTER 45

"YOU WERE INTO THAT guy," Baby said as our Uber turned off onto the Pacific Coast Highway toward Manhattan Beach.

"Oh, please." I snorted. "I'm a lawyer. Any mystique or allure men in uniform might've had for me wore off many years ago."

"Not *that* guy in uniform," she said.

"Don't be such a smart-ass."

"What? He was into you too, I think," she said. "I feel like I know him from somewhere, but I don't know where. Anyway, he seemed nice. And he's a good size for you. You'd need a big guy. He was built like a tank. I clock you two."

"I'm going to ignore your incredibly rude comments about his physical size in comparison to mine, as though that means anything at all about our romantic compatibility," I said, "and instead ask what you mean by 'I clock you two'?"

"Like, I think it's a good idea, you two being together," she mused. "Clocking something means you like it. I don't know where it comes from. Maybe it's like 'It's time for that to happen.' You could say 'I clock this handbag' and mean 'It's time for me to own this handbag, bitch!'"

"'I clock this,'" I said. "I like it. I'm going to start using it."

"Don't."

"Why not?"

"You're too old," she said. "And by the time you say it to anyone, it'll be over. People won't be saying it anymore, and you'll be even more lame."

I massaged my brow, trying to recover from being called fat, old, and lame within a single minute.

"Oh, my God." Baby sat bolt upright in her seat as we turned onto the street where my father's house sat in the row of luxury homes before the water. "There are people in the house. There are people in the house!"

CHAPTER 46

THERE WERE INDEED PEOPLE in the house. Inside and outside. In the upper window I could see a woman in a green uniform vacuuming. Three men were hauling trash toward the curb, where a neat row of twelve other garbage bags stood by the road.

"Oh, my God." Baby leaped from the car before it had even stopped rolling. "Who are they? What's happening?"

I got out of the car and chased her down. I put a hand on Baby's shoulder. "Relax. I hired a crew to come in and clean the house. The place was a bomb site."

Baby whirled around and looked at me, her eyes filled with horror. Then she took off into the house through the open door as though the place was on fire and she had to save a family of orphans inside. While I paid the cleaners and sent them on their way, she remained upstairs somewhere. I surveyed their work on the living room. My father's house had been rid of the stench of cigar smoke, stale whiskey, and rotting food that had infested it when I first entered, now smelling of floral cleaning products. There were no nameless sleepy teens in sight. The enormous kitchen benches were bare and gleaming, where clutters of pots, pans, plates, and bottles had once sprawled over them. I heard Baby come down the stairs and emerged to find her standing trembling on the spotless rug in the middle of the foyer.

"Are you okay?" I asked.

"They went into my room," she said shakily. Her eyes were huge, brimming with rageful tears. Her teeth were locked. "*They cleaned my room.* How. Could. You. Do. This?"

"How could I…" I laughed, confused by her reaction. "Baby, the house was filthy. It was like something out of *Hoarders*. There was a pancake stuck to the wall of Dad's shower. A *pancake*. When we were here earlier, I saw something scamper out the window. A possum or a raccoon or…I don't know. Normal people can't live like this."

"They touched my stuff," Baby said. "All my stuff. All my clothes are—"

"Yeah, I saw your clothes," I said. "I glanced into your room while the door was cracked open. There was three feet of clothes on the floor in there. Another month and you'd have to get around the room with a snorkel and flippers."

"You *fucking bitch*!" Baby barked.

"Whoa!"

"You don't touch my stuff," Baby screamed. Her voice was raw and wild. "You—or your cleaners or anyone associated with you—you don't ever, ever, *ever* touch my stuff!"

Baby stormed out the back door and slammed it so hard behind her that the windows looking out over the Strand shook. As she crossed away from the house, a Rollerblader with a Weimaraner on a leash almost slammed into a lamppost trying to get out of her way. I stood stunned for a long time, looking after her, then climbed the stairs to her room. With the kind of reverence reserved for an ancient temple, I crossed the threshold and stood inside on the Hoover-tracked carpet. The closet stood open, overpacked with washed, folded, and hung clothes that were threatening to burst from the shelves and hangers. The space had clearly never accommodated all of Baby's clothes at once. There was a desk against the window overlooking the distant surf that was neatly arranged with things the cleaners had had no clue what to do with: ornate candle holders and notebooks, piles of oversize sunglasses, hair clips, old iPhones with their tangled chargers.

I looked at the room around me and tried to imagine what was so precious that Baby would flip out with the kind of shock, panic, and dismay she had failed to demonstrate when we were almost killed in a car bombing only hours earlier. When I saw nothing that answered my question, I left the room and closed the door with a strange sense of certainty that I would end up paying for what I had done to the teenage girl whether I understood it or not.

CHAPTER 47

ASHTON KNEW THAT SEAN and Penny's driver was named Tom. He'd heard their father call him that. The twins had been driven around by the same withered, white-haired man since Ashton first met them at some Brentwood mansion pool party, their parents getting drunk in cabanas while the kids were taken out for gelato by the help. Ashton remembered climbing into the big passenger cabin of the limo with the smirking, pointy-faced twins and a handful of other kids. They rode all the way to Venice Beach, young Ashton trying to work out how much richer the Hanley family was than his. He'd listened while Penny bragged about the private jet her mom had bought her for her twelfth birthday. The jet's interior was all pink suede.

Ashton glanced through the darkened privacy screen of the Mercedes-Maybach S650 Pullman while they were stopped at an intersection. He'd never heard Sean or Penny call him anything but Driver. He wondered about Tom's life as a private driver to a pair of spoiled rich brats, shepherding Penny from nail salon to hairdresser to laser facial rejuvenation clinic, picking up Sean from The Abbey at 2 a.m. with coke all over his face. He wondered if Tom questioned his existence, the fairness of Sean and Penny's place in the back of the vehicle and his in the front.

Ashton sure questioned it. He questioned his own place with the two. He questioned the dangerous, humiliating games they liked to play. They played them so often that Ashton could see them coming a mile away. He watched Penny's attention prick up as they approached Lincoln Park Skate Park. Tom had gotten stuck behind a Hummer, and Penny was eyeing a small kid moving back and forth down the main skate run.

"Have a look at this little shit, will you?" Penny said.

Ashton and Sean followed her gaze. The boy, maybe eight or nine, was doing complicated flips of his skateboard at each bank of the run while a gaggle of other young kids cheered him on from the sidelines. Penny ordered Tom to pull over, just as Ashton anticipated she would.

The twins watched the boy on the run, and Ashton watched the twins. Ashton saw a flicker of something in Penny's eyes. Hateful, jealous admiration. Penny hated anyone demonstrating a hard-won skill. Her apartment downtown was cluttered with broken toys she had taken up on a whim, ruined dreams of playing the violin, mastering archery, oil painting, dressmaking. If Penny wasn't immediately an expert at something, she gave it up. Ashton had once seen her purchase a seventeen-thousand-dollar electric guitar signed by Dave Navarro that she left untouched in one of the spare rooms of her apartment for a year before having it taken to the dump.

Penny rolled down her window.

"Oh, come on." Ashton huffed. "We've got to meet Vera."

Penny ignored him. She called out to two lanky teen boys heading for the skate park with boards under their arms.

"Hey, you! Yeah, you. Come here."

The boys approached the car. The teen with tight, curly hair bent his head to look in the window.

"We ain't carryin', lady."

"I'm not looking for drugs, you idiot," Penny barked. "Are you kidding me? This is a six-hundred-thousand-dollar car. You think I have to buy my coke from two dumb-ass kids in a skate park?"

The teens looked at each other. Ashton's phone buzzed. Vera was asking where they were, impatiently sending her location, on the corner of West Fourth and South Main. He didn't know what made him more nervous: leaving Vera hanging or whatever Penny was planning to do with these kids.

"I want you two to go over there." Penny pointed. "See that kid on the skate run? The little one flipping his board? Go get his hat. Bring it back here to me."

She pulled a roll of cash from her handbag, peeled off a hundred, and waved it at the boys. The teens didn't need to think. They took off running. Ashton watched them intercept the small boy on his way back up to the top of the run, pushing and bullying the boy until he relinquished the hat.

The boys returned, laughing guiltily. Penny handed them the hundred-dollar bill and tossed the hat onto the floor of the car.

"Okay," Ashton said. "That's enough. We gotta go."

"Back off, Ash," Sean said. "We're just having fun."

"How much for you to go back and punch that kid in the face?" Penny asked the boys.

"What?" One boy laughed. "You serious? We can't do that."

"They can't do that," Ashton agreed. "Penny, leave them alone."

"I've got...ten grand here." Penny fingered the roll of cash. "I'll give you five hundred dollars for every time you hit him."

The boys glanced sideways at each other. Ashton could see scars on the knuckles of the one nearest to him, perhaps from neighborhood fights, working after-school jobs, or playing sports. He'd seen movies about kids from bad neighborhoods who skated or surfed or rode bikes to blow off steam, aggression from a bad home life, from parents who worked three jobs and still couldn't afford to put food in the fridge. His own hands were perfect, soft. Truth was, Ashton couldn't guess how another teenager got scars on his knuckles. He didn't know how they lived. He cracked his window to listen as the boys backed off and murmured to each other.

"Dude, we could just hit him once."

"Or twice, even."

"If we're gonna hit him twice we might as well hit him a bunch, yo."

"He's pretty small."

The boys looked back at the group of little kids at the top of the run who were now consoling their friend over his stolen hat.

"Are we really gonna do this, man?" the curly-haired kid asked.

"Don't be pussies," Penny said.

The boys conferred again. Ashton saw hopelessness in their eyes. Already feeling remorse for what they were about to do. What they couldn't help but do.

"Five hundred per hit?"

Penny smiled and nodded. The boys ran off across the park. Ashton sat back in his seat and watched the beating unfold, the fists raining down.

"You guys are fucking sick," he told the twins. Sean and Penny ignored him. In the front seat of the car, Tom was staring straight ahead as he always did, watching the sun set behind the smog. Ashton wanted to speak up, to ask Sean and Penny what they enjoyed so much about the violent spectacle they had created across the park. But the truth was, he knew. It was the same thing he enjoyed about the Midnight Crew games: the power, the danger, the vengeance. Ashton didn't know where the anger came from, but he felt the white-hot pleasure of release when he smashed the possessions of their victims, when he knocked over bookshelves and tore down pictures and lit things on fire. Ashton's life was full of pretty things. Expensive things. Cars and bikes and toys and gadgets, designer clothes, watches. It was as thrilling to accumulate the stuff as it was to break it. To Sean and Penny, it seemed, people were stuff too. That was the only difference.

Penny waited until the boys had finished beating the little kid and turned back toward the car, their faces hungry and fists smeared with blood. The other smaller kids had bolted from the park. The talented skater was on the ground, unmoving. The teens started jogging back toward the vehicle like happy dogs ready to receive their treat.

"Now drive," Sean said. "Quick, before they get back. "Go, Driver. Go!"

Tom started the engine. Penny and Sean erupted in laughter. Ashton saw the teenagers' mouths fall open as the car rolled away into the growing night.

CHAPTER 48

VERA SLIPPED INTO THE car and dropped her hand-bag onto the console beside her, tossing her shopping bags from boutique jewelry stores onto the floor. She threw a look around the limo's cabin that made the teens writhe in their seats at their lateness.

Sean lifted his pointy nose in the air, wouldn't meet her eyes. "We just had a little game on the way here," he said.

"A little game?" Ashton scoffed. "Benzo is dead, there's some kind of sicko after us, and these two wanted to play blood sports with grade-schoolers. We need to be really careful right now."

"Don't talk like you're in charge here, Ashton." Vera gave a thin smile. "You sound like an idiot."

Ashton worked his jaw, letting seconds pass as he recovered his dignity. "So what do we do?"

"We hit another house," Vera said.

"What?" Ashton cried.

"Yes." Penny was nodding eagerly. "I'm with you. I was thinking the exact same thing, Vera. We go hard this time.

Break some bones. Show this dumb fuck that he shouldn't mess with us."

"Shut up, Penny," Vera said. "This competition you guys seem to be having to sound like the biggest simpleton in the car is really getting on my nerves. The plan is we hit another house. We set a trap, lure this guy out."

"This is insane." Ashton shook his head.

"He must be following us," Vera said. "He's probably been following us from the moment he took Ashton's phone. He most likely emptied the phone of everything he needed before you could shut it down. He'll know who we are, where we live. He'll have all our videos. That's why we can't go to the police or to any lame-ass private investigators." She gave Ashton a withering look. "Tomorrow morning, we split up and try to shake him off. Then we come together again and make sure he's following us to the next raid. While he thinks he's watching us, we can get a good look at him."

She took out her phone and tapped away.

"I'm sending you a list of suspects," Vera said. Ashton felt his phone buzz in his pocket. "This is every male victim we've had in the last year prior to Mr. Newcombe, except for that banker we hit in November. He's in rehab."

"Did we do that?" Sean smirked. "Did we drive him to drink?"

"Maybe." Vera gave a rare genuine smile of camaraderie. "He's the guy who pissed himself, right?"

"What if it's not one of the guys we actually hit?" Ashton asked. "What if it's a relative of one of our victims? Or a friend? Or someone they hired?"

Everyone was looking at their phones. Ashton sighed at their silence.

"What is your plan, exactly?" he continued. "Once we find out who's after us?"

"Simple," Vera said. "We grab him, make him tell us exactly what he's got on us, and then we destroy everything. Cover our tracks."

"And then what?" Ashton asked. "What do we do with the guy once we have him?"

"We kill him, of course," Vera said.

CHAPTER 49

ASHTON LAUGHED. BUT EVEN to him, it sounded forced. He could see glitter dancing in the twins' eyes. They loved this kind of talk.

"We're not killing anyone," Ashton said. "That was never what this was about. The Midnight Crew is about having fun and blowing off steam, maybe scaring some people, messing with them. That's why *I* joined, anyway."

"You joined because you were angry," Vera said. "Your uncle made mincemeat of your aunt's overpriced nose job at Thanksgiving and you wanted to feel like the big man for once. Now that you've righted things in your family, you're not as angry at life." She threw her hands up. "Well, good for you, asshole. Targeting your uncle, going to psychotherapy, popping some Prozac and doing your mom's bullshit mindfulness trash has cured you. That doesn't mean you get to walk away from what we've done here, what we *are*. You can't abandon the Crew because you've lost your motivation all of a sudden. You know what that's called? That's called desertion."

"Treason." Sean nodded. "Going AWOL. You do that in

war and the army guys will put you up against a wall and shoot you."

"Don't pretend you're some kind of hard-core military guy, Sean," Ashton said. "You spend a grand a month on pedicures and anal bleaching."

"Who are we hitting?" Penny bounced in her seat. "I'm ready to go. This guy killed Benzo. We're going to find him and cut his balls off."

"You hated Benzo!" Ashton pleaded.

"It doesn't matter who we hit," Vera said. "As long as we move fast. We need to focus on damage control rather than get bogged down with the logistics."

She stopped to think for a moment, watching the downtown stores roll by the window. "There's a woman on my street with this dog. A little terrier. It barks at me every time I walk by. They'll do. We go tomorrow night."

CHAPTER 50

THAT NIGHT IN MY deceased father's house was a long, exhausting one. Still rattled from the fight with Baby, I'd spent the first few hours after she stormed out sitting in the spotless living room, texting and calling her in vain. I'd lain awake until 3 a.m., when I heard her come in. She'd ignored me on her way to her bedroom, barefoot and trailing sand on the tiles, slamming the door in my face when I tried to talk to her.

In the morning, Baby's bedroom door was still shut tight. I wandered to the rooftop of the massive house and discovered a large swimming pool stretching over its expanse. To the right of the door opening onto the roof, by a row of weather-beaten lawn chairs, stood a rusty and unused home gym draped with old, stiff beach towels.

I've been lifting weights since I was ten years old. My dad had set up a small gym in our home garage in Watkins with a treadmill and a set of dumbbells. My mother had been too gentle to guess that my father's sudden interest in getting into shape was a sign of his infidelities.

I wandered in one morning and saw him struggling to bench fifty pounds, the bar shaking and tilting, only inches from his nose. I rushed in and grabbed the bar, helped him get it up and into the rack. Like the proud, shallow, self-involved idiot that he was, he was embarrassed and instantly banished me from the garage. The banishment effectively turned his gym into a forbidden and alluring destination for a young and lonely me.

As I perused the free-weights rack next to the pool, the sensation of being watched prickled over my skin. I looked over and noticed that on the roof of the adjacent French chateau–style house, a place that appeared to be under some renovation, with scaffolding erected in the gap between the two homes, a group of tanned, long-haired men in their early twenties were crowded around their own gym equipment, keeping a careful eye on me.

I jutted my chin at them in what I intended as a friendly but tough manner, the kind of greeting two dudes might throw across a public gym. Three of the four didn't respond. The fourth put a foot up on the lip of the roof and glared at me. I guessed the fat chick playing with weights on the roof next door made a mockery of everything they stood for out there in the sunshine—health, strength, physical masculine beauty, pushing their bodies to the limit, like a bunch of modern warriors training for some unforeseen combat. I wasn't welcome here, even on my own rooftop.

One of the dudes loaded his bench press up with 220 pounds, glancing over at me as he made some comment to his bros. I went over to Dad's bench press and loaded it up with the same. As I sat on the bench, the guy lay back and pumped out five fast reps. I did the same. The bros laughed. One of them pushed his friend out of the way and loaded up another 80 pounds. I watched him work five slow, perfect reps. I loaded my weights up to 300 pounds and did the same.

Confusion hit on the opposite rooftop. The bros huddled. I sat listening to the distant waves, feeling quietly smug. While I waited for them to formulate their next move, I picked up a dumbbell and did some biceps curls.

The biggest of the bros began loading up the bench press bar. I stood and mimicked him, loading as he loaded, selecting weights as he selected them. The numbers climbed: 360, 380, 400, then 440 pounds. The big guy struggled through three reps, his whole body trembling and mouth pulled taut, baring his teeth. I cracked my knuckles, but before I could lie down, one of the dudes came to the edge of the roof.

"Don't be stupid, lady!" he yelled. "You'll hurt yourself!"

"We'll see!" I yelled back. I went to my bench. I loaded on another 20 pounds. The guys gathered at the edge of the roof and folded their arms—concern for my safety, or their own reputations, written on their stern faces.

I pumped out five slow, careful reps. My arms trembled. My chest felt hot, tight, the muscles working and straining. I felt my cheeks grow warm. I pumped out a sixth rep and heard the guys erupt in moans of awe as I fit the bar back into the rack.

I don't know what else I expected. A round of applause, maybe. A smile. A wave of admiration. But I got none of that. The guys took in my display, then turned and left the rooftop without another word or gesture, like they'd heard some kind of alarm and were evacuating.

I was alone only a moment before Baby stepped out through the big glass door leading onto the roof.

"We need to talk," she said.

CHAPTER 51

"I INVADED YOUR SPACE." I put my hands up. "I totally get it."

"No, you don't get it," Baby said. "Because as far as I know, you've never had someone walk into your life and turn absolutely everything you freakin' know upside down, including your own goddamn bedroom!"

"It needed to be done," I said. "You and Dad were living like pigs. But I should have consulted you. Or given you a chance to—"

"Don't try to side with me." Baby seethed. "I'm pissed at you. *So* pissed. So pissed I can hardly breathe, and you don't get to-to-to . . . to spray water all over my fire!"

I tried to stay silent, tapped my foot. But the words bubbled up.

"You know what, Baby," I said. "I *have* had someone walk into my life and turn absolutely everything upside down. That person was you. I've never been a mother before—do you understand that? I have no idea what I'm doing here!"

"How many times do I have to tell you? Get it through your thick skull. You are *not* my mother!"

"Well, I'm something." I shrugged helplessly. "You can't have nobody in your life taking care of you, Baby. You're a *child*."

"See, Rhonda, this is what you do," Baby sneered. "You fall back on that 'You're too young' bullshit whenever you're losing an argument."

"Well, it's true!" I said. "And I'm not losing this argument. It's not even an argument! You're just yelling at me!"

"You're yelling back!" she howled.

"I know!" I covered my eyes, took a breath. "Urgh. I know."

"I'm going to get you, Rhonda," Baby said.

"You're going to *get* me?"

"Yeah. I'm going to show you exactly how childish I can be."

She stormed off again. I reached out and caught the glass door before she could slam it, or lock me on the roof. I saw her walking down the stairs with her phone in her hands, texting furiously.

"Storming off during an argument is childish enough!" I called. "Even though it's not . . . It wasn't . . . Urgh! Baby, we can fix this. Come back and we'll fix this!"

No answer came back up through the layers of the huge house. My phone buzzed behind me on the workout bench. I picked it up. It was warm from the sun. In my email, a message with no subject header was sitting in the in-box from a name I recognized. I opened the zipped file attachment in it, and a trail of photographs began downloading. In the first, I saw the twisted dead body of Derek Benstein lying beside a darkened glass door.

CHAPTER 52

SANTA MONICA PIER WAS crowded with people slowly shuffling shoulder to shoulder, a loose parade bound for the end of the structure jutting out into the vast blue sea. Past the roller coaster and Ferris wheel, a huge, pink Styrofoam cup had been erected midway between the Bubba Gump Shrimp Co. halfway down the pier and the Marisol Mexican place at its end. The cup towered over the crowd, and an enormous straw, maybe twenty feet high, wavered in the gentle breeze off the sea.

I positioned myself on a bench by the pier rail between two sets of fishermen and watched the crowds looping slowly around the giant cup, receiving their free Miffy's Tornado Tower of Doom chocolate shakes. I analyzed every face, straightening once or twice at the sight of extremely lean men with dark glasses. It was three hours before the right man came along. I'd already gotten myself two Tornado Tower shakes, both of which sat drained on the bench beside me.

Dr. Perry Tuddy was hiding from the blazing sun under a ball cap wedged onto a tattered blond wig that was tied in a ponytail. I sidled up to him, and he flinched at the sight of me.

"Oh, dear." He expelled a resigned sigh. "Back to the container, is it?"

"That's all the fight you put up every time these guys come to abduct you?" I asked.

"Well, I'm not the kind of person who tends to kick and scream."

"You're not even going to try to run?"

"How am I going to run without spilling my shake?" He gestured to the counter, three customers ahead of us. I tried to answer but couldn't begin to approach that kind of logic.

"I'm not here to stuff you into a van," I said. "I need your help with something else. Grab your shake and one for me, yeah? I'll meet you by the taco stand."

Tuddy got the shakes, and the two of us stood in the shade, watching the sea for a while. Jet Ski riders were trailing bright pink flares in promotion of the Miffy's giveaway, and a small plane was working its way up the coastline dragging a fluttering pink banner with the company's logo.

"I know this is going to sound crazy," I told Tuddy, "but I think I'm on the trail of a killer."

CHAPTER 53

I TOLD DR. PERRY TUDDY what I knew about Ashton Willisee, describing the chance meeting with the scared, obviously lying teenager in my father's office in Koreatown and the visit to Stanford-West Academy. I told Tuddy that I thought Ashton was hiding something. The fact that he would lie about his relationship with Derek Benstein had convinced me that the boy was trying to disguise possible knowledge of what had happened to his friend.

"Let me ask you a question," Tuddy said between sips of his shake. "What has this got to do with you?"

"Nothing," I admitted. "My only connection is that Ashton came seeking my father's help and I stuck my nose in. But there's something in that kid's face. In his eyes. He's alone. He might have people around him, sure, but I feel like he's really alone in this and he needs help."

"You don't know the boy. How could you read him like that?" Tuddy asked.

"I guess because I've felt it myself." I shrugged. "When my father left, that's what it was like. I had my mother, my school friends. I even knew people whose dads had run off under similar circumstances. You know the old cliché. Went out for cigarettes and never came back. But I still felt like I was drowning, and there were a bunch of people on the shore who couldn't rescue me."

Tuddy and I watched the water. I used my long spoon to scoop chocolate chunks from the bottom of my shake.

"Okay." I sighed. "Maybe there's more to it. My little sister knows Ashton from school. I just met this girl, and we're not the best of friends yet. So maybe getting involved in this investigation, helping her friend, is something we can do together. Like when you want two kids to get along so you give them a mutual goal?"

"My grandmother used to say, if you want two cats to get along, put them in a sack and tie it up. Leave them there for a couple of hours." Tuddy looked at the water. "When you open the bag, one of them will be dead or they'll both be friends."

"That's real interesting but not very helpful right now."

"Okay, so how can I help, then?" he asked. "I mean, why chase me down, of all people?"

I laughed, a little embarrassed. "Look, it's hard to explain, but . . . I think I saw your freak flag."

"My *freak flag*?"

"Yeah," I said. I showed him my tattooed arms, gestured to my pink hair. "I mean, look at me. You can spot me a mile away. I fly my freak flag proudly. But you—you're more subtle. You keep letting the cartel lock you up like an animal. And I think that's because a part of you enjoys it, and that's real freaky, man."

He too toyed with the chocolate in the bottom of his cup.

"I'm addicted," he confessed.

"Addicted to getting abducted?"

"Not to the abduction itself," he said. "That's always traumatic. Always terrifying. It's the incarceration that my brain feeds on."

"Who the hell enjoys being locked up?" I asked.

"Me," he answered. "Have you ever heard of dopamine fasting?"

"No," I said.

"Dopamine is an organic chemical produced by your body." He turned toward me, gesturing with his straw. "It's a part of the catecholamine and phenethylamine families. It acts as a neurotransmitter so that—"

"You're losing me, Tuddy."

"It's your happy chemical," he said. "Your brain's happy juice. It's essential in helping you enjoy things. The taste of chocolate. The smell of sea air. Light and sound and eye contact. When you're locked in a dark room for a whole day, with absolutely no stimulus to release your dopamine, your brain stores it up."

"Okay," I said.

"When I spend a month alone in a shipping container, with no smells or sounds or human interaction reaching me, going through repetitive movements like making meth, it's like I shut down. I store up the dopamine in my brain. Then when I'm finally released, it's like I'm walking on sunshine. Literally *walking on sunshine*."

I watched him becoming more animated as he spoke, his eyes wide, wandering over the water before us.

"This, all this, it's like it sparkles." He gestured to the world around us. "I can smell everything. I can feel everything. The breeze on my skin is like electricity. Everything I eat tastes like it was made in the kitchen of the gods. I'm high for weeks after a release. It's like the high you get from heroin, you know? A full-body orgasm. Only it lasts days, not hours."

I stared. Tuddy stood smiling at me.

"I wouldn't know what the high from heroin is like," I said. "Would you?"

"I spent eight years researching addictive chemicals," he said. "You think I didn't mess around with my own stock now and then?" He shook his head sadly. "That's why all those companies began bidding for the patent on my methylamine alternative. They wanted to buy the product from me even though it wasn't complete."

"Because you were a liability," I concluded. "Nobody wants to work with an addict."

"That's right," he said. "In other circumstances, they would have hired me to continue my research. But I was so deeply addicted to heroin at the time, I was damaged goods. It was only the months-long incarcerations with the cartel that got me clean. The first time, I had a guard watching me twenty-four hours a day. I couldn't touch a gram."

He turned to me, his eyes glittering.

"So, yes," he concluded. "Freak. Big freak. How can I help you, my freaky friend?"

CHAPTER 54

I HANDED TUDDY MY phone, then leaned over and flipped through the photographs of Derek Benstein's crime scene for him. I hadn't looked carefully at the images myself, only scrolled through them briefly, trying not to focus.

I paused at the photographs of police officers assisting a medical examiner in removing Benstein's shirt at the scene. His torso was covered in bruises and marks. The photographer had paid particular interest to purple marks on Benstein's thigh, visible at the hem of his boxer shorts.

"Huh," Tuddy said.

"What do you see?"

"Something shocking."

"Oh." I stood back. "I'm sorry. I only—"

"That was a joke," Tuddy said. "This young man has been tortured with some kind of electrical device. Probably a cattle prod. Shocking. You get it?"

"I do." I sighed. "What tells you that?"

"These are electrical burns," he said, pointing out blue and purple welts on Benstein's body. "A cattle prod works by connecting two electrically charged prongs to the skin, thereby creating a closed electrical circuit that encompasses the human body. At the site of the connection, you get these burns. You see?"

I looked and immediately felt a little ill. "I see."

"These were very big charges," he continued. "Designed for cattle, not humans. So the extreme energy charge can't just go into the flesh from one prong and turn around and head right back out again through the other prong. It tries to find somewhere else to go in the body. This is what happens when a person is struck by lightning. It's called flashover. The charge travels through the muscle and skin and creates these bruises."

He zoomed in on a big patch of blue skin that had burst like a flower on Benstein's stomach.

"You can also see he's been starved of oxygen," Tuddy said, after enlarging the image to focus on Benstein's face. "The capillaries in his eyeballs have burst. That's consistent with sustained electrocution. Quite a good resolution in this shot to have captured that."

I walked away, went to the edge of the pier and looked at the water, sucking in the sea air. I could taste Tornado Tower shake at the back of my throat.

"Are you okay?"

"I don't spend a lot of time looking at pictures of dead bodies," I said.

"Neither do I." He shrugged. "But this young man is no longer in pain, if that's what's disturbing you."

"How do you know so much about electricity and the human body?" I asked, trying to distract my mind from the pictures of Benstein's twisted face, his bulging eyes.

"We did some experiments in my first residency with electroshock therapy and the electrical pulses that naturally occur in the brain. My professor was trying to develop a new therapy for depression. That's how I got into the study of narcotics and Alzheimer's."

"Okay," I said. I tried to take my phone back. "I think I have everything I need."

"Perhaps worth mentioning is this boy's other experimentation with electroshock." Tuddy tried to show me another photograph.

"I can't look." I held a hand up. "Just describe it to me."

"There are smaller, older marks on his thighs from a lesser charge," Tuddy said. "The electrical pulse has gone in and right back out again, creating a site injury and nothing else. Probably a stun gun. And probably self-inflicted."

"How do you figure that?" I asked.

"The thigh is a natural place for a curious person to experiment with a dangerous instrument. Away from vital organs. Fleshy, hidden from casual view. And I was a curious boy with a dangerous instrument once." He smiled. "I poured fluoro-antimonic acid on my own thigh in freshman year to impress a female. The scars are still very unsightly."

"So Benstein liked to play with a stun gun," I said. "And then someone electrocuted him to death."

"He was also shot." Tuddy thrust the phone at me again. I winced, saw only red, torn flesh. "See here?"

I snatched the phone away.

"Thanks for the help," I said, closing the images. "If I need you again, where can I find you?"

"Hopefully inside a steel box, somewhere quiet, far away,"

he said. He was watching the ocean. Sea lions were bobbing up at the end of the pier, searching for the fishermen's throwaways. I took down Tuddy's phone number as he recited it, and then I walked into the crowd, leaving the doctor to his sunshine musings. There were darker things on my mind. I was sure now that someone was enacting his sick revenge on Ashton Willisee and his friends. If I was going to stop him, I had to find out why.

CHAPTER 55

BABY WAS WAITING FOR me on the steps of our father's house when I arrived home in an Uber. She smiled sweetly as I approached. I should have listened to the niggling uneasy feeling in my belly as she tossed me a heavy set of keys.

"Let's roll," she said. "We'll take the Maz."

"Let's roll?" I asked. "Just like that?"

"Yeah." She turned and headed through the open garage door. "I've got a lead on some people who are connected with both Ashton and Benzo. You still want to go messing around that whole, like, case thing. Right?"

"Right," I said. "But you seem to be forgetting you just about ripped my head off this morning about your room."

"I know." She flicked her big sunglasses down over her eyes. "I was being stupid. That's over now. I checked out my room properly, and they didn't get to any of my private stuff. You were trying to do the right thing, so, you know." Baby took a deep breath, let it out slowly. "I forgive you."

"Oh." I laughed. "How nice."

"Don't push your luck with me, Rhonda," she said. "You do not want to get on my bad side permanently."

"Whatever you say," I said. We climbed into Dad's Maserati. I was enveloped in his smell again, smoke and sweat, fried food, bad cologne. The driver's seat was set at the perfect height and distance from the wheel for me. I felt like I was slipping on his clothes. Despite Baby's cool exterior, I was feeling upbeat about repairing our relationship, avoiding what I had assumed would be days of silent treatment punctuated by the occasional violent outburst.

"Where are we going?"

"We're going to see some very important people," Baby said, plugging her phone into the car's system. A map appeared on the console. I could see texts pinging silently into a bubble at the bottom of the screen, the number of unopened messages climbing steadily. Again the feeling pulsed through me that I was missing something. No teenager could possibly be so inundated by communication on any regular sort of day, nor would they so happily ignore the onslaught of messages Baby was now receiving. I brushed off my uncertainty, thinking that some news in her social circle must have just broken. Or maybe she was being barraged by texts in a group conversation. I headed for the address on the screen in Downtown Los Angeles as the garage door slid closed behind me.

CHAPTER 56

VERA PUSHED THE DOORBELL at 103 Redmark Avenue, Brentwood, and listened to the chimes ringing inside the big house. She straightened her skirt and flipped her hair. Though she was only four blocks from her own home, Vera felt like a different person. She liked taking on new personas. As a kid, desperate for attention, she had worn all kinds of identities with the girls in her pony club and in her swim squad. Once she had been the secret love child of an affair between her mother and Hollywood heartthrob Kurt Russell. Another time she had been fighting seizures caused by a rare and incurable tumor in her brain.

Vera liked provoking reactions in people. Awe. Sympathy. Jealousy. All her life she'd watched her father twist and wring emotions from his men, smile and laugh with them around the dinner table while they shoveled pelmeni dumplings into their mouths, or make them cower in their seats while he raged and sneered in the pool room.

It hadn't taken much to shake off the identity of Vera Petrov. To ensure she wasn't being followed by whoever was hunting them, the man who had killed Benzo and taken Ashton for a little joyride, she had set out from home and driven up into the mountains. She blasted her Porsche along old fire trails and down a narrow road behind a property owned by the Church of Scientology Celebrity Centre, security cameras following her progress as she went. By the time she was back in Brentwood, she was practicing being her new self, the girl next door just popping round for a quick and friendly favor.

When she heard footsteps on the other side of the door, she painted on a sweet smile and gazed happily at the old woman who answered.

"My name is Annabelle Cetes," she explained. "I live one street over." She pointed in the opposite direction of her mother's mansion on Redmark Avenue. "I'm so sorry to bother you, but my little brother was here in the street earlier playing with his friends, and I think he might have kicked his soccer ball up onto your roof."

"Oh, all right," the old lady said. "Come in. We can go and see from the second floor."

Vera followed the woman into the house, her upper lip stiff as she tried to mask her disgust. The houses of old people always gave her the creeps. The elderly made her think of disease, bodily fluids, dust. There were still people living in Brentwood who had bought their houses before the boom in the seventies, who didn't belong next to the sprawling ranches of the actors, oil magnates, Saudi princes, and stock-market superstars who owned the rest of the area. They were *normies,* nestling where they didn't belong, like parasites, their modest homes overshadowed by their neighbors' huge walls and trees designed to keep out the paparazzi.

Vera followed the crone to the second floor and an open window. When the old woman's back was turned, Vera slipped a tiny wireless black camera the size of a garden pea out of the pocket of her skirt and peeled the backing tape off its surface. Vera went to the window and leaned out, made a show of squinting in the afternoon light at the roof of the first floor while she stuck the camera to the outer edge of the windowsill.

"Whoops," she said brightly when the camera was in place. "I think I might have the wrong house."

With the device in place, Vera walked out, not bothering to disguise her distaste now for her surroundings. She brushed off her shoulders, straightened her spine, and she was Vera Petrov again. Without bothering to offer the old woman any kind of thanks or good-bye, Vera took a bottle of antibacterial gel out of her handbag as she exited the house and didn't look back as she sanitized her hands.

Across the street, behind a black wrought-iron gate woven with ivy, a small brown terrier was snapping angrily at her, its barks squeaky and racked with panic.

"See you tonight," Vera murmured at the animal.

CHAPTER 57

THE GPS HAD LED us to Santee Alley, the downtown fashion district. My father's Maserati was a smooth, humming, luxuriously awful ride compared to my Buick, and for the first time I had a moment to grieve my lost leopard-print lady. I stood by the window of a children's clothing store, gawking at a pair of eight-hundred-dollar shoes for toddlers as a little girl inside the store gawked at me. Between my pink hair and tattoos and oversize, well, *everything,* little kids are often fascinated by me.

Baby tapped away on her phone. She stopped to check her reflection in the window of the store, deciding to pull her curls into a puff at the very top of her head. She dropped a hip and pouted at herself as I stifled a laugh.

"We don't have an appointment," she said, stepping back to look at the next store over. "We'll have to beg our way in. So it's important that you stay out of sight."

"What is this place?" I looked up. The windows at the front of the other store were blackened. A single gold letter *U* was bolted above the heavy steel door painted black. "*U*? What's that stand for?"

"It's not *U* like *You*." Baby rolled her eyes. "It's *Ooo*—Ooo La La."

"What does it mean?"

"Nothing."

"So why does it have to be pronounced that way?"

"Because it's, like, the most relevant emerging fashion boutique in the world." She huffed. "And that's how you say it."

"I thought you said we were coming to see very important people."

"We are," she said. "Sean and Penny Hanley are just . . . *everything*."

"'*Everything*'?" I said, mimicking the reverence with which she had said the word. Baby didn't so much as crack a smile.

"Get out of the way, Rhonda." She waved me off to the side and pushed a pearl buzzer set in the wall. The *beg our way in* she had mentioned seemed to happen by ESP while she stood there pouting with her hip dropped. The door clicked as it unlocked, and I had to scramble to follow Baby into the store before the steel door shut on me.

The space inside was elaborate but confused. It seemed the store's designers hadn't known if they wanted to go for *abandoned warehouse* or *haunted Edwardian mansion*. Candelabras stood by crumbling faux brick walls, and diamond chandeliers hung on worn brown ropes from exposed pipes. There were two racks of clothes in a space that might have accommodated fifty. Behind a huge black marble counter, a young woman with a blond bob was arranging paperwork. In a corner of the room, a young man, who so closely resembled her that they were clearly twins, was slumped in a plush velvet chair, scrolling on his phone. He lifted his eyes from the screen, looked me over, laughed, and went back to his scrolling. The young woman came out from behind the counter with a similar disdain, her step quick and stern, like someone preparing to chase a beggar off their porch.

"You don't have an appointment," she said to Baby. "And who are you? I didn't see you on the security system."

She made a gesture, and two suited security guards materialized seemingly out of nowhere. My mind was racing with defenses, but Baby spoke over me.

"This is my fashion consultant, Eleanor Wave," Baby said. "I'm so sorry we didn't check in earlier. We just arrived from Paris."

The young woman gave Baby a full-body visual examination, then stood back like she'd been slapped awake. She put a hand to her chest with the kind of drama that made me want to giggle.

"I'm Penny Hanley." She offered her hand. "Oh, your cheekbones."

I waited for more. There was none. Baby nodded like someone accepting condolences at a funeral.

"Matte," Baby said. "Can we?"

"Please." Penny gestured to the racks. Baby went and shifted items of clothing along the nearest rail. Some pieces were so thin—mere strips of fabric—I assumed they were men's ties.

"Who's Matt?" I whispered, coming alongside her and pretending to sift through the clothes.

"My fashion name. Not Matt, like the man's name. Matte. With an *e* at the end. Like the finish."

"That's hilarious," I murmured.

"Don't touch the clothes. Just the hangers."

"Where are the prices?"

"There are no *prices*." Baby rolled her eyes.

"I didn't know you were into this kind of stuff," I said. I gestured to the filthy denim cutoffs Baby wore. "Those shorts look like you got them off a three-year-old hobo."

"They're supposed to look like that." Baby huffed. She turned and strolled over to Penny and her brother with one of the men's ties. Some kind of approval was given, and Baby slipped off her T-shirt, exposing her tiny upturned breasts to the entire room. There was no dressing area to speak of. Once she had it on, it appeared that the garment was not a men's tie but a strip of black fabric meant to cover her breasts horizontally like the censorship bar in a nude photograph. Baby pouted at herself in a mirror along the wall, posing in the top. Penny seemed to be on the edge of bursting out with words, holding herself back with difficulty. Finally, she gave in.

"I have to ask. Who are you repped by?"

"I'm independent," Baby said.

"Oh." Penny fanned herself like a Southern belle. "Wow. *Wow*. Sean? She's independent."

Sean looked up again, squinted at Baby, sighed and shuffled in his chair, tapping on his phone again.

He seemed to think for a moment, then gave a bored sigh. "Hire a time machine, because you're at least a year too old."

CHAPTER 58

"WELL, THOSE WERE JUST about the worst people I've ever met," I said when we were outside again. "But I think she *clocked* you, if that helps."

"That was Sean and Penny Hanley," Baby said.

"Yes, you said." I tried to keep up as she all but jogged away from the store. "They own the fashion label, do they?"

"No, they just work there," Baby said.

"They're *store clerks*?" I said. "Where do they get off having that kind of attitude?"

"They have very influential opinions in the fashion sphere," Baby said. "They only work at the store because their parents have, like, ideas about them holding real jobs for a while, I guess. That's what I heard. I don't know. Their dad's Michael Hanley, the lawyer."

"So they don't even have a background in fashion?" I dragged her to a stop.

"Why do you hate them so much?" Baby said. "Penny is beautiful, isn't she? Much more beautiful than she is online."

"They were a couple of stuck-up idiots," I said. "And I don't hate them. I don't even know them. But I hate this side of you. They looked at me like I was a walking ball of bacteria, yet here you are talking about them like they're royalty. They couldn't have been eighteen years old. You don't need to listen to people like that even if they are very important in the fashion world." My fists were clenched. I couldn't grasp what was making me so angry about Baby and her fawning over the Hanley twins. "Is that what you're into? Fashion? You want to be a model?"

"Obviously," she said. "And those two *are* royalty. They've made people's careers with a single Instagram post. Penny took a selfie with some girl she met in an elevator in London. Said she was cute. That girl is with IMG in New York now. If Sean says I look too old, believe me: it's a problem."

"Baby." I drew a long breath. "If you want to be a model, fine. That's great. But it's obvious to me that you have a talent for criminal investigation. You're observant and smart. You know how to act, how to plan. You'd make a crack private investigator or a lawyer or a cop or—"

"Oh, come on." She flipped her sunglasses down, the wall coming between us again. "You don't even know me."

"That moron in there didn't know you!" I gestured back to the store.

"He knows what he's talking about."

"And I don't?" I rubbed my eyes. "Urgh. This is so stupid. Why did you even subject me to that whole miserable experience?"

"Because Sean and Penny are another link between Ashton Willisee and Derek Benstein." She showed me her phone. I looked at pictures of the kids together. "The Hanleys used to check in regularly with Derek and Ashton all over town. Them and Vera Petrov."

"That's the girl from the school?" I pointed to a picture. "Miss Go Fuck Yourself? The one who has some dirt on you that you won't tell me about."

"That's her," Baby said cautiously.

"Okay. So the Hanley twins are friends with our guys," I said. "And?"

"So two days ago, right after the murder, they scrubbed their social media of any ties to Derek," she said. "They weren't just friends, they're now *hiding* the fact that they were friends. There's a tribute page to Derek Benstein on Popple, and they're nowhere near it. Ashton didn't want us to know he was friends with Derek. Now the Hanleys don't either."

"How did you get all these pictures of them together, then?"

"Because I've screenshotted and saved, like, everything Penny has ever done online. I went back and checked my archive."

"Why were you saving all the stuff related to that pathetic little brat?"

"Because she's my hero. I want to be just like her."

"Oh, wow," I said. I resisted another tirade only by reminding myself that Baby was less than half my age. She clearly had a lot to learn about the world and who should be considered a hero.

"It gets better. The Hanleys have also gone dark," she said. "They haven't posted on any of their accounts for the last forty-eight hours. That's a record. Armani just announced a show in Melbourne, Australia, and they haven't commented to say whether they're going. That's weird. Something is happening here. Sean and Penny are involved with whatever's going on."

"I'm not entirely convinced," I said. "All this social media stuff—I don't understand it. It's useful, but it's not concrete enough for me."

"That's because you're old and weird." She shrugged. The coldness was coming over her again. "I don't care. It's your stupid case."

"You're right. This is good work, Baby," I said. "Let's follow them. See what they do when they get off work. If you could possibly call it that."

CHAPTER 59

JACOB WALKED INTO Yellow Bar ten minutes after Vera and requested a seat at the counter, where he could watch the violent little princess in the mirror behind the rows of bottles along the bar. He ordered a vodka neat and perused the flavored oxygen canisters wasting space beside a shelf of expensive bourbons. At first he had smirked at the idea of purchasing air, but then he remembered a yacht broker in Rome he'd strangled who would probably have paid everything he had for a tiny sip of oxygen right at the end.

Vera Petrov was a girl after his own heart, he had decided. The only real predator among the children calling themselves the Midnight Crew. Though his background check on her hadn't revealed any suspicious deaths around her, Jacob could tell it was only a matter of time before she killed for the first time. She had the instinct. It was a biological thing. Vera's was a brain that was always assessing others, measuring threats, looking for opportunities for herself. She'd probably inherited it from her gangster father but trimmed off the kind of cowardice that had made him run when his criminal life got too complicated.

Vera had spied an opportunity, Jacob could tell. She had bullied and intimidated all the waitresses in her section of the establishment into fawning over and circling around her anxiously, but now she was waving them away, growling when they came close, her chin resting thoughtfully on her palm.

Jacob could see the object of her fancy. At an adjacent table, a party of middle-aged men were huddled together over a battered notebook, running through scribbled lines. Probably rappers, from the bling and the custom Nikes. On the corner of the table, a pair of leopard-print sunglasses rested unattended. Vera wanted them. He witnessed her desire in a single glance, the half second that her eyes lingered on the glasses, her refusal to look again.

Jacob guessed Vera had been stealing all her life, her first little childhood thrill. He knew she liked trophies. One of his watches had gone missing the night his family was attacked. She probably had a stash of little items at her home, tucked away safely in a box. Personal things—photographs, jewelry, handmade gifts. When Jacob had first started killing, he'd been a trophy taker. He'd liked to take driver's licenses. Eventually the collection had become too dangerous to tote around the world with him. He could've explained a couple of stray ID cards in his possession, but not fifty.

Jacob watched as Vera paid her tab in cash, dropped her handbag by the edge of the rappers' table, then scooped the sunglasses into the pocket of her jacket on her way back up from bending to retrieve it. It was an artful move. She would probably wear the sunglasses for a while and then dump them, Jacob guessed. This kind of petty theft was not where her heart lay. It was just sport.

He was in the parking lot only seconds behind her, observing the valet bringing her Porsche up from the garage as he slid into his own car. At the traffic lights they were side by side, Vera completely unaware of him as she disinfected her stolen glasses with an alcohol wipe and tried them on. She checked her reflection in the rearview mirror, smiled icily. Jacob looked at the pistol lying on the passenger seat beside him, a .45 ACP he habitually took out of the glove box and lay beside him every time he drove nowadays. He imagined himself opening his car door, leaning over, and popping Vera a few times through her window, bullets ripping through her petite frame and into the hand-stitched leather in the Porsche's driver's seat. She'd be dead before he closed the car door again. In the noise and bustle of Little Tokyo, no one would notice until she failed to drive off when the light turned green.

But he reminded himself this wasn't like one of his old jobs. This was personal. He needed to take it slow, like he had with Benzo. As much as he burned for an end to it all, he knew the years ahead would be filled with moments in which he would think of the Midnight Crew. Whether Beaty was alive or dead, healthy or unhealthy, he was going to think of them. Ashton. Benzo. Sean. Penny. Vera. He didn't want to regret not getting the fullest experience of murdering each of them for what they had done to him. To his family.

He had to make sure there was pain. Plenty of pain.

CHAPTER 60

I WAS SURPRISED BY Sean and Penny Hanley's first destination when they left work: a Walmart. From a distance, Baby and I watched them tour the hardware aisle. Sean took a shiny new hammer off a rack and weighed it in his hand, turned it, looked at the claw, and said something to his twin that made her laugh. While he twirled it, they went to the weapons section and played with a crossbow for a while but didn't seem serious about buying it. In the end, they each bought a hammer.

While Baby had seemed very enthusiastic about the mystery surrounding Ashton Willisee and his dead friend, she lost interest halfway through our tour of the Walmart. She paid all her attention to her phone, which was dinging and buzzing and making little popping noises with a frequency I had not yet witnessed. I was sure now that something was going on. In the parking lot, I watched Baby smiling at the screen while we walked back to the Maserati.

"Why would they buy two hammers?" I asked.

She said nothing.

"Even if they are building or repairing something by hand together, which I highly doubt, why wouldn't they just pass the hammer back and forth?" I continued. "Or if they're working on separate projects, what are the chances that—"

"I don't know, Rhonda. Jeez, give it a rest, will you?"

In the car, she took out some eyeliner and started applying it.

"Aren't we just going home?"

"Uh-huh." She smiled knowingly.

"Baby, what have you done?" I watched her carefully. She shrugged. Her phone was going off with such consistency that it vibrated off the seat beside her and fell onto the floor. I drove home with a darkening sense of peril, watching dazzling yellow and green billboards for liability compensation lawyers fly by the windows.

ARE YOU ON YOUR WAY TO A CATASTROPHE RIGHT NOW? one asked.

As it turned out, I was.

CHAPTER 61

THERE WERE ALREADY CROWDS two blocks from the house. Young men and women getting out of cars or sailing down the streets on bikes, cell phone screens lit up in the gathering dark. I caught a glimpse of my father's house one street away from it and saw lights on inside.

"Oh, dear." I sighed. Baby was watching me, waiting for that defeated sound. She let out a mean little laugh.

"You shouldn't have messed with my stuff," she said. "This is *my* house. Dad's house. You tried to put your stamp on it, and I'm here to show you that you can't do that."

"So let me get this straight," I said. "As revenge for me hiring strangers to come into the house and mess with your personal possessions... you've invited a thousand strangers to come into the house and mess with your personal possessions?" I asked.

"I barricaded my bedroom door." She grinned. "My stuff is safe. Yours? Well, I guess we'll just have to find out."

CHAPTER 62

THERE WERE TOO MANY teenagers in the street outside the house for the Maserati to turn onto our road. I parked, then pushed through the crowd to the front door and intercepted a skinny teen boy heading out in what was obviously my Van Halen T-shirt, the fabric dripping off him from his shoulders to his knobby knees. The crowd was crammed into the living room, music thumping so loud my eardrums pulsed. There were kids making out on the stairs and on the couches, a makeshift mosh pit at the bottom of the staircase, the scent of alcohol and weed smoke hanging like a curtain over everything. My boots crunched on plastic cups, broken glass, food wrappers, a broken lamp.

I climbed the stairs to the spare room where I had been sleeping and found my suitcase torn open, empty. A bunch of girls were sitting in the corner watching a YouTube video on my laptop. I snatched the machine away to a chorus of whines and slammed it closed, stowing it under a hutch in the hallway, and then went to check on the three million dollars of cartel money and drugs that I had hidden in my father's bathroom. A crew of boys was hanging out in there, apparently oblivious to the hidden space beneath the vanity. They were passing a bong between themselves, sitting around the bathtub like pigeons crowded into a tiny space to avoid the rain.

Baby was dancing on the pool table in the first-floor lounge when I found her. The bar had been stripped of every bottle and every glass. I saw a girl going by with a bottle of Pappy Van Winkle bourbon and took it from her before she could squeeze by me.

"Hey, bitch! That's mine!" she yelped.

"Honey, you couldn't possibly appreciate it," I said, walking on. I stood at the end of the pool table, drinking Pappy from the bottle and watching Baby dance until she noticed me. I was getting looks from all directions. They were all beautiful, sun-bronzed, and youthful creatures with metabolisms that allowed them to get by on only junk food. I was twice the age and three times the size of anyone in attendance. When Baby finally looked down at me, she had the same contempt on her features as they all did.

"Who's that?" a girl beside her asked.

"My sister!" Baby yelled over the music. "Can you believe it?"

"Whoa, crazy!"

"Yeah, crazy!"

"So if your dad was Early Bird, and you're Baby Bird, she's..." the girl said. They looked at me. Baby burst out laughing.

"Big Bird!" Baby said. They both cackled.

I stepped up to the edge of the pool table. "Enjoying the festivities?" I asked.

"Sure am." She grinned, crouching and leaning in so I could

hear her. "This is what you get for messing with my stuff, Rhonda. You shouldn't mess with me—I'm the queen!"

I nodded appreciatively. A stupid, childish, competitive spirit was twisting in me. *This is what it's like to have a sister,* I thought. I had the strange compulsion to grab a fistful of Baby's hair, throw her iPhone in the pool. A delicious meanness was growing in my heart.

"You know what's *hilarious*?" I asked.

"What?"

"I could make myself the queen of this whole party in ten minutes flat and you don't even know it."

"You think so?" She blurted out more laughter. The other kids were getting in on the game, giving me laser-beam eyes so hot they could fry an egg. I was the loser big sister. The party crasher. The fun police.

But not for long.

"Watch and learn, little girl," I told Baby. I turned and walked out of the house.

CHAPTER 63

THEY STOOD BETWEEN TWO big properties in a dark alleyway that was so overgrown with bougainvillea, from the street it was invisible. Ashton thought about the Nicole Brown and Ron Goldman murders, committed only streets away, the rear-gate access that only the killer would have known about, the alleyway secretive and overgrown with foliage. All the kids Ashton knew were overly familiar with rich-people murders—the O. J. Simpson thing, the Menendez brothers, the Manson family killings. Poor kids feared slow-driving cars with their windows rolled down. Rich kids feared hippies and disgruntled relatives.

Vera, Sean, and Penny were standing silently, listening, waiting for the terrier on the other side of the gate to find the meatball they'd laced with diazepam and go off to nighty nights.

"What's to stop this guy from leaping out and mowing us all down right now?" Ashton asked, glancing into the street. He was imagining every shadow as a tall man with a big rifle. "One gun spray and that's it. We're all done for."

"He's not like that," Vera said. "He messed around with Benzo. He was going to mess around with you before you slipped out of his grasp. He wants to take his time. He'll watch us tonight and creep up on one of us when we're alone."

"Well, that's just awesome," Ashton said. "My parents flew out to New York this morning. I'm alone tonight."

"Aww." Sean smirked under his mask. "You can come curl up on the end of my bed like the little pussy that you are, if you like. I'll get you a blankie and a bowl of milk to keep the boogeyman away."

"Go get a room at the Ritz." Penny was tucking her hair under her mask. "They have great smoked salmon at breakfast."

Vera pushed open the gate at the back of the house. The crew followed her through a lush garden, past the little terrier lying unconscious on its side on the terra-cotta tiles. Vera took out her lock-picking kit, knelt, and worked the doorknob. Ashton bet she had been picking locks since before she could walk. He'd known Vera since grade school, and she was that kind of kid—interested in doing anything that put her where she wasn't meant to be. In the empty staffroom between classes. In the out-of-bounds area under the school bleachers. In the classroom after the bell had sounded and all the teachers had gone. Even if there was nothing to do there, nothing to see, she hated being shut out. If it was gated, roped off, signposted, locked, bolted, or chained, Vera wanted in.

They opened the door and shuffled inside. Ashton's eyes adjusted to the darkness after a moment. He smelled dog and wondered how the scruffy little thing they'd passed in the dimly lit yard could infest the house with such an odor. Then he saw the rack bolted to the wall beside him. The hooks holding four leashes. One small, thin pink one.

And three heavy chain-link ones.

Ashton saw the dogs over Sean's shoulder. Three enormous figures emerged in the hallway before them, sharp ears pricked and luminescent eyes locked on the intruding teenagers.

CHAPTER 64

WHEN THE WEIGHT-LIFTING dudes' front door opened, the first thing I saw was a giant red logo on the wall. A flexed biceps, veiny and bulging, the word BRUH underneath. The armpit of the flexed arm in the logo was strangely hairy. The long-haired, beefy dude who opened the door recognized me from the rooftop weight-lifting showdown. I saw a quick grimace pass his lips—wounded pride. He seemed as surprised to see me as I was to see the long table of computers set up in the dining room behind him, monitors everywhere, wires running all over the floor. His fellow muscle-bound friends were all staring at me.

"You're a tech company?" I said.

"Yeah." The beefcake glanced back at his friends, then at the logo. "What? You think just because we lift that means we're idiots?"

"I lift." I shrugged. "I lift better than you."

"That's what you think." He puffed up. "That wasn't my best performance on the rooftop this morning. I'm recovering from bursitis."

"What's Bruh?" I asked, gesturing to the logo.

"It's an app. Tracks your protein intake, lifting schedule. Stuff like that. You can order supplements and share your progress with other bruhs." He spotted a troupe of girls going into my father's house behind me. "Party at your place, huh?"

"Yeah," I said. "You and your bruhs are invited. But you have to bring something with you."

Baby was pouring cocktails in the kitchen when I arrived back at the house with my crew of meaty tech heads. I led them through the crowd without stopping to speak with her, pushing aside kids to make way for the steel poles they were carrying. A bunch of kids on the stairs using a deodorant can as a flame thrower to amuse the crowd stopped what they were doing to follow us up to the roof, where the bruhs dropped the poles and left to get some more.

There were about a hundred young people standing around the pool, no one with so much as a toe in the water. I stood and felt sad for them, for the simple fact that being the first one to jump in the water on a sweltering night like this was social suicide to these kids. The weight-lifting coders from next door had brought the painter's scaffolding from the side of their house up the stairs and to the edge of the pool and erected it within twenty minutes. Baby appeared beside me, her eyes bleary from drink. She inhaled deeply from her vape pen, and I resisted flicking it out of her mouth.

"You said ten minutes," she said.

"You can't get good help these days," I replied.

One of the dudes had climbed to the very top of the scaffold, tested its sturdiness by rocking it back and forth. He gave me the thumbs-up and climbed down. Even with her head swimming with booze, Baby soon caught on to what I was doing.

"You wouldn't," she sneered.

"Hold my drink." I grinned.

CHAPTER 65

HEIGHT IS RELATIVE. Twenty feet experienced while standing above thick landing pads, safety-harnessed under the watchful eye of professionals, feels exactly like what it is: twenty feet. The same twenty feet experienced from the top of rickety scaffolding being buffeted by sea breezes, standing above concrete and water and the watchful gaze of a hundred drunk teenagers, feels like one hundred feet or more.

I climbed the scaffolding with difficulty, my legs trembling, mentally erasing the stupid gesture I was performing one step at a time even as I performed it. I envisioned myself climbing down. Smiling gingerly and apologizing as the bruhs disassembled the scaffolding. Melting into the crowd in embarrassment as I had at a thousand social gatherings before— senior prom, the Watkins county fair ball, a singles dance I had ventured into once. The farther up the scaffold I climbed, the deeper my regret stretched, until there I was: at the top.

The view was spectacular. The gold, glittering coast stretched to the left and right of me, sparkling arms reaching out into the black sea, Malibu to the right, Palos Verdes to the left, the city over my shoulder, dancing towers of stars. The pool below blazed neon-blue with underwater lights, and as I stood there, I realized the crowd around the pool had just about tripled. Kids were rushing into the house to gather their friends. People were standing on the walls around the rooftop, squeezed into the doorway and hall, whooping and cheering at the edges of the pool, leaning back so they wouldn't be forced into the water by the press of people.

It seemed like every single kid in attendance got out their phone and started filming all at once. Three hundred bright white lights. Even with the wind in my ears, I could hear individual jeers and insults.

"You won't do it!"

"Come on, fatty! Get down!"

"Chicken! Chicken! Chicken!"

"Thar she blows!"

I looked down and saw that Baby had folded her arms triumphantly, her head cocked, listening to the chants all around her. I took my hand off the rail and stepped to the edge of the scaffolding, my toes hanging over the gaping nothingness. I pressed my palms together like an Olympic diver.

CHAPTER 66

A SCRAMBLE, A CRASH. Vera, Sean, and Ashton backed up hard, crushing Penny, the last into the house, against the closed door. The deadbolt had clicked into place automatically, and it stuck slightly as Ashton grabbed at it over Penny's head. He heard a scatter of paws on tiles and gave up on the back door. He whirled around, followed the shadows before him into a room off the hall. The door slammed shut, and immediately there came the sound of huge paws scratching at it, wet, snapping barks coming through the wood loud and clear.

"Oh, fuck! Oh, fuck! Oh, fuck!"

"What the—"

"Turn on the light! Find a light!"

Ashton backed into a table. Sean found a light switch, revealing a spacious office, leather wing-back chairs, and a U-shaped desk. Ashton caught a glimpse of his own reflection in the big window to the street, the black skull mask hiding his tensed jaw and bulging eyes.

They looked absurd in the reflection. Four kids playing

dress-up games. Ninjas in black clothing, Sean and Penny with shiny new claw hammers and Vera with her lock-picking kit still in hand. Ashton's weapon of choice this time was a wooden baseball bat. He looked at it, gripped in his gloved fist. Even if he went out swinging like Max Muncy, he couldn't take down three huge German shepherds before one of them tore his throat out.

All at once the dogs fell silent.

A female voice called out from the hall. "Who's in there?"

"Nobody speak." Vera's whisper was hard, urgent. Ashton was glad he couldn't see her face. If she was as scared as he was, they were all dead. They needed their leader to be an unshakable pillar of certainty. But as he waited for Vera to give them a course of action, she simply didn't. She stood there, frozen, her arm stiff when he grabbed it.

"Tell us what to do! What the fuck do we do? We're trapped!"

"Shut up." She pushed him off.

"Who's in there? Answer me!" the voice called from beyond the door.

Ashton heard a sound that made his throat constrict and his stomach lurch. A loud double crunch, metal grinding on metal.

Sean recognized the sound as well.

"That was a shotgun," Sean said. His voice steadily rose in pitch. "She just pumped a fucking shotgun. There are three attack dogs and a chick with a shotgun out there, Vera! What do we—"

"I'm calling the police!" the voice said.

"You don't want to do that!" Vera shouted back.

"We're dead." Penny was at the window, looking down over the drop to the concrete below. "We're all dead. We're all dead. We're all dead."

Sean grabbed Vera's shoulder. "Vera, we—"

"I'm thinking!" Vera ripped Sean's hand off her, bending it backward so that his fingers cracked as the boy howled. "Get your filthy fucking hands off me!"

Ashton looked at the walls, the shelves by the door, searching in his insane panic for an escape hidden somewhere, anywhere, even in the books standing in neat rows. *The Handbook of Guard Dog Training. Canine Behavior for the High-Stress Environment. The Other End of the Leash.* He saw nothing that made him feel any better.

"I'm dialing now!" the voice called. "You assholes move a muscle and I'll fire through the door!"

"Put the phone down, lady!" Vera shouted. She was fishing in her pocket. As Ashton watched, she took out a small gold lighter and held it up to the door, flipped it open and ground the wheel.

"What are you doing?" he asked.

She ignored him. "You hear that, bitch?" Vera asked, flicking the lighter open and shut. "You hear that?"

Ashton, Sean, and Penny stood back as Vera went to the drapes, held the lighter to the bottom of one.

"Vera!" Penny cried.

"I'm lighting this place up!" Vera called. "You smell the smoke yet? I'm lighting the curtains! I'm lighting the papers on the desk!"

"You're going to kill us!" Sean said.

"Listen, woman!" Vera went to the door, put her ear to

it. Yellow flame was creeping up the curtain, rippling slowly across the surface of the desk. "You better think about your priorities. You leave us in here and the room will burn. By the time the cops and the fire department get here, you'll have four dead kids on your hands. You want to try to explain that? Smart thing to do is call off the dogs, let us go now, and try to save your house before everything you own is toast and your ass is in jail. Up to you."

Silence. The only sound was the crackling of the growing flames, the occasional whimpering of one of the dogs behind the door. Ashton watched black smoke coiling against the ceiling. Penny started coughing.

"It's getting hot in here!" Vera called, gripping the door handle.

The door opened. Ashton felt relief rush over him. Until he saw Vera reaching for the gun hidden in the waistband of her jeans.

CHAPTER 67

I JUMPED.

Freeze-frame.

Time locked into place.

The wind rushed, warm and loud, past my ears. The impossibly bright blue surface of the pool soared up at me. For a long time it felt like I hung in midair, falling and yet not falling, a floating balloon suspended just above the unbroken surface of the water. A sound came up from the crowd, the sharp intake of three hundred gasps. My arms and legs were flung out and my eyes were bulging as I descended.

Later, I would see footage of the fall. Kids can do all kinds of things with videos on their phones these days. Like a great, round star, I descended in slow motion over the pool, floated down frame by frame, my belly rippling, my thighs jiggling, my pudgy fingers gripping at nothing, struggling for purchase. My stomach hit the surface of the water first, sent an undulating wave out in a perfect circle from the center of the pool. Then the rest of me hit. Asteroid slamming into Earth. Water balloon hitting concrete. The pool spewed water in return, walls surging ten feet high, directly upward, a display reminiscent of the Fountains of Bellagio in Las Vegas. The water sucked toward me and then rose and bellowed outward, soaking the first three rows of people completely and everyone behind them to the waist. The giant wave rolled out over the rooftop and flooded through the door to the house and down the stairs. I was swallowed whole beneath the surface of the pool.

Under the water, I heard nothing, saw nothing. When I righted and broke the surface, my ear canals cleared, but there was no sound. I stood and wiped the water from my eyes, looking around. The silence seemed to hang. Then three hundred kids all raised their arms and let out the greatest, loudest cheer I had ever heard.

Fifty kids jumped into the pool with me in one united motion. There was no consensus. No starting gun. They all just dropped their phones and jumped. Kids were all around me suddenly, whooping and splashing and trying to lift me. More kids piled into the pool as the seconds passed. The rooftop was flooded again. Screaming and laughing and cheering filled the air.

I was an instant hero. My plan had worked. Like a thousand youth icons before me, I'd made a spectacular, dangerous, and stupid gesture, and in response the teenage mob had accepted me as their queen.

There was only one figure outside the pool who was standing still. Who was not grinning. Who was not shouting praise at me. That figure was Baby, and in the chaos and noise she soon disappeared.

CHAPTER 68

VERA THREW OPEN THE door. She knew she had lost touch with reality, and that disconnecting in this way was a good thing. Disassociating. It would help her make decisions faster, go into a fully instinctual mode to protect herself. She had already decided as she stood there in the room slowly being consumed by fire that it was fine if Ashton, Sean, and Penny didn't get out of this mess alive. She cared about only herself. It was time to fight, then flee.

She pivoted, stepping into the hall and bringing the gun up in one smooth motion. The lights were on. The space seemed smaller now than it had in the darkness. A tall woman stood there in a robe with a pump-action shotgun held with the barrel pointing upward. Vera fired twice. Aimed low. Hit the woman in the stomach. A self-defense strategy, if she needed it later. *I panicked. I closed my eyes and fired.*

She blasted the dogs without really aiming. Vera didn't really like dogs, but she respected them. They were loyal. Predictable. Dependable. She hit one in the leg, and the others bolted, startled by the white light and the noise of her gun and the sound of their owner hitting the floor. The smell of blood. Vera ran for the back door, twisted the deadbolt, and yanked it open, running out into the cold night air before the woman with the bullets in her guts even realized what had happened to her.

When Vera turned and looked over her shoulder from two blocks away, she saw three masked figures behind her. Her crew had escaped. That was a plus, she supposed. Less cleanup. When they all stopped in the dark outside some mansion, she realized that Sean, Penny, and Ashton were huffing like they'd run a marathon. Her own pulse had hardly risen at all.

"Well," she said. "That was unexpected."

"What was unexpected?" Sean's voice was low, dangerous. "The three attack dogs? The shotgun? Or the four of us now suddenly facing murder charges?"

"Attempted murder at best." Vera snorted. "She'll be fine. I hit her in the stomach. Maybe she'll have to wear a bag for the rest of her life, but there's no need to get all dramatic."

Vera could smell smoke on the wind. In the distance, sirens wailed. She pulled off her mask and folded it, tucked it into her pocket, and slipped the gun back into her waistband.

"You're weirdly quiet," she said to Ashton. "I've been standing here bracing myself for your classic moaning and whimpering. Have at it."

"I have nothing to say," the boy said.

Vera waited, but he didn't continue. She looked at them all, felt the tide turning against her in their silence. She was the only one unmasked, and they were standing there, hiding their contempt behind plastic and cloth. Typical. *All mutineers are cowards,* she thought.

"Listen," she said. "If you guys think—"

Her words were cut off by a sound, a sharp pop on the sidewalk at their feet. Sparks. They all looked. Another pop and Penny collapsed like a folding chair.

"Oh, God," she wailed. "I've been shot! Help me, I've been—"

Vera didn't stay to hear the rest. She threw herself behind a car as more gunshots went off all around them.

CHAPTER 69

I'D DONE THREE LAPS of the house, trying to find Baby, toured the Strand all the way to Hermosa Beach, my clothes drenched and heavy and my hair plastered to my skull. When my phone buzzed, I looked down at it, clutching the device in my fist without a dry pocket to put it in. A Twitter account I hadn't used in six years was being tagged in a new post. The teens from the party had found me and were linking me to the video of my dive. It was going viral. A tweet attached to the video read:

Bell E Flopp just OWNED a house party at Manhattan Beach! EPIC!

I stood on the beach and looked up and down the stretch of darkness, watching the waves crash, feeling helpless. A couple of girls walking up the beach stopped and pointed at me.

"Yo, there she is!"

"It's her! It's Bell!"

I gave an awkward wave, politely refused selfies.

When I finally found Baby, she was sitting on the ramp of a lifeguard tower, vaping as the wind tousled her hair. Her phone was glowing on the ramp beside her. She spotted me and stood.

"Don't run off again," I said. "My clothes are wet. I'm getting chafed like you wouldn't believe."

"You were right." She threw her hands up. "You're queen of the house. Queen of the internet. Queen of the world. You win, Rhonda. Now go away and leave me alone."

I was glad she was still angry and not crying. Angry meant we could talk, that the responses would be rapid-fire instead of sullen and wading through misery. If I played my cards right, I hoped I could bring her around to my side of the argument without her being embarrassed by her tears. An angry teenage client had always been a lot easier to handle than a sad one. But then nothing about Baby had adhered to the principles of managing teenagers that I had followed since I had been one myself. She was my sister. She shared my blood. And yet she was the one kid on the planet I couldn't possibly understand.

"I'm not trying to win anything against you, Baby," I said. "We're on the same team here."

"Whatever."

"'Whatever,'" I mimicked, sighing.

I watched the waves crashing in, white foam appearing and then dissolving into the blackness.

"Here's the thing," I said. "I'm not going anywhere. You can push me and push me and push me, but I'm not going to go away. Dad's gone out of our lives for good, and I'm here to stay. And those are two realities you have to deal with."

Baby didn't respond. She sucked hard on the vape.

"Have you even cried about him dying yet?"

"No," she said. She turned away, but I saw her lip tremble. "I'd rather cry about *you* being here."

I didn't take offense. Baby wouldn't meet my eyes.

"Have *you* cried about him dying yet?" she asked.

"I haven't," I admitted. "But look, I didn't know the guy like you did."

She chewed her nails.

"Losing him is harder for you than it is for me. You didn't have a proper mom," I said. "My mom was great. Is great. After Dad left, she married a guy named Tony. Total opposite of Dad. You probably feel like you're on your own in the world. But you're not. You've got me. I'm not the enemy."

Baby didn't respond.

"Do you want a hug?" I asked.

She seemed to consider it. I was betting anger, confusion, and tears were sparkling in her eyes. "I don't want to hug you. You're all wet. And I don't know you. We haven't even figured out who you're supposed to be in my life. You're here trying to be, like, my sister right now. But one minute you're trying to be cool and then you're telling me not to listen to the Hanley twins about my age. It's like you don't know if you're my friend or, like, my boss."

"It's going to be fine, Baby. All of it. When we get back to Colorado, you—"

"When I *what*?" Her head whipped around to look at me. "Colorado?"

"Well, yeah," I said. "We'll have to go back there. You can't stay here by yourself, and I have a job. I have a condo. I have friends, and—"

"*I* have a job! *I* have friends!" Baby yowled. Her eyes were huge. "Don't they matter at all?"

"They do," I reasoned. "But I mean, you're young. You'll make new friends. Your life is not as—"

"Not as important as yours." She nodded.

"No, that's not—"

"I'm not going to Colorado," Baby said. "If you try to take me there, I'll run away and you'll *never* find me."

A punch of terror directly to my chest. Baby had already run off on me twice. I knew her threat was real.

"Hey, hey, Bell!" someone called. I turned and saw two gangly boys with long black hair jogging across the beach toward us, their silhouettes almost alien in their angularity against the lights of the house.

"Are you Bell E Flopp?"

"I guess so," I said. "No selfies, guys."

"Some dudes are going through your stuff back at the house," one of the kids said.

"It's okay. Everybody's going through my stuff." I sighed. "Everything important is tucked away. Don't worry."

"No, we mean, like, badass guys." The boy nearest me swept his hair behind his ears and out of the wind. "Like gangsters. They're old. Like, forty maybe? And they're really looking for something. They're breaking stuff and throwing things around. They pushed some girl down the stairs."

"Have they got flowers on their shirts?" I asked.

"Yeah. And real bad tattoos." The boy nodded.

Baby and I looked at each other. For once, we were instantly on the same team. She rose, and we ran toward the house.

CHAPTER 70

PENNY, SEAN, AND ASHTON were crouched behind one car with Vera behind another. Bullets skittered off the curb and the sandstone wall nearby. Vera figured the shooter had to be in the trees on a nearby hillside.

"We're gonna die here," Sean said. Penny was moaning beside him.

Vera thought about running, leaving the three of them for the gunman. It was a strategic move. He would likely try to keep the others pinned, keep the bigger target in hand rather than pursue her. But she couldn't be sure of that. Was it time to be loyal to her crew or risk going out on her own? She held her breath, crouched, and sprang forward, leaping the gap between the two cars to join the rest of the Midnight Crew. Sparks flew as a volley of shots popped into the bumpers of the cars beside her.

"Penny, you need to shut up," Vera said. "You sound like a dying cat." She took out her phone and turned on its flashlight, examined her friend's ankle.

"It's shrapnel," Vera concluded.

"I've been shot," Penny whined. "He shot me. He shot me!"

"I said, it's shrapnel," Vera said. "Stop losing your fucking mind."

"How would you know that? Are you a fucking gun expert?" Sean asked.

"I know because her foot is still attached," Vera growled. "He's not shooting at us with a BB gun."

The crew was silent. Vera needed to rally them. There were times for abandoning the flock and times for using them as cover. Safety in numbers. She swallowed hard, forced herself to soften her tone.

"I've seen a gunshot wound before," Vera said. "My dad brought a guy home once who took a hit in a robbery. They had a deadbeat doctor treat him in our garage. That wound was from a 9mm gun. Whatever he's shooting at us with, it's bigger than that."

"What the hell are we gonna do here?" Sean asked. "If we break cover, he's going to kill us."

"If he wanted us dead, we'd be dead," Vera said. "He's playing with us. He just wants to watch us squirm. In a couple of minutes emergency services are going to be swarming all over this place, and we'll be trapped here like sitting ducks."

"I can't go to jail." Sean ripped his mask off, gripped his hair in both hands. "I'll kill myself before they put me in there."

"You're all being so dramatic." Vera laughed suddenly. She looked at Ashton, but he was still worryingly silent. Vera didn't like that. She knew he was planning something. He was too stupid to think and talk at the same time. Maybe the boy would run off on his own, abandon them all. It would be the first smart thing he did in years. She couldn't let him do that. She needed to make a gesture. Show them she was still in control.

Vera slowly rose. Then, with more confidence, she stepped out into the street between the cars. She could hear Penny screaming in protest. Sean begging her to come back. But the only sound that was important was the pocking of bullets at her feet. Each time a bullet hit, she tried not to flinch. Not to glance down at the sparks hitting the asphalt. The window of the car behind her blew out, the bullet missing her shoulder by mere inches. Vera knew he could hit her if he wanted to, but she wasn't going to play his game. She lifted up her arms, her pistol in one hand, and smiled broadly in the light of the streetlamps in the direction where she guessed the shooter was hiding.

"Let's go, motherfucker!" she roared. "I'm right here!"

Lights came on in a house behind her. Then at the house next to that. The sirens in the distance had grown much louder. Smoke was flooding the streets, smudging the streetlamps. She heard voices shouting. A bullet hit the car beside her. Sean shouted out in terror. Vera bit her tongue to stifle a surprised sound as the pistol in her hand was ripped from her fingers by a passing bullet, the shot clanging hard against the muzzle, sending shock waves up her arm and into her shoulder.

"I'm coming for you!" she called.

Lights came on in the house next to where she had guessed the killer was hiding. The firing stopped. Vera smiled triumphantly as dogs barked and people stirred in the properties nearby.

It was Ashton's hands that gripped her shoulders, turned

her to go. She picked up her still-intact gun. Vera looked back into the darkness and fought the desire to run up there, to shoot wildly ahead of her into the trees. Instead, she followed her crew as they disappeared into the night.

She knew the real confrontation wasn't too far away.

CHAPTER 71

AS SOON AS I stepped through the door off the Strand into my father's house, every kid in the building erupted into cheers. Those who actually saw me started it, and the sound carried onward and upward through the levels to the rooftop. I noticed the Bruh guys walking out through the living room toward the front door carrying pieces of scaffolding. A smart choice. It wouldn't have been long before teen boys tried to top my dive with backflips and tumbles of their own.

Vegas and two of his guys had discovered the door to Baby's bedroom that she had hidden ingeniously behind a bookcase on the third floor. The bookcase lay on its side, pushed over carelessly, books and trinkets spilled out onto the carpet. This was a quieter space in the house. The door to my father's bedroom I'd passed on my way up the stairs had been closed, I assumed because teens were making out in there or worse.

Vegas was sitting on Baby's bed next to an incredibly nervous-looking teenage girl with spiky black hair. His two thugs were leaning against the window, seemingly waiting for us to arrive. Vegas's hair was tied back in a ponytail, and his boots were a startling fuchsia-dyed leather branded with patterns of violets.

"Jesus. What size shoe are you?" I said, trying to take all the danger out of the room, to show that I wasn't afraid. "If I didn't know you were the world's most disgusting human being, I'd think of buying those gorgeous things right off your feet."

Vegas glanced down at his boots, uncrossed his legs, and planted his feet on the carpet.

"We've finished messing around, Rhonda," Vegas said. "It's time to transition our relationship into reduction mode."

"You're firing me?" I looked at Baby, made like I was miffed. "But I'm your key assets holder!"

"Very funny, Rhonda." Vegas smiled. He reached out with his long arm and scooted the teenage girl a little closer to him, hugged her waist in tight with his. Her eyes were wide, pleading with me. "But I'm being serious now. I want to terminate our relationship, and the only way I can do that is if you tell me where my stuff is."

I stood in Baby's bedroom and looked the men in their eyes, each of them in turn. All I had to do was tell them where the cash and drugs were hidden. In seconds, they could walk downstairs and retrieve what they wanted.

But I knew that if I let them do that, there would be no reason for them to keep Baby and me alive. There would be nothing to stop them from opening fire on us. On any of the hundreds of kids in the house.

"You're a businessman," I said. "We can negotiate. But not under these conditions. Let the girl go and we—"

"You don't get to negotiate." Vegas smiled again. "You don't have any leverage in this situation. You'll either give me what

I want now or you'll give me what I want after I've demon-strated what you have to lose."

I could see the ivory-inset grip of a revolver sticking out of his back pocket. He didn't need to touch the gun. I under-stood he could whip it out and plant a bullet in the guts of the girl beside him before I could cross the room to stop him.

I tried to think, but my brain was thrumming with panic. Vegas was cool. Calm. He stroked the girl's waist.

"I just want to say," Vegas continued, "I think it's so unfor-tunate that you have burned your bridge with me in this way. Your father and I were building something great. We *had* built something great." He glanced around the enormous room, at Baby's elaborate four-poster bed and the giant leather ottoman dominating the floor space before the walk-in closet. "I have a daughter. She didn't grow up with a bedroom like this. Earl only wanted what was best for you, Baby. And you, Rhonda. You've come in and destroyed what was a very profitable relationship."

"Maybe we can salvage things," I said. "Let that girl come over here to me and we'll talk."

The girl piped up, her smile trembling. "I really would like to go. It's been real cool hanging out, but—"

"Quiet, honey." Vegas snuggled her closer. The girl wriggled, tried to lean away. "The adults are talking."

The cartel boss turned to me. When I didn't budge, he nodded at one of his men.

"Maybe I need to put a bit more pressure on the situation," he said.

CHAPTER 72

THE GOON WENT FOR Baby, as I knew he would. In the same way she had been in the Denny's parking lot, Baby looked like the vulnerable one in our duo, a waiflike and reedy young girl. But she was ready this time. I hadn't noticed her hand creeping along the doorframe to a shelf on the wall, packed with loose items the cleaners had gathered there.

She grabbed a snow globe and smashed it into the goon's face as he reached for her. Her blow was quick, sharp, and true, aimed right between his hands at his nose. The heavy wooden base of the globe pulverized his upper lip against his teeth.

It was clear to me in that instant that Baby had never been violent with anyone before. As soon as she'd landed the blow the girl dropped her weapon, grabbed her own mouth, and howled in sympathy for her victim and in horror at what she had done. I stepped in, blocking the guy as he recovered and shoving him into the desk.

Vegas watched all this from the bed. His remaining goon watched from the window. Both had hard, unsurprised stares, like they'd assumed all along I would only deepen the danger-ous debt between us. They seemed all too willing to extract payment when I finished ringing up my tab.

I waited for Vegas's second man to come for me, but before he could, something outside the window caught his attention, and he gave a frustrated sigh. The ceiling was lit by red and blue lights. Downstairs I heard kids screaming warnings, flee-ing out the door to the Strand and the beach. For the first time since I had entered the room, Vegas's eyes left me and watched the kids barreling down the stairs, leaping over the toppled bookcase in the hall like antelope fleeing a pack of lions.

Vegas didn't say anything. He just stood and slipped by me, glancing at me as he went, the promise of future violence so clear in his eyes that I felt my stomach clench tightly and the blood rush to my head. As his goons followed him, one cupping his bleeding face and the other helping him along, the girl on the bed burst into tears.

CHAPTER 73

THE FIRST TIME I ever saw the police disperse an unruly crowd, I was standing on a platform with a bunch of other angsty teens watching the authorities try to contain a small riot at a Sepultura concert. I now stood on the threshold of my father's house, watching the long arm of the law clear the Manhattan Beach streets, badges and buckles reflecting the red and blue lights of their cars.

The cops swept at the kids in rows like a vacuum trying to clean up after a beanbag had exploded. Now and then they got some kids, but every time they cornered some between the houses or in the street, others would seem to float upward and billow out, tumbling beyond reach and pooling back together. There were a couple of bad eggs jumping on the hoods of cars and throwing beer bottles at the officers, but all in all, the entire crowd was gone within fifteen minutes.

Officer David Summerly's approach was less intimidating this time. I missed his earlier commanding stride toward me. He walked up and stood on the stoop, his hands on his hips, the two of us blocking the main entrance to the house entirely.

"I'm going to get you this time," he said.

"You sound like some kind of supervillain," I remarked, stepping back so I could admire him in all his uniformed finery again.

"You might have wriggled out of a charge for the exploding car, but you can't wriggle out of this," he said. "This party is disturbing the peace, plain and simple. There must have been five hundred kids in there."

"Five hundred?" I asked, reluctantly proud of Baby and her efforts. "You think?"

"I can charge you with disturbing the peace, and also charge you for every single instance of illicit drug use on your property," he said. "I just had a look through the beachfront windows. There are so many pills scattered around in there you could open up a pharmacy."

"Well, I hate to break your heart," I said, "but you're not going to put the cuffs on me tonight, Summerly. At least not for a crime."

He rolled his eyes, waiting. I couldn't keep the grin off my face as I replied.

"The owner of this domicile is deceased," I said. "I haven't yet filed the paperwork to claim the property as my own. I don't know if I ever will. But until then, no one can authorize a search of the premises, and you can't do one yourself because you can't prove anything illegal happened inside."

"Yes, I can," he blurted. He gestured to the street. "All these kids came out of this house!"

"Have you got any proof of that? Photographs or video maybe?"

"Probably. It's probably on the patrol cars' dash cams. On the officers' body cams."

"Are you personally going to verify that footage in a court of law? With paid experts?" I asked. He paused, thinking. I continued. "Because the way I see it, all these kids showed up and caused a ruckus *around* this house. But you have absolutely no proof at this very moment that any of them were ever inside or that the presence of all these rambunctious youths has anything at all to do with me. I'm only as guilty as those people next door." I pointed to the Bruh house. At the houses across the street. "Or them. Or them."

"A party has clearly occurred on these premises." He waved an arm through the open door, at the beer cups and used condoms and broken glass and pizza boxes everywhere, the fallen earrings and lost shoes and torn T-shirts that rain down during good parties the world over.

"Maybe I just live like this." I shrugged.

Summerly gaped at me. "You just *live* like this?" he said. "Every morning you get up and throw handfuls of glitter and pills and condoms everywhere? These..." He bent and picked up an item lying at my feet by the door's threshold. It was a huge pair of novelty sunglasses with a plastic penis glued where the nose would go. "These are yours?"

I took the sunglasses and put them on. The plastic penis stuck out from my face six inches and wobbled as I smiled up at him. "They sure are," I said.

Summerly managed to hold it together for a moment before he burst out laughing. "Lady, if you really do live this way, I want to be a part of that life." He adjusted his belt, stretched his back. "There's probably enough stuff on the floor in there to cure my backache for the next twelve years."

We continued to smile at each other. I took the penis sunglasses off and thought about saying something further. But I didn't. While everything in my world was wildly out of control, I had just enough sense to wrangle back anything that might interrupt the delicious moment Summerly and I were sharing.

He stepped down to the sidewalk. When he turned back, I was sure he caught me checking out his butt again, but it didn't matter, because what he said blew apart any and all concern that might have existed before he opened his mouth.

"You know," he said, pointing at me, "I really like you."

My mouth fell open. I couldn't find the words to reply. I just stood there with my jaw hanging as he went back out onto the street.

CHAPTER 74

WHEN DRIVER ARRIVED, Sean took the keys to the Pullman from him and told him to go away. He did. Good staff were like that. They nodded silently and did exactly as they were told, no questions asked. There were no weird looks about Penny sitting crying on the curb with her leg soaked in blood, the two of them dressed in black and obviously rattled. Over the years, Driver had picked up Sean from highway gas stations between LA and Mexico in the middle of the night, from outside the houses of big-deal politicians in nothing but his underwear after someone's wife returned home early from a weekend away with the gals. Sean watched the old man walk away with his hands in his pockets and wondered what regular people did when they couldn't buy silence.

"You can't drive," Penny wailed as her brother helped her into the front seat.

"I can drive," he said as he slid into the driver's seat and searched for where to put the key. "I drove to a bodega last year when the house lady was sick."

"Take me somewhere nice," Penny said. "I can't go to a

regular emergency room. That's how you catch things. Call ahead and get us a private room."

"We're going home, and I'm calling you a vet," Sean said.

"What?"

"That's what you do when you get shot," Sean said. "You call a vet. We can't go to a hospital. The police will be involved."

"So call me a deadbeat doctor!" Penny said. "Like Vera's dad did with that guy."

"You think I have a list of dodgy doctors in my phone?" he snapped, shoving the shifter and pulling awkwardly out from the curb. "A vet will be cheaper. A vet we can buy, any vet at all. No problem."

"Ask Vera for—"

"She needs to know we can handle this ourselves," Sean said. "Now shut up. I'm trying to concentrate here."

It was on Sunset, outside the white walls of the Archer School for Girls, that they noticed the black BMW in their rearview mirror. The driver was in shadow, but he had stopped his vehicle close enough behind Sean and Penny to hide his headlights against the trunk of their car. Uncomfortably close. A gesture that commanded attention. The twins sat watching, waiting. The engine of the car behind them revved.

"It's not him." Sean reached over to put a hand on his sister's knee, a rare gesture of comfort and affection. "Vera said he would just watch us tonight. Too risky to come after us with all the chaos back there."

"Who is it, then?" She turned with difficulty in her seat, stared through the big empty car out the back window. "Is it . . . is it a gang?"

"Not in that car."

"We're about to get carjacked. Lock the doors."

The doors were already locked. The light changed. He accelerated slowly, and the BMW stayed right behind them.

"Turn onto the 405. North on it, not south." Penny's voice was low, strangely calm. "Speed up. We'll outrun him."

For once, Sean did what she said. That's when he knew he was in real trouble. Penny was talking sense, and he was listening. With a white-knuckle grip on the wheel, he turned onto the freeway, eased his foot down on the accelerator.

Penny was right. He couldn't drive. He had spent about as much time driving as he had doing all the other things that regular people did. Cleaning. Filing paperwork. Calling their mother. He didn't look before he changed lanes, almost sending a green Saab careening into the center divider. The Saab driver leaned on the horn. He heard shouts, winced, felt humiliated. The BMW was right on their tail, the high beams on, making the rearview mirror blaze at the corner of his vision. The Pullman wasn't built for speed. It was big, heavy, low, built for gliding with style.

"We're going to be fine," Penny said. "We're going to get out of this."

"Call 911," Sean said.

"We can't," she said. "This was a bad idea. Turn off the freeway again. We'll lose him in the hills."

He did as she instructed, and after a while, the road narrowed, began to wind through the hills. Trees here and there around them, leaning and black. Sean gained space between him and the black car, losing it again as he slowed hard for corners. The killer knew he couldn't drive. He was probably back there laughing at him, a shark following lazily behind a struggling swimmer. Sean was drowning, catching glimpses of the shore as he came up to gulp air, the city below appearing between the hills and clumps of vegetation.

"We shouldn't have come up here," Sean said.

"Shut up! Pay attention to what you're doing!"

"He brought Ashton up here. This is his hunting ground. This is exactly what he wanted us to do. We're falling into his trap. Call someone, Penny, for fuck's sake. Call anyone!"

"I've got no reception!" She looked up from her phone to him, her eyes wild. Then she spotted something on the road. "Stop, stop, stop!"

CHAPTER 75

SEAN SWERVED RIGHT TOWARD a hill, but the tires slid in the gravel, fishtailing, hooking around the deer harmlessly as it stood frozen in the road like a marble statue. The Pullman was so long it ground over the edge of the road, up and over the low bank of vegetation marking the drop-off, rocks scraping the underbelly. Sean felt them gouging the surface beneath his feet. The gold, sparkling city below was suddenly right in front of them, and they were plunging absurdly toward it.

There was no screaming. In the detached, hellish panic that gripped him as the car tumbled down the ravine, he realized that he wanted to scream but couldn't. The sound caught in his throat like a painful bubble.

He must have blacked out, because when he woke, the car was crumpled against a tree, a branch piercing its roof. Hissing, creaking, popping sounds were issuing from the car all around him. He tried to figure out how the hell he'd gotten there but could only grip on to the memory of Vera and Ash and Penny standing in the street, Penny bloody and torn,

Vera telling them to go home and hunker down for the night, that it was safe now. Penny shoved hard against him as she crawled out through the windshield, stepping on his crotch to get herself free from the wrecked vehicle.

She was gone for thirty seconds. He lay there counting them. Thirty seconds in which she tried to make her escape alone before remembering that her only sibling, the being who had shared a womb with her for nine months, needed her. She came back and leaned through the squashed window on the passenger side.

"Give me your hand."

Penny pulled him free. They held each other in the dimness, listening to their pursuer crunching through the shrubs and stones toward them.

"Go, go, go." He pushed at Penny, but she was rigid with terror, walking straight legged, slipping and stumbling in the loose rocks. Sean thought about pulling her to the ground, trying to hide. But all his senses were telling him the hunter behind them was closing in. The same natural electrical impulses were shooting through his brain that blasted through a rabbit's mind when it saw the eyes of a wolf emerging from the undergrowth. They needed to run, run, run.

A puttering sound filled the quiet ravine, like gloved hands clapping, and Penny screamed. Sean knew the killer had sprayed the brush around them with bullets, his suppressor dulling the sound from the houses below. He tried to keep Penny moving, but she slumped against her brother, went down clutching her side.

She was in too much pain to make a sound. He followed her hand to the hole just under her ribs on the right side.

Warm, wet, drenching his wrist and arm in seconds. Sean had a choice to make now. Die with her or survive alone.

"Don..." she managed. "Sean, don't le..."

The footsteps were coming. Sean squeezed Penny's hand, already consoling himself about what he was going to do. It had been her idea anyway to join the Midnight Crew. She'd been Vera's friend from the dance academy when they were in grade school. Really it was she who had gotten them into this mess in the first place. He told himself that these excuses and others would be at hand later, in therapy, when he tried to get over the guilt of leaving his sister to die without him.

The killer was close. Sean could hear him breathing. Maybe readying the gun to fire blindly at them again. If Sean was wounded, that would be it. It would all be over. He wasn't ready for it to end yet. Soldiers left each other behind all the time in war. Pushed on. Survived to fight again. He had no time to be honorable now, or to make her understand why he wasn't.

"I love you," he told Penny, because he supposed that might help. He looked her in the eyes when he said it, which was brave of him, he thought.

Then he turned and ran.

CHAPTER 76

THE EDGE OF THE road lit up white, softly at first and then blazing as the car passed in the night. Sean watched it from where he hid in the bushes ten feet back from the asphalt, down an embankment on the hillside. He had considered waiting until daylight to move again, but the pain in his knees and hips from crouching, too frightened to move, was becoming unbearable. Even turning his head to peer through the gaps in the scrub oaks sent rocks and sand crumbling from beneath him. Instead he listened and watched the road.

He had lost the killer while the man dealt with Penny. There had been a kind of yelp and gurgle on the wind, and then nothing. Sean had made his way sideways up along the edge of a ravine, guessing the killer would predict he'd follow the slope of the earth. He was smart. He was going to survive this. Leaving Penny behind had been the right move—he knew that now, because her sacrifice had bought him time, security. Now all he had to do was get the attention of a passing motorist and he was home free. And the cars were coming with greater and greater frequency. His Hublot, the glass now cracked, told him it was 4 a.m. Normal people would be on the road at this time. Cleaners arrived at work. Bartenders departed. He looked around and saw no movement on the hillside.

Sean shifted onto his haunches, gripped the earth, and crawled forward into the shelter of the next clump of bushes, closer to the edge of the road.

A truck rumbled along the ridge in the distance. He watched, ready to spring. When it was right next to him, he saw two fat Hispanic men sitting in the cab, a Saint Joseph cameo hanging from the rearview mirror. Sean sunk back into the bush. He didn't want to spend the first precious seconds of his escape trying to explain the need to step on the gas in broken Spanish to a pair of idiots. He watched the truck go by. The crunch of its tires on the road ahead masked all but the final moments of the killer's approach.

CHAPTER 77

SEAN HEARD THE LAST footstep in the gravel. He turned, just far enough to catch the blur of a big hand sweeping up to grab a hunk of his hair, the other gripping his shoulder hard. He was yanked backward, hitting the ground with a thunderous impact that knocked the wind out of him.

He opened his eyes and tried to suck in air. Sean remembered the feeling from a summer day at Malibu Beach. A wave had tumbled him into the sand, and the pressure on his lungs had been terrifying in the seconds it took for him to reach the water's surface again. When he breathed this time, though, something was different. Only one lung inflated, the air struggling through his lips, as thick as honey.

He reached up and gripped the tree branch protruding from the left side of his chest, sticking out from his smashed ribs by two feet or more. He thought about how, in movies, actors managed full conversations while impaled like this through the back, but he could move his lips only silently.

An old man stepped around Sean, stood in front of him, looking at the wooden spike with a kind of quiet satisfaction.

In his dying moments, Sean watched the killer's face and tried to recognize him. He wanted to know which of the Midnight Crew victims he had been, which night of fun and laughter had brought such undeserved cruelty down on him and Penny. But the old man seemed to be just an old man, like so many other indistinct, unimportant people who had fluttered in and out of Sean's life.

Sean died with his feet struggling in the dirt, his heart torn in half, and some nameless nobody staring at him in the growing dawn.

CHAPTER 78

IT WAS FIVE IN the morning when the knock came at the door. I had been shifting around the house restlessly, gathering little Baggies of drugs from among the debris of the party in a kind of grim treasure hunt and emptying their contents into the toilet. During my scavenging I found a smattering of strange items brought by the teens for purposes known only to them—an inflatable sex doll, a unicycle, a bucket of twigs, and several cans of sausage and beans.

At 3 a.m., Baby had appeared behind me in the kitchen, sniffing the air like a gopher just emerging from the earth. She had been sitting on the concrete wall at the edge of the Strand, drinking colorful flavored vodkas with some remaining teens, while I rattled around the house. I knew she was in for the hangover of her life, but I didn't go out there and call her in. She had taken on the strange new woman in her life for Queen of the Party and lost. Her most sacred space, her bedroom, had been invaded by commercial cleaners and drug lords, and her father was only a few days dead. She needed to get it out of her system.

"What is that smell?" She groaned.

"Spam." I showed her the pan I had been laboring over.

Four thick slices of the tinned meat were bubbling in butter on the Teflon.

"Oh, God." Baby gagged. "That's not right."

"It's right by me." I shrugged.

She slid onto a bench and shoved aside a bunch of junk to clear a path between us. "I'm feeling very emotional," she said, after watching me cook for a while.

"You don't say?" I smiled.

"I hit a guy in the face with a snow globe." Her words were slurred. "I've never hit anyone. With anything. Ever. And I hit *that guy*. In the *face*. With a *snow globe*."

I glanced over. Her lip was trembling.

"Rhonda, I didn't even know his name!"

I couldn't stifle a laugh. She started laughing with me.

"You want some Spam?"

"Oh, hell no. Are you crazy?" She watched me sit and start eating. "You're just going to sit there and eat it like that? No toast? No pancakes? No eggs? Just fried slices of Spam?"

"I don't like anything to interfere with the taste of my Spam," I said.

She watched with a horrified look on her face for a while, then reached over and plucked a juicy slice from the side of my plate. Within minutes, I was frying myself more Spam while Baby devoured the original batch.

The knock at the door came maybe fifteen minutes after Baby had slouched off to bed. I opened the front door and found Officer David Summerly standing there. I hadn't realized just how present the man was in my fragmented brain until I laid eyes on him again. I had been thinking about him ever since he'd left, while I'd pottered around the house alone, even while Baby and I had eaten and laughed together. The officer's collar was unbuttoned, and he was tapping his hat against the thigh of his trousers.

"You didn't say anything back," he said.

"When?"

"When I said I liked you."

"Oh." I gazed over his shoulder, tried to look nonchalant. Probably failed. "I guess I figured that was just an LA thing. We're on Hollywood's doorstep here, you know. People get dramatic."

Summerly laughed. "Well, it's not an LA thing, Rhonda. I wasn't being dramatic. I was being real."

He stepped up from the front walkway, onto the stoop. I didn't budge from the doorway.

"I see a lot of crazy stuff in my line of work," he said. "Nothing surprises me much anymore. But you talking your way out of both jams you got yourself into over the past couple of days, that was really something else. That was like verbal...legal...gymnastics."

"I'm pretty flexible," I said. "Why don't you get in here and I'll show you a couple more of my moves?"

We both laughed at the cheesiness of our banter, the silliness of needing to exchange words at all when our bodies were busy doing all the talking for us. He was advancing into the entryway. I was walking back, drawing him in, both our hands already restless, ready to grab at clothes, to pop buttons and pull zippers and explore the hard, warm skin beneath. I closed the door behind him, and Officer Summerly's hand found mine in the early-morning darkness of the foyer as I led him toward the stairs.

CHAPTER 79

VERA WALKED INTO HER house from the back entrance, climbed the stairs, and quietly shut the door to her bedroom. She hadn't been explicitly told by her father to stay at home and care for her mother during his absence, but it was expected that the hens would huddle together for safety when the rooster was away. It was a ridiculous rule. Vera wasn't a frightened chicken but a lone wolf capable of hunting and surviving on her own. The light under her mother's bedroom door had told Vera that she was up, even at 4 a.m., probably watching religious programs and fiddling with a battered Bible.

She went to her laptop, pushed it open, and clicked on the app that controlled her hidden cameras. The rooftop of the old woman's house was the best angle, but she had hidden a couple of other cameras in trees along the street outside the property with the dogs. The feed was live, showing a cluster of fire and emergency-response vehicles currently jamming up traffic, the typical gathering of neighbors and gawkers outside the police tape. Vera could have searched the internet for news about whether the woman with the dogs was dead, but she didn't. It didn't matter. She would tell Sean, Penny, and Ashton that the woman had survived with only flesh wounds, and they'd be too weak to check for themselves, the way they'd been with the young girl who had collapsed at the Palos Verdes raid.

She rolled the footage back and watched the emergency trucks disappear and the neighbors recede, the street folding back into night. She stopped when she saw her crew bursting out of the gate into the little hidden alleyway, running like jail breakers onto the street. Their humiliating retreat had marked the end of the escapade, so she followed the footage carefully further back, all the way to the start. She stopped and played the tape. The four of them arriving, slipping under the cover of the leaves and vines around the alleyway, mere minutes passing between their disappearance from view and the lights inside the house flicking on as the woman was alerted by her dogs.

Vera waited. As the action played out inside the house, a car rolled slowly down the street, on screen for only two seconds before it disappeared. She rolled the footage back, took a screenshot of the car, and stared at it. An old, beaten-up panel van, maybe dark-blue or green, the back windows blocked with patterned curtains. One of those "If the van's a-rockin', don't come a-knockin'" type vehicles.

No, that wasn't him.

Vera knew the man had used a white van to abduct Ashton. A panel van with the windows blocked was also a perfectly serviceable vehicle for an abduction. But there was no need for two grab vans. And this vehicle was too distinct, too memorable. It was probably the last remnant of some aging hippie's former life before they sold their soul to Wall Street and bought a seven-bedder with a screening room in the hills behind the Getty.

No, Vera knew she should be looking for something with discreet sophistication. Something that wouldn't look out of place rolling around the neighborhood at night. He didn't want to be pulled over and searched with an enormous rifle perched on the passenger seat, a series of telescopic lenses in the back, surveillance material on a bunch of rich teenagers stuffed into the glove box. He wouldn't bring his grab van. He'd bring his everyday car.

No other cars passed in the street while the failed raid played out. Vera tapped her nails on her desk and thought. Maybe he wasn't following behind. Maybe he'd kept just ahead of them, anticipating their moves, keeping them in his rearview mirror as they headed for the target.

Vera rewound the footage back further, to those moments when the four of them stood in the alley, waiting for the terrier to succumb to the diazepam. Further again, until the street was silent, just seconds before they would appear on screen. A car rolled by. Vera stopped the film and screenshot the image, blew it up.

She knew a little about cars. If there was one status symbol among Russian mobsters, it was their mode of transportation. She googled some BMWs and found the model—the Gran Tourer. Jet-black. The website advertised that instead of a trunk, the car had a big cargo space for kids' scooters and sports bags, nets behind the front seats for their iPads and crap. A family man. A man with kids, killing kids. Vera smiled. This was very interesting.

She opened the list of Midnight Crew victims on her desktop and deleted all the childless couples. There were four men remaining. One of them had been her target: the jerk from the mall who had stolen her and Ashton's parking spot. She'd been having a terrible day. The mall valets had been on break, and then the stolen spot had pushed her over the edge. Vera sat back and thought. The mall guy was the same guy with the kid who had collapsed. Jacob Kanular. But she remembered his car from the mall: a blue sedan of some kind, whizzing into the space ahead of them. Not a BMW. She selected the Kanular family from the list and rested her finger on the Delete button.

Then she stopped.

A white van. A blue sedan. Was there another car? Had the sedan been his? Or was it the car his wife usually drove?

She remembered the Kanular guy glaring at her over the duct tape wound around his head, his black eyes strangely calm, calculating. She googled the Kanulars' address and selected Street View. Outside the house, Google had caught someone coming home, one door of the four-car garage rolled halfway down, a pair of legs, jeans, and boots, standing by the trunk of a vehicle.

She saw the black, blue, and white BMW symbol on the trunk of the car and smiled.

CHAPTER 80

OFFICER DAVID SUMMERLY LAY beside me in the late-morning light, the gold hair on his chest glowing in the sunshine from the open window as he fiddled with the edge of the sheet and stared up at the ceiling. He was probably turning over the same idle things in his mind that I was, the same strange questions and possibilities that had opened up after we unexpectedly fell into bed together before sunrise. How he was going to get out of the house without running into Baby, who was loudly clattering around in the kitchen below. Whether we would see each other again. How to discern if the morning's recent activities meant anything—what we had shared both before and after the "I really like you" moment, the intimate whisperings we'd had in the bathroom as he'd watched me in the shower. Those words that had come before we fell asleep, excited murmurings, soft laughter.

The hand that was fooling with the sheet wandered up the pillow and toyed with a strand of my pink hair. Something crashed in the kitchen, and we heard Baby's curse echo through the big house. She sounded hungover and desperate, rattling around, shifting bottles and opening and slamming the fridge.

"Is there any more Spam?" she roared through the big empty house.

"I know that kid, you know," Summerly said.

"Really?"

"Yeah," he said. "I responded to the thing at the school a couple of years ago."

"What thing at the school?"

"Nobody told you?" He paused for a moment to think. "Oh. I shouldn't, then. But...if you're her guardian, maybe it's relevant."

I had told Summerly some of my situation with Baby in the hours since he'd shown up. I had come to a crossroads now. I could trust Baby to have handled her past and leave it where it lay, unexposed to me, or I could open her box of secrets and see if there was anything in there that concerned me.

"What happened?" I asked, knowing even as I said it that I was betraying Baby's trust.

"She kissed a teacher," Summerly said. He was looking at a photograph on the dresser near the window of Baby as a kindergartener. "She got confused, I guess. She was thirteen. She might have thought the guy was flirting with her or something, wanted to be her boyfriend. You know how teenage girls dream up these things sometimes. Man, I've dragged enough runaways out of dangerous situations they got themselves into based on dreams and fantasies. I couldn't tell you."

"Same." I nodded. "How did it happen?"

"Story is, she was the teacher's pet. He'd kept her back on her own after class that day to compliment her on her work, and she just launched herself at him and kissed him."

"Whoa," I said. "Are you guys sure that's how it played out?"

"Yeah." Summerly nodded. "We looked into it. He did not, as it turned out, want to be her boyfriend. Not at all."

"Oh, God. And he didn't know it was coming?"

"No," Summerly said. "The whole thing took him completely by surprise. And she was so upset and embarrassed about having done it and been rejected that this male teacher thought, *Oh, dear. I better let the school authorities know.* Because he's thinking, next thing you know Baby'll be saying *he* kissed *her*."

"That's the way it usually goes."

"Mmm-hmm," Summerly said. "So he made damned sure his boss heard his version of events first."

"I see," I said.

"So the school authorities brought the police in just to make sure everything was dealt with correctly. They didn't want a lawsuit on their hands. My superior officer handled it. I assisted. We questioned Baby and the teacher. They both said the same thing. She got confused. Tried to plant one on him in the classroom."

"Oh, Baby." I covered my eyes. I could feel my sister's hurt and humiliation burning up my throat from deep in my chest. "How did our dad handle it?"

"He was…" Summerly paused to remember. "You could tell he didn't know what to do. He sort of brushed it off, told her it was no big deal, didn't answer any of our follow-up calls. He wasn't one of those very experienced dads."

Funny, I thought. *It wasn't his first time, being responsible for a troubled thirteen-year-old girl.*

"How the hell did the other kids find out?" I asked. "When we were at the school, another girl there seemed to know about it."

"You know how it is." Summerly shrugged. "People talk. Kids overhear them. How is she? Is she okay?"

"How does she seem?" I asked. As if on cue, the sound of glass smashing came from downstairs followed by more cursing from Baby. "It's a weird time with her dad gone and me being in her face, as old and lame and completely intrusive as I am."

With the room around us still trashed from the party, and Baby's activities downstairs becoming louder and louder, it seemed impossible to stay in bed. I got up and pulled on a T-shirt and boxers and threw Officer Summerly's shirt at him.

"I'll distract her while you sneak out the back," I told him.

"Who are the teenagers now?" He smirked. His phone bleeped, and he took it from the nightstand, checked the screen. "Will I meet you later for..."

"For what?" I asked. But he had become consumed by what he was reading. I threw his hat at him.

"I was going to say coffee, but I've got to go." He pulled his shirt on. "I've got a call out past Upper Canyonback."

"Where?"

"It's..." He waved vaguely north.

"What is your beat, exactly?" I asked. "First you turn up at Stanford-West Academy, then you're here in Manhattan Beach. Now you're getting called to a canyon?"

"I cover for a lot of guys," he said, slipping his shoes on quickly. "I've got to go."

He wouldn't meet my eyes as he headed for the stairs. I was left with the distinct sensation that I had just been lied to.

CHAPTER 81

WHEN I FOUND BABY, she was trying to sweep up the broken pieces of a beer bottle on the kitchen floor, standing barefoot, surrounded by shards. I walked over piles of crumpled party detritus and shooed her away.

"Let me handle this," I said.

"Was that the guy?" she said.

I looked up. Summerly was just disappearing up the Strand, as visible as any mountain-size man would be slipping between the beautiful people outside.

"What guy?"

"Oh, come on." Baby slapped me playfully. "You just had that cop in your room, didn't you? The one with the ass!"

"Baby." I sighed.

"This is so romantic!" she squealed.

"Is it?"

"Yeah." Her eyes were dazzling with excitement. "You two are perfect for each other! Oh, wow. And if you're spending all your time with him, you won't be messing with my life."

"Who says I'm going to spend a minute more with that

guy?" I asked, sweeping the glass into a dustpan, pouring it into the trash can.

"What, don't you like him?"

I was beginning to see the Baby who, at thirteen, had gotten herself all tied up in knots about a teacher having a romantic interest in her. This was yet another unfamiliar side to the girl who had proved to be the most unpredictable teenager of my life, the one I was responsible for. This sudden gushing fascination with my love life defied her usual surly, sarcastic, apparently wizened outlook.

"Baby," I said, "despite what you might think about over-weight and socially defunct women from the howling depths of Colorado, we are perfectly capable of sleeping with random guys without needing them to rescue us from crushing loneliness by getting romantically involved. Now go take a shower," I instructed. "I'll make coffee."

The doorbell rang. Baby tottered over in the bemused fashion of a girl only just coming to terms with both the worst hangover of her young life and the idea that I, of all people, was more sexually liberated than she was. She opened the door to Ashton Willisee. His exhausted, terrified face made me drop the dustpan into the trash can at my feet.

"I need help," Ashton said.

CHAPTER 82

THE BOY SMELLED OF smoke. One of the knees of his black jeans was torn, and I could see a cube of safety glass, the kind used in car windows, wedged into his boot. Ashton walked in stiffly and went to the spacious living room, numbly staring at the party junk on the couch as though he didn't know how to solve the intricate problem of shoving it aside to sit down. Baby assisted.

"We killed someone," Ashton said.

"What the fu—" Baby wheeled around, her eyes wide and locked on me.

I put a hand up as I sat down across from the boy in an armchair. "Ashton, don't say another word," I said. "Whatever you've done, you don't need to make it worse by blurting out something that might count in court as a confession to people you barely know."

Baby's eyes somehow grew even larger. "He just said he—"

"He's shell-shocked, panicked, maybe injured," I said to Baby. "He needs his parents and a legal representative on hand as soon as possible. Ashton, I want you to call your parents now and—"

"I don't have my phone," he said. While Baby was becoming more excited by the second, Ashton on the other hand seemed to be calming, easing himself back into the leather couch and fixing his mussed hair. "And I don't want a lawyer. Last night my friends and I broke into a house in Brentwood, and while we were there, we got trapped. We set the place on fire to escape. We killed the lady who lives there."

I held my head in my hands, my thoughts racing to find a way to contain the situation legally, even if Ashton insisted on blathering all the details of his crime to Baby and me. Baby curled up on the couch sideways, facing Ashton, her phone glowing as her thumbs danced over the screen.

"I'm going to jail," Ashton said.

"Well, not for murder," Baby said. We both looked at her. She was chewing a nail as she scrolled one-handed. "'A home invasion in Brentwood last night has left a woman with multiple gunshot wounds and neighbors terrorized.' Looks like half her house burned down, but she's still alive. She's in stable condition at Santa Monica Med Center."

All the air seemed to go out of Ashton. There was silence as Baby continued to scroll.

"You killed two dogs," she finally said. She looked up from the phone at the boy beside her. "You asshole."

"I didn't mean to kill or hurt anybody," he said. "And what happened last night wasn't my fault. When it started, when I got into all this, we were just trying to scare people."

"I'm really going to advise you to stop talking now," I said.

"I don't have any choice," Ashton said. "I have to tell someone what we've been doing because he's coming. He's going to kill me. And if I don't let the secret out now, no one will ever know."

CHAPTER 83

ASHTON TOLD US EVERYTHING. I sat and watched the boy physically unfold as his story did, his posture loosening, his hands—which had been tucked tightly into his armpits—slowly emerging and beginning to illustrate in the air.

It had started with another excruciating Thanksgiving dinner. In the hours after sunset at his parents' vacation home in Carpinteria, before Ashton was allowed to join the local kids on the beach, during the insufferable cocktail swigging and hard laughing of socialites with deep tans and painfully white teeth. He'd stood on the balcony and watched his uncle Ray argue with his wife, Francine, then his uncle's big hand smacked the side of Francine's head in the dark beyond the palm trees. The strike had made no sound in Ashton's world, was swallowed up like a scream in space. When he went downstairs and tried to explain what he'd seen, the adults smirked and shrugged or wandered away, changing the subject the way they had with just about everything unpalatable he'd brought up over the years.

As Ashton spoke, I saw the anger rise in his throat and temples, and I recognized a pain in him that I had witnessed many times across my career working with troubled youth. The unmistakable hurt of a child ignored, a child discovering that justice didn't always play out in the real world.

In that moment, Ashton had realized every story he'd ever been told in his life was a lie. The wolf eats Grandma. The witch eats the children. The robber dashes away from the cop. Sometimes in life people didn't get what they deserved, and that ugly truth so rocked the boy's world that he began to obsess over the slap. The sound of it in the night. The looks on his parents' faces. It stopped being about Aunt Francine and Uncle Ray and started being about everything. The whole unfair, awful, stupid world.

Turning to Vera, Benzo, Sean, and Penny had been the natural move, he told us. Ashton thought of the crew as his "angry" friends. There were other kids in his life—mostly the children of his parents' wealthy friends, princes and princesses of worthy empires—but they were just as dim-witted and shallow as his parents and hopelessly immune to discontent. The members of the Midnight Crew were capable of hate. They *listened* to Ashton when he spoke about feeling alone, feeling like just another of his parents' accessories— a toy that had been fun to tote around when he was small and cute and could be dressed like a doll but eventually had grown tiresome as he got older. He was a troublesome boy. He wanted to talk about legal reform and taxes and poverty and things that made his parents and their guests very uncomfortable. They couldn't throw money at him and make him shut up. That was annoying.

Vera had texted their group, saying, We should do something ourselves.

Ashton had sent a laughing emoji, and for a while there had been silence. He'd got the feeling, a sixth sense, that the others were talking on some other group text thread without him. Then Vera had texted again.

Let's meet up. I can tell you about our game.

CHAPTER 84

THE GAME WAS EVERYTHING Ashton had wanted. One big, loud, violent release. They called themselves the Midnight Crew. They wore a uniform. Moved in sync, like ninjas or black ops soldiers.

The look on his uncle Ray's terrified face when he and his friends stormed into the bedroom and threw on the lights had given Ashton a deep, stomach-clenching, skin-tingling pleasure that he'd been able to call upon even months afterward. They locked his aunt in the bathroom and tied Uncle Ray to his desk, then stripped, taunted, and belittled him, leaving him bloodied and sobbing and drooling onto his paperwork as they ransacked his house. Ashton jumped on the bed, threw a can of beer from the fridge at a mirror in the guest room, and heard the giggles rippling up from inside him at the delicious smashing sounds.

The righteous violence released his tense shoulder and neck muscles so that the next morning he was actually walking straighter. Thinking clearer. He was braver, smarter, fiercer. He felt tough. Capable. He snapped at a guy in a café who tried to cut ahead of him in line, sent him shuffling away. He fired his acting coach and personal trainer, and demanded his father's secretary find him better ones. Ashton was finally the big man. He was in touch with his primal, powerful self. He couldn't wait to wear the black skull mask again that Vera had given him. He wished he could wear it every hour of the day and night.

The next raids followed quickly. Ashton barely listened to the justifications for the victims they chose. Some guy had cat-called Penny outside a construction site. A woman had turned Vera away from a dance club. All he had to know was that these were bad people who didn't know their place. Ashton told himself he was doing a good thing—dishing out justice, teaching people respect, humility. But he hardly needed any convincing. He was having so much fun.

Aunt Francine left Uncle Ray. Ashton heard talk at the next party that she had moved to London and started trading expensive antique pottery, had a younger guy living in her apartment—a *much* younger guy. He had seen his uncle once afterward, at a christening. Ray had looked pale and thin.

As I sat listening to Ashton, my mind bounced between pity and fury at the child before me. A part of me wanted to scream at him that the "righteous anger" that had led him down his violent path was just the selfish whining of a spoiled brat who too early had gotten bored of being rich and didn't know what to do with all his pent-up energy. But another part of me knew that it didn't matter how much money a kid had, how big his house was, or how many toys his parents paid the holiday decorators to wrap and arrange artfully under the tree. If a parent ignored, abandoned, or abused their child, an angry seed was planted that could grow into a poisonous tree. I knew that whether a parent was rich and snubbed their kid for expensive wine or they were poor and snubbed them for cheap crack, the message to the kid was the same:

You're not as important to me as my next high.

The slap Ashton witnessed that had so outraged him wasn't as important as the parents who hadn't listened to that outrage. I'd been dealing with the fallout of ignored kids in courtrooms for a decade, defending girls and boys who had gone out looking for the attention and acceptance they didn't get at home, looking in all the wrong kinds of places, with all the wrong kinds of people.

"How did your little game get this out of control?" I asked when Ashton had finished his story. Ashton looked up at me, gripped the torn knees of his jeans.

"We messed with the wrong guy," he said.

CHAPTER 85

I SAT THINKING. Baby scrolled and tapped on her phone. I knew that even though she seemed distracted, she had been soaking up everything, probably confirming or discounting what Ashton said with searches online. He explained Derek Benstein's death and the terrifying encounter he had had with the killer outside the house in Brentwood the night before. It was a lot to take in.

Ashton was watching me hopefully, and even though I hadn't decided how best to help him, I knew I needed to begin throwing ideas around just to ease the tension before it consumed him again.

"Whoever this guy is," I said, "he's on your list, and he's got a big-ass rifle. He's probably military or ex-military, if what you've said about his sharpshooting skills is correct. So we just look at the list of all the houses you hit and find a military family."

"That's fine if he's one of our victims. But it doesn't help if the person we're looking for is a friend or associate of someone we targeted," Ashton said. "Or someone they hired."

"Excuse me for butting in." Baby put a hand up. "But isn't finding the guy who's hunting you a problem for the police? Rhonda, we should turn Ashton in. There's probably a big reward, which I think should probably go to me because it was my idea to do it."

"Are you kidding me right now, Baby?" Ashton turned to her in shock.

"Nope," she said.

"We go way back, you and me," he said.

"I go way back with the cute lacrosse player from school. This guy?" She gestured to him. "I don't know this guy at all."

"I didn't come here to hand myself in," Ashton said, turning to me. "I came here for your help. I'm sorry. You have no idea how sorry I am for everything we did. It's like I'm someone else or...under the mask I was seeing through different eyes. But I can see now. What we did was wrong. So wrong. But at the same time, I don't want to die for it."

"No, Ashton, you don't want to pay for it." Baby scoffed. "You don't want to do time, so you're hoping Rhonda will stick up for you. Make this all go away. That's what rich kids do. Well, you should have thought about that before you *broke the law*."

I put my own hand up. "Baby, don't be a smart-ass. You don't get to lecture people about being spoiled when you're sitting on a twenty-thousand-dollar couch in your dad's fifteen-million-dollar house. And the party you hosted here last night shows you're much more Courtney Love than Mother Teresa."

"I don't know who either of those people are," Baby said.

"But I do know that if someone busted in here, tied me to a chair, and broke all of my worldly possessions, I'd probably want to clamp a car battery to his nipples too."

"Baby, *outside*," I snapped. She followed me in a huff as I got up and went to the Strand, slamming the door behind us.

CHAPTER 86

AS SOON AS WE got outside, Baby took her phone out and started tapping on it.

"Put that away and look at me."

"In a second."

"What are you doing?" I leaned over. "Are you googling Courtney Love?"

"No." Baby scrolled. "She seems cool, though."

"Derek Benstein didn't have a car battery clamped to his nipples," I said, pushing her phone down. "He was tortured with a cattle prod and then shot to death, probably while begging for his life."

"How was I supposed to know that?" Baby took out her vape pen and put it to her lips. It wobbled in her mouth as she spoke. "Online it just said he was electrocuted. He's dead. What's the difference?"

"The difference is that I've seen those crime-scene photographs," I said. "And his death was horrific. It was prolonged, violent, and sickening."

"How did you—"

"Never mind." I grabbed the vape and threw it into a nearby bush before she could take another drag. "What I'm telling you is that Ashton has come to us admitting he's done terrible things and saying he's sorry. He's asking for help. It doesn't matter what a person has done; when they ask for help turning things around, you've got to set aside everything that happened before that moment and try to start fresh."

"You're nice," Baby said, plucking the vape from the ground and bringing it to her lips. I sighed, the fight going out of me for trivial things when I was trying to communicate such important themes. "I guess you've probably had some nasty kids come to you wanting you to go into the ring for them in the courtroom."

"I have," I said.

"Rapists and killers and stuff."

"That's right."

"And how did you know which ones really were sorry and which ones were just playing you for a sap?" Baby asked.

I tried to answer, but no words would come.

"I don't trust this guy." She nodded toward the house. "Yeah, I knew him back when we were kids, but this is some heavy stuff right here."

"You're still a kid," I said. "And news flash! You don't trust anyone. You don't trust me, and I'm your own flesh and blood."

"Well, what does that even mean?" she asked.

I stepped back and exhaled slowly, reminded myself that I was trying to talk about family trust and loyalty to a child whose mother had dumped her on her uninterested father's doorstep.

"Let's just not call the police yet," I said.

Baby got some kind of alert on her phone. Something was going on in her internet world, a disruption only she could sense as she went back to flicking and scrolling.

"Let's get more information and see what kind of danger we would be putting Ashton in if we did that. We don't know if this guy is watching him right now. If he senses Ashton's about to be locked up, out of reach, he might make a move."

"I'd say you're right," Baby said, exhaling smoke at her phone screen. "He'll probably move on Ashton next."

"What? Why?"

"Because Sean and Penny Hanley are dead," Baby said. She turned her phone toward me. I saw a car crushed against a tree, the hood streaked with blood. "Only Ashton and Vera are left."

CHAPTER 87

VERA WALKED UP THE cobblestone driveway, smoothing her curls back and smiling her best girl-next-door smile again. Jacob Kanular's house seemed smaller in the daylight. The dark hours stretched things, created long shadows and yawning spaces in closets and at the ends of halls that frightened little children. Vera wondered if Jacob's daughter had been scared of the dark. If she ever would be again.

It was the wife's social media profile that had given Vera everything she needed. Jacob was a dark vacant space online — a stray elbow visible in the corner of a selfie Neina had taken with their grinning daughter, Beatrice, or a reflected outline in a window beside the slender woman as she snapped a sunrise. Neina, whose sculpture page on Instagram had tens of thousands of followers, had posted a brief note about Beaty's condition the day after Vera and her crew invaded the house.

Pray for us. Beaty in hospital after severe asthma attack. All shipments/commissions postponed until further notice.

An earlier Instagram post about participating in an upcoming exhibition at the Palos Verdes Art Center had given Vera the ruse she needed to get through the gates. She tucked her clipboard under her arm and went to the huge front double doors of the house, the same doors she had run through with her crew only a few nights before. She tried to look eager when Neina opened the door and a little surprised at her bedraggled, exhausted appearance.

"Annabelle Cetes." Vera put out a hand.

"Is this going to take long?" Neina asked. "I'm really busy here."

"I just need a couple of snaps of the pieces you planned to exhibit for the program and the online marketing scheme." Vera brandished the little camera hanging around her neck.

"This was too awkward to try to explain through the intercom." Neina leaned in the doorway, sighed. "But the pieces I put together for the exhibition were destroyed. There was a...an accident here at the house. I won't be participating in the exhibit. I explained all this to—"

"Oh, I'm so sorry," Vera gushed. She pulled out the clipboard and flipped the pages on it. "This is so weird. You're still on my list. I should have been told about this. God, how embarrassing. I'm so sorry."

Vera squinted in the sunlight, wiped invisible sweat from her temple.

Take the hint, lady, she thought. But the killer's wife didn't budge from the doorway.

"Hoo!" Vera said. "A real hot one today, isn't it?"

"Was there anything else?" Neina asked.

"Do you think I could come in for a moment and make a call back to the office, see what's going on? It's so hot out here."

Neina looked back into the house. Vera smiled sweetly again. She knew Jacob wasn't home. In case he was following her, Vera had driven through a series of parking lots and alleyways in Culver City before heading to the Kanulars' address. She'd then texted Sean, saying she was going to meet with Ashton at Soho House, in case he had her dead friend's phone. She'd even sent her phone to the restaurant by courier in case Jacob was tracking her device. She'd watched the Kanular house from the hillside for half an hour for any sign of him before approaching but had only seen Neina through the huge windows facing the sea, rattling around the house and gathering her things.

It seemed now that the woman was reluctant to be alone in the big house with a stranger. Vera concentrated, positively beamed innocence and genuine warmth while fanning her cheeks in the oppressive California heat.

Don't let me drop dead of heatstroke on your doorstep, bitch, she thought. *You already have one fragile little girl in a coma to worry about.*

"Can't you—" Neina began.

"I'll only be a moment," Vera said.

She stepped back reluctantly as Vera followed into the huge foyer.

CHAPTER 88

THE KANULAR HOUSE HAD been cleaned since the Midnight Crew's rampage. The only indications left of their presence were the strangely bare shelves, where books or sculptures had stood, and the smell of fresh paint in the air.

Vera followed Neina into the big living room, looking at the back of the woman's skull, thinking about the shape of it beneath her chopped dark hair, the delicious force it would take to crack it. There was a suitcase spread open on the couch, another clipped closed and standing ready in the hall leading to the bedrooms. Neina was leaving. Vera guessed a husband running around enacting his grisly revenge on a bunch of teenagers when he should have been sitting beside their dying child would put a strain on any marriage. That's assuming Neina knew what was going on. How smart was she?

Vera watched the woman carefully as she settled on the arm of the couch. She made a show of playing with her phone. Made a fake call and huffed as it wasn't answered.

"Do you think I could trouble you for a glass of water?" she asked.

Neina seemed to stifle a sigh but went to the kitchen. Vera followed. When Neina took a glass from the cupboard and then to the sink, Vera let her hand wander across the counter toward the knife block.

"Oh, sorry." She laughed. "Uh, maybe a cold one? Do you mind?"

Neina rolled her eyes and went to the fridge, turning her back on her visitor.

CHAPTER 89

SOMETHING ABOUT THE HOSPITAL room felt different as soon as Jacob walked in. Though the flowers and greeting cards at his daughter's bedside were the same, he sensed a shift in the air as if a window had been opened somewhere, letting the room finally breathe. Jacob knew the smell of death, and he also knew the scent of life. He went to the bedside and sat beside his child, took Beaty's limp fingers in his.

There was blood under Jacob's nails. He noticed a splinter, probably from the tree branch he had used to impale Sean Hanley, embedded in one of his knuckles. He picked at it and, while he was focused on it, almost missed the sensation of Beaty's fingers moving in his. Her hand gripped his for an instant—no more than a flutter, but the movement shot a bolt of painful energy through Jacob. He looked at her passive face and saw no signs of wakefulness.

Finally, finally, some of his work out there in the world, hunting down the ones who had done this, was bringing some life back into his little girl. Three of them were gone, and their passing was bringing Beaty home one step at a time.

He stood and brushed off the legs of his dirty jeans, fixed his hair. He'd walked into the hospital looking like he'd been scrabbling up the sides of rocky ravines hunting wild animals, but his appearance hadn't raised eyebrows. The halls were full of men and women who looked bedraggled and worn and dirty from days and weeks spent refusing to leave the sides of the sick and dying.

He had to find someone, tell them Beaty was coming back. He would get them to order more brain scans. He kissed Beaty and walked into the hall, grabbed his phone as it buzzed in his pocket. Neina's name flashed on the screen.

"She moved," he said before his wife could speak. He tried flagging down a doctor walking busily past in the hall before him. "I felt Beaty's hand move."

"Can you come back to the house, please?" Neina's voice was tight, strangely low, like she was afraid of being over-heard. "The police are here."

"What?" Jacob stopped walking.

"There was another home invasion last night in Brentwood, up north. A woman got shot. The police know about what happened to us."

Jacob looked back at the door to his daughter's room. A painful prickling was creeping out from the center of his chest. His old instincts warning him.

"Do they know…" he said. Neina was silent for a long time, and in his thoughts he screamed at her words that he could never say out loud.

Do they know what I've been doing?

"Just come here," Neina said. "Now, Jacob."

"I'm on my way," he said.

He hung up, looked back down the hall. The old Jacob, the hit man for hire, the shadow who had walked the earth with only a backpack and a gun and a desire for blood, said one word to him: *Run*. Beaty would be okay, or she wouldn't. Neina would be okay, or she wouldn't. If he decided to go now, to slip away from the hospital, out of the city, and into the ether again, there would be no coming back, no dropping in now and then, no watching his little family from afar. He either abandoned them completely now or stayed to fight through whatever implications his revenge would have on his existence as a father and a husband.

He tapped the phone against his leg, watched a man with a toddler girl hugged against his hip using the nearby vending machine. The little girl was slapping the glass as the colorful treats glowed in the bright lights.

Could he have his vengeance *and* go back to the life he had built himself here with Neina and Beaty? Or was having both of those things simply too much to hope for?

Jacob decided he had not lost hope yet.

He turned and headed for the parking lot.

CHAPTER 90

NEINA KANULAR PUT THE phone down on the tiles beside her face and stifled a scream. She was pressed face-down on the floor of the kitchen, the teenage girl's bootheel pressing into the tender place beneath her shoulder blades, the muscles knotted and bunched, trying to protect the bones beneath. Neina rolled onto her side and clutched at the deep slash wound the girl had cut across her chest, the tiles around her already smeared and streaked with blood. She scrambled into the corner of the kitchen.

"Jacob's coming," she said. She cowered on the floor and tried to remain calm. "It's him you want, right?"

The girl didn't answer. She was using the knife to flick photographs stuck to the refrigerator door onto the floor. Beaty and her friends in sleeping bags on the living room floor, camped out watching a horror movie. Beaty and Jacob at the helm of a small sailboat.

"If he comes and sees there are no cop cars out front, he'll know something is up," Neina said. "You'll need me to get him in the door."

"I don't need you for anything," the girl said. She shifted the knife in her grip. "You've served your purpose."

She advanced toward the older woman. Neina dragged herself to her feet, backed against the wall, an animal cornered.

"Now, don't scream," the girl said.

CHAPTER 91

AT A GAS STATION off the 405 heading north, I kept Ashton in my sights as he walked into the main building to buy some snacks. I filled up the little orange Jeep I had borrowed from the Bruhs. The huge biceps logo emblazoned on the side of the vehicle wasn't the most subtle thing in the world, particularly as we didn't know if the man hunting Ashton and his crew was following and watching us. But I'd turned the keys in the car knowing it was unlikely to explode on us, which was more than I could say for my father's Maserati.

I watched the teenage boy inside the gas station. He guzzled a bottle of water and shoveled the contents of a bag of Cheetos into his mouth as he walked to the counter to pay for an armful of snacks. It had been a big night.

Baby leaned against the car beside me, her eyes hidden behind her huge sunglasses. I knew she was nervous, and not only because we were on the run from killers. In Baby's world, she was probably equally terrified that at any moment Ashton would tell me about how she'd kissed her teacher. The kiss was almost certainly "the thing" they had talked about in the hall outside my father's office. I was sure I had heard Baby in the back seat of the Jeep growl something like "If you say anything" at the other teenager as we drove. When I'd glanced up, she'd been making a cutting motion at her neck and Ashton had looked distinctly uncomfortable.

Now Baby was rubbing her shoulders, trying to ease out some of the tension as I pumped the gas.

"This is the worst idea I ever heard of," Baby said finally.

"When the heat is on, you go underground," I said. "We've got a Mexican drug cartel after us *and* some kind of revenge-bent psycho after Ashton. Neither of those parties is going to pursue us all the way to Colorado, or if they do, we'll have plenty of time to lose them and form a plan to keep ourselves safe when we get there."

"Yeah, that'll be really easy to do with us driving around in a bright orange car with a giant armpit printed on it." Baby gazed at the freeway, the cars zooming past, a huge pink bill-board advertising Jennifer Lopez's new film. "Let's assume we get there safely. Then what? We, like, hide out in your shitty condo until this all blows over? Just crawl under the beds with your thousands of cats meowing and pawing at our faces? Get real, Rhonda. This isn't going to just blow over. We ought to stay here and fight."

"Okay, hold up. First of all, my condo is awesome. And what's with the cats? Why would you think I have thousands of cats?"

Baby shook her head.

"Oh, I see." I nodded. "I keep thousands of cats because I'm so fat and lonely I just sit at home waiting for a man to come along and marry me?"

"You're missing the point," she said.

"Look, Vegas is a businessman. Or so he keeps telling us. Hopefully, if he's weighing risk versus reward, he'll find it far more rewarding to go back to the beach house and try to find the money and drugs there while we're gone rather than come after us," I said. "He might even be successful after a while."

"So you did hide it in the house," Baby said, chewing her lip.

"The search will keep them entertained," I continued. "Those guys want their stuff more than they want us. That's their priority. So we set them up to get busted while they're searching. That's one problem solved. As for whoever is after Ashton and his friends, without him in the picture, the killer will have only Vera to focus on. We can call the police and negotiate Ashton's surrender, and while we're at it, we tell them this guy is going to be watching her, and—"

My words were cut off by a wail of sirens. Two squad cars and an unmarked sedan with a flashing light bar in the windshield pulled into the gas station, surrounding us, the last to arrive screeching to a halt only feet from Ashton as he exited the building. He dropped his armful of snacks, shattering a glass bottle of soda on the concrete. Men and women congregating around the automatic doors backed up against the wall, their hands up.

Officer David Summerly was the last person I expected to see exit the lead unmarked vehicle and walk across the station toward me. He took a pair of cuffs from his belt and snapped one onto my wrist.

"Rhonda Bird," he said, "you're under arrest."

CHAPTER 92

JACOB WAS RUSTY. That was his problem. He'd gotten worn down and slightly crooked, like an armchair flopped into too many times over too many years. Creaking and cracking. He was getting old. Jacob had made mistakes, and the biggest of them was falling in love, building a family. As he drove through the streets of Palos Verdes, slamming his foot on the accelerator of the BMW and hooking into turns like a race-car driver, he scolded himself. A family not unlike his own, two parents and a young girl, hurled themselves out of a crosswalk and onto the grass beneath a palm tree as he roared past.

When Jacob had been a killer for hire, he'd loved no one, nothing. He had obeyed the rules of men like him, in the last years of the Cold War, that glorious time before CCTV cameras and DNA and civilians with cell phones. Never walk into a room with only one entrance and exit. Keep your back to the wall and your gun loaded. Always have a backup plan, a bug-out bag, a safe house. Keep your body taut and tight. Practice holds and escape maneuvers whenever a spare moment presents itself—in traffic, in the bathroom, in a shitty motel room in Thailand across the road from the sprawling resort where the target lay relaxing in their final hours of life.

Jacob had abandoned all of it when he met Neina, told himself he wasn't that man anymore. But that man would never die. He wasn't as sharp anymore. Maybe he was carrying a couple of extra pounds. And his guns had been packed away, useless, in a cupboard in a basement. But the plan should never have changed. The old rules should have been obeyed.

Jacob crested the hill and pulled over, looked down at the house perched on the outcrop of cliffs looking over the vast, sparkling sea. The sun was hanging low over the horizon, making the windows of the house blaze pink. Jacob was glad he couldn't see inside now. He knew as he sat there watching that there were no officers sitting around Neina on the couches, playing good cop to her while they tried to pry out what she knew. The gate to the property was open, and there were no cars in the driveway.

Which meant Neina was dead.

Rusty. Stupid. He'd allowed himself to be lured. Not lured into a trap but away from the only thing in the world more precious to him than his wife.

Jacob stepped on the gas and spun the wheels, heading back toward the hospital.

CHAPTER 93

ONE OF THE PATROL cops, I saw, was trying to grab Baby, with Ashton surely next, while Summerly shoved me toward his sedan.

"What the hell is this?" I yelled as he shoved me into the back seat. I waited, barely containing my fury, while he walked around the front of the car and got in. "Are you kidding me? You're arresting me for what?"

"I can hear you, Rhonda. You don't have to shout." He winced, rubbing his ear. "There are only two of us in the car, you know."

"Where are you taking those kids?"

"Just calm down." Summerly turned the wheel and headed out of the lot. "We're all going to the West LA station. They can service us there."

"Service us? What the hell is going on?"

"I've been lying to you, Rhonda," Summerly said. "I'm not a patrol cop."

I stared out the window at the gridlocked traffic. Somewhere behind us, I imagined, Baby and Ashton were being loaded into the patrol cars. It would have been tight with me in the back seat and the two of them squished in with me, but I wanted the kids by my side. The pendulum that had been swinging between being Baby's mother and sister now had me feeling the hot, flustered stress of a mother duck with her ducklings loose from the flock, toppling and turning down river rapids.

"I'm a detective," Summerly said. "Gang and Narcotics Division."

"Well, congratulations!" I sneered, the new threat of danger creeping up my spine. "What has that got to do with me?"

"Oh, I don't know," Summerly said. "Do you happen to know someone around here who might have millions of dollars of cartel cash and drugs in their possession somewhere?"

I bit my lip.

"You're not under arrest for possession." Summerly watched me in the rearview mirror with his warm brown eyes. "But I gotta tell ya, if I didn't like you so much I'd be tempted."

"Well, what the hell am I under arrest for?"

"Nothing," he said. "We were making a show of taking you into custody so that the guy working for Martin Vegas who was sitting in the yellow Camaro at the gas station where we picked you up would know you guys were off-limits."

"You . . ." I tried to think. "What guy? There was a guy?"

"You didn't notice?" Summerly said. "The car was bright yellow."

"I was a little distracted."

"Drug dealers have terrible taste in cars." He shook his head.

"And clothes too," I agreed.

I felt strangely deflated. Stupid and gullible. Since I arrived in Los Angeles, I had been playing with the big bad kids, and I'd just been revealed to both them and myself as the odd one out. I'd thought I was putting the pieces of the puzzle together, and all this time it had been shifting around me as I stumbled along. I sagged into the seat, crushing my chained hands against the leather.

"So you've been onto me since the car bombing?" I asked.

"No, we've been onto you since Earl died," Summerly replied. He blasted the horn at a vehicle ahead of us holding up the lane while I tried to collect my thoughts. "Rhonda, your dad was working for us."

CHAPTER 94

VERA FELT NUMB. That was good. Once, when she was about eight, she'd crept to her father's office and lingered outside the door, listening to Evgeni Petrov describe his first kill to an associate. The anticipation of what it would feel like had been so great, he'd said, that the act itself passed over him as seamlessly and unremarkably as the act of pouring a cup of coffee or making the bed.

Vera had always wondered what her first real kill would feel like, whether she would work through it mechanically, like her father had, or whether she would connect with what she was doing emotionally, something she assumed would make her weak and vulnerable. But killing Neina Kanular had been like smacking a mosquito. She'd fought a little. Been difficult to catch, to pin down. But then the superefficient death strike, right on target, had given Vera a little ripple of satisfaction and nothing more.

She had the mind for it. The soul. She really was Daddy's girl.

Vera walked now through the hospital halls and took the elevator to the fifth floor. Neina hadn't given up any further information on her daughter's location, but Vera knew the girl wouldn't be hard to find. She used the mirrors in the elevators to wipe a blood smear from her neck and tuck her wild curls back in. Though Vera was sure she had buried Neina's death somewhere deep in the dark corners of her mind, her eyes seemed a little wild to her. She closed them, breathed, tried to reset. A family with a stroller got onto the elevator at the third floor, and Vera cooed at the smiley baby.

Vera walked confidently onto the ward and turned left into the first room as though she knew exactly where she was going. She shoved back a curtain to reveal an old man with a neurosurgery scar sleeping with his mouth hanging open. She turned and walked out, checked the next two rooms: two teen boys sitting on a bed playing with their phones while a woman took a phone call by the windows, another old man reading a newspaper.

Three more rooms revealed nothing more. Vera pretended to read a chart on the wall about visitation hours while she thumbed the safety off the pistol inside her bag. She didn't want to use the weapon, but she was running out of time, and she knew that if Jacob returned earlier than she expected, she would need to be ready. Her hope was to slip in and out, leaving the kid for her father to find, pale and lifeless in the bed, still warm to the touch. Vera had always thought it was wonderful in movies when the parent arrived just seconds too late to save the child. The closer the margin, the better the tragedy.

She turned into the next room and found a bedside cabinet crowded with cards and flowers, the bay where the bed should be sitting empty.

She went and snatched up the nearest card.

Dear Beaty, We hope that you...

Vera threw the card on the floor.

Outside the room, an orderly in a blue uniform was cleaning off a whiteboard with a cloth and spray.

"I'm looking for my sister." Vera smiled, her hand on the gun in her bag. "Could you please help me?"

CHAPTER 95

ASHTON SAW RHONDA BIRD being driven away in an unmarked cop car, then stood and looked around him at the scene that remained: a squad car pulling out slowly to join the traffic heading in the other direction on the 405, with the people who had paused to gawk now resuming their activities. Baby was standing beside the open door of the second squad car while a silver-haired officer tried to corral her into the vehicle.

Two things struck him. The first was that everybody seemed to have completely forgotten his existence. This meant that whatever Rhonda and Baby were being arrested for, it had nothing to do with the Midnight Crew. The second was that the officer at the front of the remaining squad car had slid into the vehicle, leaving her partner alone to deal with getting Baby into the back of the car, and the old patrol cop was struggling with the outraged teen.

Ashton gathered up his pile of snacks. The temptation to walk away pulsed in him, heavy and urgent. He could walk to the edge of the gas station and disappear down an alley into the streets, get a cab home. But all that waited for him out there was a killer who had only him and Vera left to track down.

At least here he had an ally. He had thought Vera would protect him, that she and the other members of the Crew had been the kind of team who would be there for him when things got scary. He'd been wrong. Maybe it was time to start hanging out with a different crowd.

Ashton walked up behind the older officer and gave him a nudge on the back of the ankle with his shoe.

"Hey, man."

The officer turned.

"Catch this."

Ashton threw all his snacks at the officer at once. Two bags of Ruffles, a Hot Pocket, a can of nuts, and two doughnuts. A crackling explosion of color and crinkled confectionery packaging. He didn't need to tell Baby what to do. While the old man struggled to catch the barrage of treats, the teenagers bolted.

CHAPTER 96

I SAT QUIETLY FOR a moment. My father, an under-cover operative? Whatever was clogging the traffic suddenly released and we were on our way again.

"My dad was—"

"Not a hero," Summerly said. "Before you go too far down that track. He was not working with the police out of a sense of honor and justice and service to the community."

"Oh."

"We had a tracker planted in a shipment of drugs coming up from Mexico, and your dad received it," he said. "We got him dead to rights. He agreed to work with us in a sting on Martin Vegas. All he wanted was to stay out of jail and take care of Baby, so we cut him a deal."

"Oh, he didn't want to stay out of jail to care for Baby," I sneered. The anger was boiling up inside me, hotter and hotter. "He wanted to stay out of jail because they don't serve whiskey there. Is Perry Tuddy in on all this?"

"Of course," Summerly said.

"So all his bullshit about enjoying being locked up by the cartel was just a lie?"

"Nope," Summerly said. "That guy is a genuine nutcase. He gets himself locked up by the cartel almost intentionally because he enjoys it for some weird reason. But we approached him after he was last released and asked him if he wouldn't mind us placing a tracker on him too, to see where the cartel took him. And, yeah, even though he likes being locked up, I still felt conflicted about it. What kind of jerk lets a guy rot in a shipping container in the middle of the desert just to make a case?"

"I don't know. The same kind of guy who would sleep with a woman just to make a case?"

Summerly jerked the wheel and slammed on the brakes. The car's bumper barely missed scraping the concrete barrier at the side of the road. He turned and stared at me.

"You can't honestly believe that's what I did."

"I don't know." I shrugged. "It's hard to believe you have any genuine feelings for me while I'm cuffed in the back of your police car, Dave."

"You're only back there for show," he said. "How would it look to Vegas's guys if I tossed you the keys and we both swung through Miffy's for a shake?"

"Just about as bad as it does for us to be sitting here by the side of the road having a heart-to-heart."

"Well, I don't care." Summerly snorted and locked eyes on me. "Rhonda, I haven't met a person like you in . . ."

He thought about it. I waited.

"In all my life."

"How romantic. I've lost feeling in my fingers and I really need to pee. Can we get moving?"

"I was kind of hoping you and me could hang out after all this. Go out on a real date."

"You'll be lucky if I don't put your head through the wind-shield of this car as soon as you take these cuffs off," I said.

"I mean…" He turned, looked at me in the rearview. "I mean, I was kind of hoping you felt the same."

"I don't know how I feel about you. For me, it was just something that happened. I haven't thought about it yet. I haven't had a chance to!"

"Oh, so it's okay for it to have been just something that happened for you, but not for me?" He smirked. "Nice."

"I don't care what kind of something happened, as long as it wasn't something for the sake of searching my house for Vegas's drugs and money while I was asleep."

"Well, it wasn't." Summerly huffed.

"Well, good," I snapped.

We sat in silence.

The yellow Camaro drove by us on the freeway, the driver's head swiveling toward us as he passed. "That was him. He saw us. Vegas's guy will report back that Baby and I are locked up and out of reach. You can let me go now."

"Not until you tell us where Vegas's drugs and money are."

I sighed. "If I do that, I'll be admitting that I have it."

"Tuddy says you took the meth from the shipping container," Summerly said.

"Yeah, well you've only got his word on that. There may be footage from the camera inside the container, but I assume that was a cartel camera and not something you planted," I said. "You've got about as much of a chance proving that I committed a felony as you do proving that the earth is flat."

"Rhonda, I'm not going to charge you with possession of the drugs and cash." Summerly looked me right in the eyes.

"But if you don't tell me where it all is, I can't protect you from Vegas."

"And you can't catch him either," I said.

Summerly didn't reply. He was asking me to trust him. Not only about the hours we had shared together but also about my future, about whether I would spend it behind bars or wandering around in the free world. He was asking me to trust that he wouldn't charge me for failing to surrender the drugs and cash to police even as I sat in his car in cuffs that he himself had snapped onto my wrists.

I didn't like the powerless feeling of the metal restricting my movement, the reek of the back of the police vehicle, where probably wrongdoers of every shape and form had sat before me, contemplating the very thing that I was contemplating: how their families would survive in the outside world without them. Because there was no escaping the fact that Baby would go into foster care without a legal guardian to care for her. She thought her life was hard in *my* custody? I tried to imagine her arriving on the doorstep of a crowded group home or a suburban house packed to the rafters with neglected toddlers and teenage runaways.

"Take me to the station," I said. "I want to speak to Baby."

"Rhonda, I need you to tell me where—"

"I've done enough talking," I said.

CHAPTER 97

VERA FOLLOWED THE SIGNS to the children's ward on the second floor. Colorful drawings were taped to the walls, and misshapen artwork made from pipe cleaners and cotton balls hung from the ceiling like weird descending spiders. She gripped the gun in her handbag and went from room to room, peering in to look for bed 29. Vera didn't know why the girl had been moved, but she wondered if Jacob had called ahead and requested it.

If that was the case, it meant that Jacob had found his wife in a pool of her own blood on the kitchen floor, and he would be on his way back now, so she didn't have much time. Trying to hide his daughter instead of calling building security and the police meant Jacob had not alerted the hospital authorities of her plan. It meant he wanted to fight. He wanted Vera to himself.

She smiled. She wanted him too.

Vera found the girl in an empty room, the light from the crack in the curtains falling across her soft face. There was a dullness and a sunken quality to her features that told Vera the girl wasn't out of the coma yet, that behind the closed eyelids and long dark lashes there probably wasn't much going on.

In a way, that was a shame. Neina had known what was coming. Vera had seen her thoughts shuddering through her face as she lost her grip on the earth and began to leave her body. All the days that she wouldn't experience, days that had been promised to her—birthdays and anniversaries and simple evenings staring at the rolling sea with her loving family by her side. Sunrises and sunsets. Neina had known then that she'd enjoyed her very last meal. She'd made her last phone call. She'd chosen her last outfit. This was it. This painful and terrifying and fury-filled end was hers, and there was not a thing she could do about it.

Vera wouldn't get to see all those emotions race through Beaty, the knowledge that Vera was the all-powerful force that had chosen when to bring her life to a close. But that was okay. More victims would come. More delicious ends. Vera had crossed into the bad world, and there was no going back.

Vera climbed onto the bed, straddled the girl, and wrapped her fingers around Beaty's thin neck.

The machines started ticking and singing around her. A part of Vera's mind knew this was a bad plan. That killing her this way would bring nurses and doctors, and she'd have to dispense with them too. But she had to take Beaty. Then Jacob. She'd worry about plans later. She was good at this. It had always been in her. She was so good at killing she didn't need an exit strategy. This was her entry into a new life.

The girl bucked and twisted underneath her, the gagging, jerking dance of the unconscious body deprived of air. The girl's eyes flew open. Vera held on. She'd imagined killing someone this way a few times before. This kind of death would be perfect for her mother. A slow, drowning, intimate death. Vera felt her whole body come alive with pleasure.

A slamming door cut the euphoric feeling short. Two nurses burst in, their squeals of surprise and horror making Vera retract her hands from the girl's throat as though her skin was hot. She leaned over and fumbled in the handbag she had thrown on the table beside the bed while Beaty coughed and spluttered. Vera grabbed her gun and fired twice, hitting a nurse with each bullet. They lay still on the ground.

Outside the door, chaos was growing. People had heard the gunshots and were shouting out, trying to get a sense of what had happened in the room, too afraid to come look. They knew, of course. The distinct sound of a gun in a crowded public building meant only one thing in the modern United States. Vera heard running footsteps, alarms beginning to sound. But as she focused back on strangling the invalid girl, all she was really listening to was the sound of Beaty's final gasps for air as the life drained out of her underneath Vera's hands.

And then he was there. Jacob came into the room silently and quickly, striking so fast that his movement was a blur at the corner of Vera's vision. He wrapped an arm around her neck, dragged her backward, and threw her against the wall. The gun clattered onto the floor between the two dead nurses. Vera righted herself and locked eyes with the man in the dimly lit room.

CHAPTER 98

THE TWO TEENAGERS RAN through the streets. Above them, tall, thin palm trees looked like dark prison bars against the orange sunset sky.

They didn't talk. Baby tried to turn down an alleyway, but Ashton grabbed her hand and pulled her in a different direction; after that, there seemed no reason to let go of her fingers. They were warm in his, and he needed something to hold on to.

Baby eventually took her hand back when they stopped on a street corner to lean against a fence, huffing with effort. The sweat on her forehead shone like a mist of diamonds.

"We need a plan," Baby said. "You've got an assassin after you. I've got the police and a cartel on my tail."

"I can't believe this is happening." Ashton tried to suck in air, but his chest was tight. "It was never meant to be like this. I'm not this person."

"You can have a mental breakdown about it later." Baby held a hand up. "Right now, we've got to get off the streets."

"Can you call Rhonda?" Ashton asked. "She knew what to do. She can tell us what to do."

"The police would have taken her phone, probably," Baby said. "It's just us now."

Ashton shivered. The words hit him hard. *It's just us now.* At least it meant Baby was going to stick with him. He hardly knew her, couldn't trust her, but she was all he had. They were two kids on the run, and he'd never felt more like a kid: confused, angry, on the verge of tears, so completely out of his depth. Ashton knew how stories like these ended. They ended on lonely highways with the car littered with police bullets or they ended with the kids in jail for the rest of their lives.

"But Rhonda—"

"She can't help us," Baby snapped. "Her big plan was to go to Colorado and hide. She was right about one thing. We need to get out of the city." The girl wheeled around on Ashton. "You're rich. You've got money. We go to a bank and you get as much cash out as possible. We go to an airport and hire a pilot to take us to, like, Bermuda or something. Maybe a private jet. Have you got a private jet?"

"No," Ashton said. "And I'm not as rich as you think. My parents are rich. I've got access to a couple of thousand bucks or so of pocket money, but that's it."

"What? Are you kidding me?"

"I overspent a while back." Ashton could feel his neck and jaw becoming hot. "They put me on lockdown. I get two thou a week spending money. That's it."

Baby chewed her lip, shook her head in disgust. Her thoughts seemed to be racing.

"I might know where we can get three million bucks," she said. "That should keep us safe for a while."

"Jesus," Ashton said. "You think? We could buy a boutique hotel to hole up in. Maybe a passable yacht."

"Getting the cash will be dangerous, though," Baby said, his attempt at humor shot down with a single glance. She grabbed his hand again, and Ashton felt his stomach plunge. "Come on," she said. "This way."

CHAPTER 99

"GODDAMNIT." SUMMERLY YANKED THE wheel
again. We had been driving along in stony silence when his
phone rang. He'd listened to the call and then thrown the
phone onto the dash of the car. "Baby got away."

"What?" I sat up. "Got away how? Where is she?"

"I don't know." Summerly flicked the sirens on. "They were
putting her in the car at the gas station when some kid came
up and got in the middle of everything. The two ran off
together."

"Ashton," I said.

"Who?"

"Never mind. She's gone. She's out there alone. We've got
to go back and find her."

"I'm trying." Summerly leaned on the horn as drivers ahead
of him panicked and tried to get out of his way in various
different directions, blocking the lanes even further.

I could only sit back and burn with frustration, wondering
what Baby's plan was. I guessed she would be afraid and angry
at me for abandoning her, even though the arrest wasn't my

fault. Maybe she would split off from Ashton, or she would take him along, but in either case, she wouldn't let the older boy be in charge of keeping them safe—she didn't trust him, didn't trust anyone, and would be thinking quickly about the best route to safety. Yes, that's what she would do. I didn't know Baby completely, but I thought I knew how she would act under duress.

I felt confident that she would go back to the house for the drug cartel money. There'd been a sharpness in her eyes at the gas station when she realized that I'd given her a clue to the whereabouts of the cash.

So you did hide it in the house, she'd said.

Baby and possibly Ashton would almost certainly head to the house. Vegas and his guys were probably heading there too, now that he knew I was under arrest and out of the picture.

I opened my mouth, almost told Summerly that I was near certain Baby would be heading back to Manhattan Beach. But like my young sister, my trust had been ground down to nothing. If I sent the police back to the house, I risked surrounding Baby with cops just as she left the premises with a bag full of cash and possibly the cartel drugs, since I'd stuffed the meth into the duffel too. It was a situation even I couldn't see myself arguing her out of.

Maybe the best thing I could do at this point would be to help Baby get in and out of the house quickly, before Vegas and his guys turned up. The longer Baby and Ashton searched for the money, the longer they would be in danger. I had to tell them where to find it.

I worked my phone out of my back pocket and tried to

visualize the screen, but there was no telling if I had been successful in swiping it open. I took a moment to lament the days when phones had actual buttons that beeped when pressed. I tossed my phone onto the seat beside me and stared helplessly at it. In the front of the car, Summerly's phone rang again and he reached for it and answered.

"What? Where? How many?"

He was distracted. I shuffled sideways and lay down on the seat, my mouth to the phone.

"Hey, Siri," I murmured.

"Yes?" the robotic female voice answered.

"Text Baby."

"What do you want to say?"

"Under vanity."

"Your text says, 'Under vanity.' Would you like to send it?"

"Oh, my God," Summerly said from the front seat. He gave a hard sigh as he swung the wheel again, cutting through traffic and off an exit ramp.

"Where are we going?" I asked.

"Change of plans," he said. "I've been called elsewhere. Baby's gonna have to wait. There's an active shooter on the loose."

CHAPTER 100

THE BLOND GIRL, VERA, launched herself at Jacob. She hit him in the stomach with her shoulder but didn't even knock the wind out of him.

Jacob twisted and threw her against the other wall of the little room, smashing down a little shelf of books and a whiteboard covered with magnets, paper, and pens. They scrambled together against the wall, knocking a vase of flowers off the bedside table and onto the floor.

Vera screamed with rage and pain as Jacob picked her up again and threw her into the hallway. He took a moment to roll his shoulders, flex his triceps. He was going to take his time, enjoy this. For Beaty. For Neina.

Vera scrambled away up the hall, her hand bleeding, leaving little wet prints. Jacob walked up, tried to straddle her, but she whipped around and slashed at his leg with something thin and sharp, a piece of glass from the broken vase. He bent and punched at her face, missed, hit the floor, felt her sharp nails gouge across the side of his head and into his eye. She moved fast and had good aim, the natural instincts of a predator.

Jacob gathered himself, grabbed Vera's wrist, and bashed it against the linoleum until the shard of glass came free. She wriggled out of his grip and got up, ran around a corner and down a short hall, scattering terrified hospital staff and visitors. Jacob followed. He drew his gun and blasted three times into a door, one bullet hitting an inch from her shoulder as she barged through.

An old man in a thin paper gown came out of his room, eyed Jacob, and retreated into the darkness again, flashing his sagging underwear as he went.

Jacob pushed through the doors and found himself in a huge operating theater. On the operating table a man lay unconscious, his chest spread open and innards exposed under white lights. The surgical staff cowered as Vera snatched a scalpel off the abandoned tray table. She brandished the scalpel in one hand and beckoned Jacob with the other.

CHAPTER 101

"WHAT'S 'VANITY'?" BABY ASKED. She stood in the kitchen of the Manhattan Beach house, the cupboards all around her emptied of pots and pans, plates and glasses, all of it now mixed with the party debris on the floor and countertops, a sea of mess. Ashton was in the hall nearby, going through a cabinet of silverware and dumping the drawers' contents on the floor.

"It's, like, your self-esteem, I guess? If you're vain, you think you're cool."

"'Under vanity,'" Baby said, looking at her phone.

"What?"

"I got this text from Rhonda that just says, 'Under vanity.' It's probably autocorrect. Unless she's trying to tell me that I'm too full of myself? But it's not really the time for—"

Ashton's eyes widened. "The bathrooms. Come on!"

The teens ran to the stairs. Halfway up, they heard the front door burst open. Baby shoved Ashton down, and the two huddled, listening. Slowly, they crept back down a couple of steps and peered around the banister at what they could see of the foyer.

A single boot appeared. Blue ostrich skin with a skull-shaped cap on the toe. Martin Vegas dropped the twisted and bent handle of the front door on the tiles at his feet.

"Go." Baby pushed at Ashton to head upstairs. "Go, go, go."

CHAPTER 102

THE PARKING LOT OF the hospital was in chaos. Summerly's sedan nosed its way in between the vehicles of medical staff and hospital visitors trying to flee the scene. A woman running with an IV pole rolling along beside her was almost knocked down by a man in an orderly's uniform who had jumped the curb with his green four-wheel drive. I could see other patients and civilians standing at windows inside the hospital, watching the activity in the parking lot, their hands pressed against the glass.

Summerly's phone had continued to ring as he drove, but he left it wailing alone on the seat beside him. The radio crackled with updates, which he now and then responded to.

"Unit Five at the scene. We're getting reports on the identities of the shooters," a voice on the radio said. *"Two suspects. One male, fifties. Female, late teens. The guy has been identified as Jacob Kanular. He's a local. Family man. Has a kid in critical care. Over."*

"This is Summerly. Who's the girl? Over."

"A witness recognized her as one Vera Petrov."

"Oh, my God," I said. "He found her."

"You say something?" Summerly put his radio down and looked at me.

"I know the girl," I said. "Vera. Well, I mean, I don't know her. But I'm pretty sure I know why that guy, Kanular, is after her."

"You know why they're shooting at people?" Summerly asked.

"They're not after random people," I said. "Kanular is after Vera."

"That doesn't make any sense. Witnesses are saying they're both shooters," Summerly said. "People inside the hospital have told officers on the scene that the girl killed two nurses."

I shook my head. Terror and dread washed over me.

"I don't get it." Summerly slammed on the brakes and put the car into park. A woman ran past us with a tiny baby in her arms. "How do you know the shooters, Rhonda? What's your link to all this?"

"Never mind," I said. "I don't have time to explain. Uncuff me, and let's get inside."

"You're not going anywhere." Summerly pulled his gun from a shoulder holster. A couple of officers running through the lot used the car as a shield for a second, bracing themselves to make a run for the hospital's automatic doors. I saw their hot breath on the glass only inches from my face.

"Dave, you've got to let me out," I said. "At least uncuff me!"

"You're not a cop, Rhonda. Stay in the car."

Summerly got out and ran toward the hospital. I growled with frustration, turned and kicked the window of the car out. I knew there was a spare handcuff key in the glove box of every squad car in Colorado, just in case there was a traffic accident and an officer was ever hauled away with their key before a suspect could be freed from the back seat. I hoped LAPD detectives had the same rules. I struggled forward and kicked as hard as I could at the inside of the door.

CHAPTER 103

JACOB RAN AT VERA. He batted the scalpel away, took a deep cut across the palm of his hand in doing it, but the pain didn't register. He was in killer mode. His body was shutting down all unnecessary senses, focused only on survival, on neutralizing the threat.

Vera couldn't beat him physically, but she was doing a good job outsmarting him. The second he had knocked the scalpel from her hand, her wrist seized in his big fingers, Vera's other hand was coming at his face with some kind of steel hook, another instrument she had snatched from the floor as he'd dragged her along. He slammed her into the steel cupboards, felt the *thunk* of the hook as she embedded it deep in his shoulder. She scrambled out of his bloody hands like a wet cat, impossibly strong and nimble, slipping out into the hall again.

He followed her, drawing his gun from the waistband of his jeans where he had tucked it as he entered the operating theater. The desire to use his hands on Vera had been too strong to ignore.

A chair swung out of nowhere into his field of vision. He lifted an arm and blocked it. The attacker was not Vera. Some civilian hero in a pink shirt hoping to save the day. Jacob almost laughed. If there was one thing he knew, it was that a man who tried to separate two fighting dogs was going to get bitten. He reached out, grabbed the guy by his salmon-colored lapel, and landed a punch in his stomach that folded him in half like a deck chair. A plastic ID tag and pen clattered onto the floor as Jacob dropped the guy in the doorway. The badge crunched under Jacob's boot as he walked on. Some kind of medical consultant, he guessed. A surgeon maybe. It didn't matter. Everybody went down if you hit them hard enough. Jacob turned and shot the guy in the ankle to keep him down.

Screams came from behind a door marked as a nurses' lounge. Jacob went inside and found Vera there, clutching a plump woman in scrubs around the throat, the teenager's small arm a pale noose by which the older woman hung. Vera pushed a cutlery fork against the woman's neck, jutting her chin at Jacob defiantly as she backed her hostage away.

"Think about it," Vera said. "Stop and think about it. You won't kill an innocent woman just to get to me."

"Don't be so sure, little girl," Jacob said. He shot a trembling orderly in the chest. Vera dropped her hostage, staggering back as Jacob surged forward to fire again. The bullet entered Vera in the arm, sending her flying back. Jacob might have grabbed the girl then, but a pair of male nurses who had been huddling behind a table made a run for it, cutting between them, giving Vera the seconds she needed to shoulder her way through the lounge's other door, back into the hallway.

CHAPTER 104

ASHTON AND BABY SLIPPED into the guest bathroom on the third floor and shut the door as quietly as they could. The space was larger than most regular bedrooms but seemed impossibly small, their heavy breathing echoing off the ceiling. Ashton caught a glimpse of his face in the huge mirror. His cheeks were drained of blood, the whites of his eyes stark. Baby's shaking hands fluttered over the sink, almost knocking over a bottle of perfume, which she grabbed just as it slipped over the edge of the counter.

"*Under* vanity," she breathed, ripping open the doors under the sink. "This thing is called a vanity. But it's not here. It's not here. I don't see anything."

"How many bathrooms does your place have?"

"Six. But this is the room Rhonda has been sleeping in."

"Doesn't mean it's the vanity she was talking about."

"Shit," Baby said. "But I know it's not in my bathroom. At least I think it's not."

"Where are the others?"

"There're two on the ground floor. We can't go down there

now." As though to confirm her words, they heard a crash from the lower floor as one of the gang members smashed through something, a bookcase or cabinet. "There's one on the roof, next to the pool. And my dad's bedroom is on the next floor down."

Baby ran to the door, slipped silently out into the bedroom. Ashton followed closely behind her, marveling at her fearlessness. She peeked out into the hall and crept down the staircase before even glancing back to make sure he was behind her.

She's one of those girls, Ashton thought. *The ones who just assume you'll follow.* The ones who walked ahead of him into parties like they hadn't arrived in the same limo. The ones who tossed their handbags at him at the airport and expected him to catch. He was following Baby as though on a string. He was so distracted by his self-reflections that he didn't even see the cartel guy with a cast on his hand and a gun tattoo on his face turn into the second-floor hall as Ashton reached the lower landing.

Ashton and Gunmouth faced each other, the cartel henchman so stunned he didn't even lift the enormous shiny silver gun he carried at his hip.

"Hey!" the man said, raising the hand strapped tightly into a dirty fiberglass cast. Ashton leaped across the hall and threw himself into the bedroom with Baby, slamming the door shut.

"They're here!" Gunmouth shouted from beyond the door. *"Ellos están aquí!"*

CHAPTER 105

A HOSPITAL IS A busy place. At every hour of the day and night people sit in seats in hallways drinking coffee, crying, talking, chewing their nails, waiting for news. Orderlies mop floors, delivery people transport flowers, as nurses and doctors rush back and forth. Overhead, announcements are made in gentle tones, while machines bleep and screech and click in every room in every hallway.

So when I walked in to find the hospital seemingly empty, a sense of unreality gripped me, made me pause. The speakers nestled into the ceiling of the big foyer were playing a repetitive, high-pitched *whoop* sound. People had dropped bags and other belongings as they ran—a coffee spilled here, a teddy bear discarded there, telltale signs of panic. On a seat in front of the admissions desk, a cell phone was ringing, and the sound of another chimed from the bathrooms to my left. I followed the empty hall until I found two police officers, who swiveled and pointed their guns at me.

"Get down! Get down! Get down!"

"She's with me." Summerly appeared beside me, a troupe of

officers at his side. He was trying to strap a bulletproof vest to his thick chest. "I told you to wait outside."

"You did," I said.

"But you're here. Which means somebody let you out or you ripped my car open like a sardine can."

"I'm sure it's fixable," I lied. The detective's car door had collapsed under my boot by the fourth kick. I had been squatting about 350 pounds for months. It never stood a chance. "Where are they?"

"We think they're in the cafeteria, in a seating area above it," he said, then shook his head, catching himself sharing details of the operation with me. "But look, this is not your scene."

"I want to help."

"I know you do." He nodded tersely. "You're that kind of person. I get it. But, Rhonda, you don't just get to pick and choose which situations to insert yourself into."

"Yeah, I do," I said. "And I've picked this one because there's a teenage girl up there who needs help, and that's what I do and I'm good at it. And I'm not just *inserting* myself into this situation. I'm *barging* in. Because I'm good at that too."

I shoved past him, waiting to hear him order his officers after me. But those words didn't come. When I turned and looked after a few seconds, I realized Detective Dave Summerly was beside me, marching toward the double doors at the end of the hall that led into the cafeteria.

"You're crazy," he said. I thought I saw a flicker of a smile at the corner of his lips. "Damn crazy woman."

CHAPTER 106

ASHTON THREW HIMSELF AGAINST the door. The handle rattled, and after a few seconds a thump came against the wood as Gunmouth heaved himself against the opposite side of the door. Baby joined Ashton, throwing all her weight against their side. After a few moments of silence, they heard a click.

"Get down!" Baby shouted.

Four bullets smashed through the door, a fragment of a second after Ashton had hit the carpet. He barely managed to keep the door shut as the man in the hall threw himself against it again. Baby ran to a bedside table and shoved it sideways against the door. Ashton dragged over the dresser.

"*Dar la vuelta al lado!*"

"They're going around the side!" Baby cried. "Go, Ashton!"

Ashton dove into the bathroom, throwing open the doors of the cabinet beneath the sink. Deodorant cans, cologne bottles, face cloths, soap packets.

Nothing else.

"It's not here!" As he rose and turned, he knocked the

wooden facade at the bottom of the cabinet with his toe. It tilted inward, one corner popping out. He wrenched the wood away, then shoved his hand into the dark space and felt fabric.

He dragged the bag out from beneath the vanity and ran into the bedroom in time to hear gunshots. He saw Baby cowering against the pile of furniture they had shoved against the door as bullets pierced the wood above the makeshift barricade.

"Come on! Come on!" He grabbed her hand. They shoved open the bedroom's large window together. Beneath part of it was a huge bougainvillea bush, dense with razor-sharp thorns. Ashton looked down the side of the house and saw Martin Vegas and two of his guys clambering over the small fence separating the back half of the property from the front.

"I can't do it," Baby said. She gripped his hand, backing toward the door of the bedroom, where the man with the gun tattoo was shouldering through the door, splintering it slowly, the furniture barricade shifting on the carpet with every shove.

"I've got you," Ashton said. He gathered her up and helped her climb onto the window casing.

They closed their eyes, held hands, and jumped.

CHAPTER 107

JACOB AND VERA WERE alone together in the wide mezzanine seating area perched above the cafeteria. Vera knew this was the place where one of them would die. She could smell it, like an approaching storm, the smell of a coming force that would sweep the earth and carry one of them away with it. Inevitable, unstoppable. Jacob had come through the double doors from the hallway and now stood between the tables and scattered chairs. As she'd hoped, he put his gun down on the nearest tabletop and smiled at her.

She wanted it to be equal. The end. Two killers coming together, discovering which of them was the strongest using only their hands. There had been enough playing around with weapons, enough chasing and running away. Vera gripped the bullet hole in her arm, gave it a final squeeze, and let it go. She would bleed while they battled. So would he. Their blood would mark the floor beneath them, the tables, the walls. When they were done, the cafeteria would look like a bear pit.

"You've been doing this a while, haven't you?" she said.

"You're not just some dad who's pissed. There were others before Benzo and Sean and Penny."

"Plenty of others," he said. "I've been doing it since before you were born."

"What are the chances?" Vera asked. She laughed and felt blood dribble on her lip. "We choose some asshole from a shopping mall parking lot and he turns out to be a real psycho."

"We're more common than people think," he said, and they both smiled. Because they had recognized the thing in each other that made them different. Not something extra but a lack of something. They were empty people.

She went to him. He grabbed her throat and squeezed, and for a moment he had total control, until she kicked the wound she'd given him earlier, almost as if she had planned it, ground her heel into the glass cut in his thigh while she grabbed at his head. They wrestled, knocked over a table, smashed plates and glasses onto the floor. She reached for a weapon, something, all thoughts of fighting it out with him bare-handed abandoned as Jacob continued to grip her throat, her brain crying out for air.

Then he slipped.

There must have been something on the floor. Coffee, it smelled like. His leg slid out, and Vera's feet touched the floor for the first time in seconds—long, terrifying seconds. She felt her adversary falling, and she went with it. They crashed into the glass barrier of the mezzanine, shattering a pane of it. Vera dug her heels into the floor, pushing Jacob out over the edge as he gripped the floor with his bloody hands, glass grinding under his palms.

Vera pulled herself to her feet, stood above him. He'd been so frightening. So powerful. And now he was just an old man hanging from a ledge by his gnarled, bloody fingers. She lifted her boot and placed it gently on top of his knuckles as Jacob's wide eyes looked up at her.

CHAPTER 108

ASHTON AND BABY HIT the ground hard, the duffel bag buffering them from the nasty thorns of the bougainvillea, but there was a moment of blackness as Ashton struggled to maintain consciousness after his head smacked the ground. Ringing, white lights, muffled voices. A few seconds passed before the flaming, tearing, screaming pain. Then Baby dragged him up, Ashton's feet pounding the pavement crookedly as they sprinted for the front of the house.

He was wide-awake now, hearing the hum of the garage door opening remotely—Baby's doing. He sucked air into his lungs as he ducked under the rising door and then jumped into the Maserati beside her. She squeezed her eyes shut as she turned the key in the engine, then when the car started, she paused to blow out a terrified breath and threw the car into reverse.

The still-moving garage door scraped along the length of the roof as they backed out and turned into the street. The tires screeched, and the back window collapsed in a shower of glass shards as bullets zinged off the frame of the car.

"Hold on," Baby said as she slammed her foot down on the accelerator.

CHAPTER 109

"WAIT!" I CRIED.

Vera looked at me. Beneath her, Jacob Kanular gripped wildly at the edge of the mezzanine with his free hand, broken glass making a good handhold on the floor impossible. Vera's bright blond curls were red and black in parts, matted with blood. Unknown emotions crossed her face as she took in the sight of me and Dave Summerly standing at the edge of the huge dining area.

Officers began spreading out around the room with guns drawn, aiming where the other shooter hung, one hand now wrapped roughly around a barrier pole with the other wedged beneath Vera's boot. A female officer was slowly climbing the open stairs leading to the mezzanine, on Vera's right, her pistol drawn, blocking the girl's exit on that side. But there was no one yet at Vera's back, still leaving her an escape through the hallway doors behind her. I had to delay the girl until she was completely surrounded.

Vera stood watching me, stunned, but in mere seconds the shock dissolved, and I saw her calculating how to manage the new situation unfolding around her. My presence and what it meant. I put my hands up and stepped forward cautiously.

"Vera," I said. "I—"

"Don't even start." Vera held up a finger. I saw a flash of something in her. Confident and cutting and sure of herself. A woman who could see the next ten moves I planned to make and didn't have time for any of them. "Don't say my name like you know me. You don't know anything about me."

"I don't have to know you to know what this is," I said, gesturing to her, the man beneath her, the cops falling into position around her.

"Oh, yeah? What is this?"

"This is a terrible situation that's going to get an awful lot worse if we're not careful. You've got time to think this through. Plenty of time."

"No, I don't." Vera smiled, letting her eyes dart to Detective Summerly behind me. "And I'm not going to fall for your delaying tactics. We both know the door is closing. This is good-bye."

"Vera," I said, "I care about what happens here."

She laughed hard, shuffling her feet, making Jacob grind his teeth as he instinctively kept clinging to the very edge of the mezzanine.

I felt Summerly's hand on my shoulder, pushing me forward a little. "Keep at it," he murmured. "You're doing great."

"I care about you, Vera," I said.

"Are you kidding me?" She snorted. "You met me once!"

"Nope," I said. I shook my head, and I meant it. "I've met you a thousand times before. You're every kid I've ever walked into a courtroom with. You're every boy and girl I've sat with in interview rooms, in bedrooms, in prison cells. I've met so many kids like you, Vera. Kids who found themselves in the kind of mess that can't be gotten out of. This is a pretty good mess you've made—don't get me wrong. Spectacular. But you can get out of it. All you have to do is take the help I'm offering you right now."

Vera looked down at the man hanging from the mezzanine. I saw her weight shift so that she crushed his fingers harder. Jacob yowled, grabbed at the mezzanine's barrier pole again with his other hand, slipped in the blood, and swung gently. Vera seemed to be considering her options.

The female cop to her right was five feet closer now, her gun leveled at Vera's head. Vera had made her decision.

I didn't expect what happened next.

The girl smiled sweetly. A little sadly. Like she was giving in.

"Okay." Vera nodded. She lifted her boot and eased back a step. I watched her raise her hands. "I'll take the help."

I rushed forward. The female cop did too. Behind me, I heard Summerly's footsteps as we all ran toward the falling man who had let go.

For an instant, we completely forgot about Vera.

It was exactly what she'd planned.

CHAPTER **110**

I REACHED JACOB FIRST. I fell as he fell, clipping me with his weight. We both sprawled on the floor, with him draped over my thighs. I grabbed his uninjured hand. It was wet, slippery. I leaned sideways and dragged myself out from under him. It was the only thing that saved my life. Because Vera had backed up not to escape but to grab a gun from somewhere behind her. She first fired into the shoulder of the female cop on her right but immediately then leaned over the edge of the mezzanine and fired at the man I held by the hand. I'm sure she wasn't bothered about also maybe killing me in the process.

She fired twice. The first bullet whizzed between our heads and pounded into the linoleum floor. The second shot was on target. I heard it zip past my ear, a sound like paper tearing. And then I saw his head buck, and a hole appear out of nowhere in his flat, wide forehead. I felt the mist of his blood on my cheeks and chin.

Jacob's body went limp. I heard footsteps running, officers coming to assist the female officer on the stairs, quickly carry her out, as Jacob slipped away, his hand seeming to grip mine for a long time before his eyes rolled upward. I hung my head over him, too scared to look up in case Vera decided to fire again.

I heard doors swinging open and shut as she ran through them. The footsteps of officers in pursuit. But I knew there was no point in running after her. I had seen in Vera's falsely sweet and innocent smile the confidence of a girl with a plan. I'd thought it was relief that I had given her, a sense that she was going to be taken care of now, that I would help unpick the tangled web she was so hopelessly coiled up in. But it was just the grin of a spider watching the last group of insects step into its trap, safe and secured, exactly where she wanted them.

When I dragged myself to my feet, I was alone. The cafeteria sprawled around me, signs of the violence that had occurred here only minutes before written in the broken glass and blood and spilled drinks on the floor. In the yawning space beneath the mezzanine, the killer named Jacob Kanular stared up at me, unseeing. I felt the failure of being unable to save him, or Vera, reach deep inside me, into my bones, and carve its mark.

CHAPTER 111

THEY FLED. BABY GRIPPED the wheel and Ashton hung on to his seat belt with gritted teeth as Baby took the car through the streets, blasting through red lights, cars honking and swerving in their rearview mirror. On the corner of Manhattan Beach Boulevard and Aviation, a minibus driver jerked the wheel and careened across the intersection into a lamppost to avoid their path. A man flipping and twirling a lime-green sign advertising two for one Baja fish tacos dove into a bush at the sight of the two teenagers speeding toward the sidewalk. The Maserati missed the curb by mere inches as Baby corrected and got them back on the right path.

It was only on the 110 heading north that she finally eased off the accelerator. Ashton unclenched his jaw with difficulty. In silence they rode, glancing now and then at the rearview mirror.

"I think we lost them," Ashton said.

"Don't jinx it," Baby said.

Ten minutes passed. Fifteen. The road behind them emptied, then refilled with cars. None of them were mirrored chrome or violent purple or any other bright shade of the drug dealer rainbow. None of the cartel guys seemed to be following them.

"I think we lost them," Ashton repeated. The teens looked at each other. Ashton felt laughs ripple up his throat, and then suddenly they both were laughing hard, swiping at tears, banging their fists on the dashboard, and whooping. He real-ized for the first time that he was drenched in sweat, his body cooling from the adrenaline.

"Well? Get the bag, man. Show me the goddamn money," Baby said.

"Show me the moneyyyyyy!" Ashton cried.

"Show! Me! The moneyyyyyy!" Baby crowed, blasting the horn. Ashton dragged the bag into his lap and pulled out a wad of bills as thick as a block of cheddar cheese. He ripped the elastic band from the stack and threw it up, letting the cash rain down all over the two of them in the car.

Baby laughed. He loved the sound of it, low and smoky, a cool girl's laugh. He remembered that laugh from school. Back when everything was uncomplicated, pure, wonderful. Being with Baby was taking him back to happier times.

"What are we gonna do now?" Baby said.

A silence descended on them. Ashton gathered up some money, felt it in his fingers, began stacking the bills back to-gether. He pulled one of the packages of meth out of the bag and turned it over in his hands, tossed it onto the back seat.

"The smart thing for us to do is to find Rhonda," Baby said. "Ask her where to go. We use some of the money to keep ourselves safe for now. We dump this car. Buy a new one. Hole up in a hotel. We buy some phones to call her and wait for her to come get us. She comes, helps us negotiate your surrender, and then packs me up to live with her and her cats forever in some loser town in Loserville."

Baby eased out a long, slow sigh. Ashton kept stacking up the cash.

"That's the smart thing to do," he agreed.

They drove in silence for a while.

"I don't feel like being smart right now, though," Baby said eventually.

"Neither do I."

"This might be, like, my last night of freedom," she said. "And yours literally."

"Yeah, like, *literally*."

"I don't *feel like* going to Colorado." Baby looked at him. "And I'm sure you don't *feel like* going to jail for the next twenty years."

They smiled at each other.

"Vegas?" Baby asked. Ashton threw the money into the air again.

"Vegas, Baby!" He laughed.

Baby floored it. The engine thrummed. They didn't look in the rearview mirror again.

CHAPTER 112

DAVE SUMMERLY FOUND ME at his car, dialing and redialing Baby, my hands sweaty and my heart racing.

"The Bruhs just called me," I said without looking up.

"Who?"

"The Bruhs!" I snapped. There was still blood on my fingers. Vera Petrov's blood maybe, or Jacob Kanular's. Both of them were killers—I'd seen Vera kill Jacob, and she'd shot two nurses, shot a police officer; Jacob had surely taken the lives of Derek Benstein, Sean and Penny Hanley, and possibly three or four innocent civilians inside the hospital. I wiped off my phone screen with the edge of my T-shirt, beginning to panic.

"I don't know what you're say—"

"My neighbors at the Manhattan Beach house, Dave," I said, trying to regulate my breathing. "They said they heard gunshots inside and saw Baby and Ashton flee in my dad's Maserati. They're on the run out there somewhere, and they probably have three million dollars on them."

"They *what*?" Summerly stepped back, shook his head. "She knew where the money was?"

"I told her."

"Jesus, Rhonda!"

"I knew she'd go for the money. When she escaped your officers at the gas station, I thought she'd go home and collect it, and I was right. It's a good thing I told her where the money was or she would have been caught trying to find it by the cartel guys."

"You just *knew* she'd do that?" Summerly asked.

"She's my sister," I said. I realized as I said the words that the battle between whether I would see myself as Baby's mother or sister had been won, for now. Maybe I would always swing between the two roles, but at that moment I was thinking and feeling like her sibling, like her ally and friend and co-conspirator. It was Baby and me against the world now. We needed to be on the same team. "We've got to find her."

"Well, if you think you've got this sister-sister ESP thing going on with her, you figure out where she is now, and we'll try to snatch her up before the cartel does," he said.

"Don't you have to try to catch Vera Petrov?"

"The pursuit has been taken off my hands." His shrug was labored. "I've been stood down, for now. Seems I let a civilian lawyer into the danger zone around an active shooter and she got an inch and a half away from having her head blown off."

"Oh, Dave. I'm sorry."

"Doesn't matter." He gripped my shoulder. "You almost had her, Rhonda. I saw it in her eyes. She thought about coming with you. If we ever had a chance of connecting with Petrov, that was the moment. I think you did good, and I'll defend my decision to let you help."

I leaned into him a little. His hand ran along the back of my arm, a small, swift gesture that reminded me of our bodies twisting, his breath on my ear, my foot running up his calf.

"I'm coming with you," he said. "We're gonna find these kids. Where do two reckless kids with nothing to lose go with three million bucks and a Maserati?"

Baby's voice traveled back to me from a couple of days earlier, the first time she had asked about the location of the money.

You think I'm going to take it all, drive to Vegas, and have a wild time?

Dave seemed to know what I was thinking.

"Rhonda, they wouldn't," he said.

"Don't bet on it," I said. "Ashton thinks he's going to jail for the rest of his life, and Baby thinks I'm going to abduct her and lock her in my cattery of social doom."

"Your what?"

"Never mind."

Night had fallen. I looked helplessly at the lamps as they sprang to life all over the parking lot, shuddering on in the reflections on the windshields of cars, making the plastic crime-scene tape shine like tinsel. I thought of Baby driving through the night with the cartel behind her. If they were clever, Martin Vegas and his guys would let Baby and Ashton get a little ahead of them. Hang back, so the kids would think they'd gotten away. Vegas and his boys would wait for the teens to relax, before pouncing on them when the opportunity arose.

I saw it as the obvious strategy, but I was older, wiser, and savvier than the kids. I knew Baby and Ashton would probably fall for it, meaning that every second ticking by as I stood there was sending my sister farther and farther away from me, and closer and closer to danger.

"How do we catch them?" I said. "They have a huge head start."

"I might know a way," Summerly said.

CHAPTER 113

AT NIGHT, FROM THREE thousand feet above the desert beyond Victorville, the I-15 from Los Angeles to Las Vegas looked like the ocean. There were long stretches of nothingness, bare roads, then here and there clusters of gold lights floated in the blackness like little meetings of fishermen. Streams of slow-traveling red dots wound gently through the desert basin, the taillights of people leaving the coast for the city of cards and dice.

In the sixties, the mob used the desert outside Vegas as a dumping ground for whacked guys, and serial killers used it to pick up hitchhikers heading from the Midwest to be singers and actresses in LA. Desert highways always made me think of lonely ghosts, and tonight I was hoping my sister wouldn't become one of them.

Summerly hunched over his phone in the seat in front of me as he connected it to a cable in his headset, punching in a call before he'd secured the unit over his ears again. "I need CHP keeping an eye on 15 near Barstow, at the turnoff for route 127, and at the state border, just before Primm," he yelled as the helicopter blades thumped outside our windows. Then, once his headset was in place, he continued in a quieter tone. "Yes, that's what I said. No, you don't need his approval. You've got mine. I wasn't stood down, I was...I've just been reassigned. Just set it up! It's two kids in a black Maserati!"

My headset clicked as Dr. Tuddy was patched through from his seat next to the helicopter's pilot. I saw his shaggy brown hair shift as he tilted his head back toward me.

"Beautiful night for an air pursuit!" he said, his voice barely audible through the headset.

"You're so good to loan us your chopper!" I said.

"This is one of many toys I bought with the patent money," he said. I saw his shoulders rise and fall as he sighed. "It's not the best of my collection. I also have a Bell 47G from 1946. It still runs! I'd have suggested we take that one, but there's no way it would cope with our collective weight."

"There's also no way I'm getting into a seventy-five-year-old helicopter!" I yelled. "Are you nuts?"

Dave ended his call and sat back.

"Vera's gone," he said. I reached out and put my hand on his knee. I had the cold, awful feeling deep in the pit of my stomach that we would hear from her again. She was not a nimble and crafty fox, darting into the night to hunt chickens another day, a nuisance that would be dealt with the next time it appeared. She was a rampaging tiger going to ground in the jungle, a creature who wouldn't and couldn't stay hidden for long. I had the feeling that Vera had gotten a taste for blood, and wherever she ended up next, people would start to disappear.

"We weren't dealing with a kid there," Summerly said, as though he could read my thoughts. "She wasn't a child making a mistake. She was a killer with training wheels."

"And now they're off," I agreed.

He nodded.

"I'm sorry," I said. "I should have—"

"You couldn't have known, Rhonda." He waved a hand. "You did your best, and that was pretty amazing, even if it didn't work out."

He reached into his pocket and took out a handkerchief. I wasn't crying but took it anyway. Only when I looked down did I realize it was for the blood still on my hands, on my face.

"They said Jacob Kanular had a kid inside the hospital?" I asked.

Summerly nodded. "They're saying his ten-year-old daughter came in after a severe asthma attack. She's been in a coma. A unit went to the house a couple of hours ago and found her mom dead. Knife wounds."

"If that poor little girl wakes up, they're going to have to tell her that both her parents are dead," I said.

"She's awake," Summerly said. He was scrolling through his phone. "She's on her way to another hospital. I've got a report here that says she's cooperating with police as best she can."

I looked out the window. Summerly reached over and rubbed my knee.

"You can't save them all, Rhonda," he said.

"I know," I said. "I know. But I like to try when I can. It feels good. It feels like I'm helping some version of me when I was that age. In some stupid way it's almost like if I help enough of them, I'll get back there, through time, to myself. I'll be able to undo all the pain."

"That's a nice thought." He smiled at me. But I didn't have the strength to return it. Baby and Ashton were down there somewhere in the dark, and our hopes of finding them seemed to be ticking away with every turn of the rotors above our heads. The land below was a mess of scattered lights, as unreachable as distant stars.

"How the hell are we going to find them?" I asked helplessly.

CHAPTER 114

BABY TOOK HER RIGHT hand off the wheel and reached out to grab Ashton's arm, shaking him awake. All the terror and pain had left him weak to the temptations of sleep. The hypnotic shadows of rocky terrain drifting by had taken him deep into slumber.

"Police," she said.

"Oh, man." Ashton sat up, rubbed his eyes. In the distance a cluster of California Highway Patrol vehicles sat on the wide median between the two lanes of the freeway heading in each direction, but all of them were pointed toward their east-bound lanes. The taillights of cars ahead brightened as they slowed on approach.

"Is it a roadblock?"

"Whatever it is, it's for us. It's gotta be."

"I'm getting off the road." Baby swung the wheel at an exit and made a couple of turns to get her to the opposite side of the interstate, where the CHP wasn't watching. She doused the headlights and rolled unseen. Abruptly, the front wheels crunched on gravel, began to shudder over rocks.

"This thing wasn't designed for off-roading, Baby!"

"Hang on."

They crept through the blackness more slowly, sagebrush shunting under the bumper.

"You'll blow the tires!"

"Shut up, Ashton!"

"There are ravines out here. Crevasses!"

"Don't be such a wimp," Baby yelled. "It's a crevasse or a jail cell. Which would you prefer?"

In time, Ashton looked back to see a single pair of headlights behind them, blinking out too.

"Oh, shit, it's them. It's them. They're back there. Speed up! Speed up!"

He held her wrist. Together they felt the rocks, shrubs, and broken stumps of Joshua trees crash and thump under the vehicle. Ashton watched the lights of the slowed vehicles on the highway disappear when a huge pair of headlights flicked on only feet behind their vehicle.

Baby screamed. The sound was strangled out by terror as the car behind smashed into their rear bumper, shoving the car sideways. Desert dust coiled and spun in the blinding light.

"Get ready to run!" Baby cried.

Ashton looked ahead. A torn and rotting billboard loomed into view and then collapsed, folding around the car as they plowed through it, bringing the Maserati to a crunching halt.

Ashton barely had time to read the sunbaked lettering:

ROCK-A-HOOLA WATERPARK.

CHAPTER 115

THEY CRAWLED FROM THE wreckage. Ashton's blood was rushing so hard and fast through his veins that new injuries did not register in his mind—a nail scraping along his arm from the billboard frame, a sharp stone slicing the skin from his ankle as he stumbled in the dark, cutting almost to the bone. He grabbed Baby's hand, and they raced over the cracked and tilted concrete of what had once been a wide, bare walkway between the attractions of the water park. Ashton followed her through the doorway of a crumbling building under a broken neon sign that read TICKETS.

"What is this place?" Ashton breathed.

"It's an old water park. Abandoned. I used to come out here with some skater boys."

"You would hang out here?" Ashton scoffed. The darkness inside the building made it impossible to see the room around him, but he could smell its contents clearly: stagnant water, urine, human feces, old beer. He kicked a blanket out from under his feet and crouched behind the counter, holding the rusted frame of what he guessed was an empty fridge. He could just make out the patterns of spray-painted artwork on the walls. "Who hangs out at a haunted water park for kicks?"

"The pools make great skate ramps." Baby shoved at him. "Keep your head down."

They waited. Sure enough, in the moonlight, they made out the shapes of four men emerging from behind where the Maserati was nestled in the collapsed billboard. They were walking. *Bad men always walk,* Ashton thought. They didn't need to run. The water park was like an island in the middle of the desert. The kids could shelter here, or they could take their chances out there in the darkness where there was no cover, nowhere to hide. All Vegas and his crew had to do was hunt them from building to building until they locked them down.

When a voice drifted toward them from the group of shadows, Baby and Ashton gripped each other in the cool darkness.

"We just want our stuff!"

It was Vegas who had spoken. His deep, honey-smooth voice was as calm as a man calling his children inside from playing in the garden. Ashton almost felt like going to him. He sounded safe. Confident.

"It's in the car!" Baby yelled.

"Shhh! Are you crazy?"

"The sound will bounce off the buildings," Baby said. She was right. Vegas's men shifted at the sound of her words but didn't turn toward the ticket kiosk. There was a pause, then one of them turned and walked back toward the Maserati.

"They'll go now," Baby said. "You watch. They'll leave us alone. They don't want to hurt two stupid kids."

"We're too much trouble," Ashton agreed, shuddering with fear. "Not smart. Not worth the effort."

They waited. The man returned from the car with the duffel bag. In the dim moonlight the cartel men checked the bag, then one of them shouldered it.

Then the men fanned out across the park.

CHAPTER 116

ASHTON COULD SEE HIS death clearly. He'd seen it in flashes as he lay in the back of the van when he was abducted, his wrists bound and the lights of the highway rolling over his helpless body. He'd seen his parents standing over a stainless-steel morgue table, clutching each other, trying to identify his twisted and broken remains.

Ashton had seen a dead body once. He'd pressed against the glass as their limo drove slowly by a car wreck on the way to his dad's surprise fiftieth birthday at the Fairmont. All he'd glimpsed was a shattered knee poking out from the back seat area, but Ashton knew the person was dead from the leisurely pace of the emergency responders pulling tarps from their truck to cover the scene. He'd thought at the time how weird it was that people were just bodies in the end. Flesh and bones.

He was going to die out here in the desert. If they found him at all, he was going to be scraped up, packaged, and tossed away. When he was gone, there would be reports of his involvement in the Midnight Crew. They would sit uncomfortably next to photographs of him on the Stanford-West Academy lacrosse team and the honor roll. Eventually it would all prove so unpalatable that his family and friends would stop talking about him altogether, and that would be it. He would exist as a family myth shared by distant cousins about their relative who was murdered by members of a drug cartel.

"We can't let this happen," Ashton relayed to Baby, crouched shivering beside him. "It can't all end like this."

Whatever Baby's death dream was, whatever her vision was of what she'd leave behind if Vegas and his boys killed them, Ashton's words seemed to give her strength.

She nodded, and they ran through the back doors of the kiosk.

CHAPTER 117

THEY WERE NOT THE only living things in the water park. Ashton heard things moving in the dark as they made their way, as silently as possible, along the walkway between a bumper car enclosure and a pile of broken café furniture. Animals. He imagined desert foxes scurrying out of the shadows, rats sniffing along walls, rattlesnakes unfurling on the stones.

Baby climbed through a shattered fence, and they ran through a kiddie pool almost entirely overgrown with razor-sharp desert plants.

Ahead of them, the gentle curves of a roller coaster rose from behind a pool ringed by giant concrete elephants, coils of dried paint falling from their shoulders like flayed skin.

"Listen." Ashton dragged Baby to a stop. "They're going to search for us building to building. We have to think smart. Go somewhere unexpected."

He pointed up at the roller coaster. A single train, three cars long, was stuck on the tracks twenty feet from the ground, probably dragged back up the line by hooligans hanging out in the park at night. Baby nodded. They turned and ran.

"Hey!"

From the battered, graffitied remains of a hot dog hut, a figure cloaked in a blanket emerged in the moonlight.

"You little assholes, keep it down!"

"Shhh!" Baby waved desperately at the vagrant. "Go back insi—"

The night erupted with white light. Ashton hadn't realized there were members of Vegas's crew so close behind them. The homeless man in the blanket bucked and twisted as the bullets tore through him, his body falling in a heap. Another figure, a woman, emerged from the hut and was also shot down, her squeal high and wild, animalistic.

Ashton grabbed Baby's wrist to hold her back as she instinctively leaped forward to help the victims.

"Come on! Come on!"

A scent of fire was on the breeze. Vegas and his guys were going to smoke them out. Ashton and Baby rounded a corner and were confronted by the sight of an ancient carousel set alight, flames climbing up candy-cane poles to consume grinning dolphins, sharks, and mermaids. Beyond the carousel, another hot dog stand was just catching fire.

They raced along a line of palm trees, climbing onto the roller-coaster platform. Ashton hesitated before he put his foot on the track, inexplicably worried it would be electrified even though the controls on the driver's desk at the side of the track were almost completely covered in weeds.

"We'll climb up there." He pointed up the steep rise, toward a row of carriages stuck on the track. "They'll never look for us up there."

He put a hand out and found Baby frozen, her hands protecting her neck.

"I can't do it."

"Yes, you can! Come on! We've got to go!"

"They're going to light the whole place up." Baby stammered, "Look. Look. There's fire on the other side. They're going to trap us!" Her shirt clung to her body with sweat, her stomach sucking in and out as she struggled to breathe. "We don't have a gun. We don't have anything!"

"Baby, I've got you." Ashton climbed up off the tracks and onto the platform. He had his arms open to hold her when the bullets cut him down.

CHAPTER 118

THE FIRST SHOT HIT Ashton in the lower back. Baby watched him arch backward sharply, his eyes wide and mouth gaping. The second bullet seemed to shove him forward, slamming into his shoulder from behind. He fell into her, and they went down on the rotting, peeling wood. Baby held him, expecting the next shots to take her, for it all to end in a single, fire-red burst of pain as a bullet cleaved its way into her skull.

But it didn't.

The gunfire kept coming, but it was from behind her now.

Baby saw Officer Summerly step up onto the platform, taking cover behind the driver's control desk as he shot at the cartel guy who'd appeared at the other end of the platform. Baby squeezed her eyes shut against the white light popping at the corners of her vision. Ashton didn't seem to be breathing. She told herself she needed to let go of him, but her fingers wouldn't unlock from around his arms and shoulders.

She came to herself eventually, forcing her legs to move. Baby dragged Ashton down off the platform, onto the ancient detritus in the dirt: cigarette butts, a lost ball cap, flattened scraps of paper cups. While more gunshots zinged over their heads, she shook the boy, held Ashton's face, and yelled at him to wake up and stick to what they had set out to do in the darkness. That it couldn't end this way. Not like this.

She pressed her fingers into his neck.

He was gone.

Baby was aware of movement. Two cartel guys were trying to advance toward Summerly. Silence then drifted out over the roller-coaster platform, and Baby lifted her head in time to see the police officer pursuing Gunmouth into the dark.

Another of the cartel guys lay flopped on the stairs up to the roller coaster, his mouth open and leaking blood, the height restriction sign hanging above him on a rusty chain, swinging and pocked with bullet holes.

The sound of footsteps made Baby turn and look over her shoulder. Martin Vegas stepped onto the tracks twenty feet behind her. His footfalls were soft, measured, the casual stroll of someone completely assured of his situation. Yet they seemed to shake the entire structure.

Vegas had a long silver revolver in his hand, hanging by his thigh.

"It doesn't have to go this way, you know," he called out to Baby. "I'm always on the lookout for girls like you."

Baby couldn't say anything. Her skin prickled.

"You've got that look," Vegas said. "It's very marketable. A personal asset you're not making use of. Young. Fresh. Put a California girl like you in a Mercedes convertible, maybe a surfer dude in the passenger seat, and I can move mountains. You'd get a cut of everything we make."

"Fuck you," Baby snarled.

"This isn't clever," Vegas said, chiding. "Look at your situation. It's win-lose. If you choose to lose, you don't get to play again."

He drew the hammer back on the revolver. Baby refused to look at the weapon. It didn't matter how big the gun was, how sickening the sound was of the cylinder turning and aligning the bullet with the barrel. If she was going to die, it would be between the two of them in those very last seconds. Baby watched Vegas drawing them out, savoring them, the way he had probably dozens of times before.

It was this indulgence that cost him his life.

CHAPTER 119

I'D SCALED THE STRUCTURE behind the roller-coaster platform as quietly as possible in the darkness, but with every inch I advanced, I was sure Baby or Vegas was going to hear me. The rotting wooden beams and struts creaked, crumbling and groaning under my weight. As I hauled myself up onto the tracks, I felt the whole wooden frame rock back and forth in its fittings thirty feet below. If the scaffolding I'd leaped from at the Manhattan Beach house had been terrifyingly rickety, the old roller coaster was about as sturdy as a kid's cardboard construction. I swung a leg over into the first car of the roller-coaster train and tumbled in, throwing my weight forward. Nothing happened. I saw below me, in the moonlight streaming through holes in the station roof, Vegas aiming a gun at Baby.

I could only hope Baby would get out of the way in time. I leaned back, threw myself forward again, felt the carriage's rusty wheels grind on the track. Another shove and something snapped.

The train screamed down the tracks. My stomach lurched.

I gripped the silver lap bar and yowled as the looming figure of Martin Vegas twisted around, spotting me soaring toward him in the car without time to leap out of the way.

A heavy, thundering crunch and Vegas disappeared under the coaster wheels, shoving the car upward and to the side, throwing me onto the platform with enough force to tear the skin from my forearms and rip holes in the knees of my jeans.

I rolled and crawled to the edge of the platform. I didn't look back at the twisted body of the gangster for long. A shattered arm poking out from under the car, gravely still, was all I needed to confirm that Martin Vegas was at least too broken to do any more harm to us.

The car had stopped an inch or two from where Baby was cowering over the body of Ashton Willisee. I reached down, and with difficulty, she let go of her friend and let me haul her up.

We held each other, two sisters bloodied and bruised and shaking. In the distance, beyond the crumbling frame of a burning pool house, I saw Dave Summerly and Dr. Tuddy coming together, the big cop embracing the thin scientist with smiling relief now that the fight had ended.

CHAPTER 120

AS SHE HAD DONE the night before, Vera crept into her house in Brentwood and walked past her mother's bedroom. There was no telltale white light shining under the door this time. Her mother was in the first-floor living room being questioned by police officers.

Vera had come home to find the house surrounded. The police had been waiting in the shadows beneath trees, leaning and looking through the cracks in curtains in her neighbors' houses, waiting for Vera to return. Stupid. If they knew anything about her father, they'd have known that having a discreet way of entering and exiting the family home was the first priority of any Russian gangster worth his—or her—salt.

Vera had slipped onto her neighbor's property, unlatched the gate that led under the decking of his aboveground pool, and walked in a crouch through the crawl space, past the pool filter, and into the space under the decking of her own home's pool. From there she had accessed the basement through a hidden panel and quietly climbed the stairs to the first floor.

Vera had caught her father entering and exiting the house this way maybe a dozen times, either when the police were looking to question him or when he'd been out too late with his men and didn't want to answer her mother's questions.

She went to her bedroom, opened the closet, and brought down an empty backpack. It was a little unnerving not to have a plan. She liked plans. Liked to have direction, rules, a goal. Vera didn't know what her life would be like by the time the sun rose. All she knew was that her day had been filled with killing, and she'd never felt more exhilarated than she did now, packing her passport, wallet, and gun into the bag. She wanted more days like this one.

Vera went to the desk and unlocked the bottom drawer, where she kept her trinkets from the Midnight Crew games. The photograph of Mr. Newcombe on the ski trip with his boyfriend. Neina Kanular's ponytail. Jacob Kanular's watch. She took Jacob's watch and put it in her bag. She wanted to remember the old killer. The one who had set her free. The rest didn't mean anything anymore.

Vera went to the hall, looked down over the banister at the officers standing in the kitchen doorway drinking coffee. One of them was using her father's favorite mug. Vera thought about taking her gun out, shooting him where he stood. It was an easy shot. But now was the time to be smart and slip away into the dark.

She'd be back, when the time was right.

CHAPTER 121

I DRESSED FOR MY father's funeral in an Opeth T-shirt with a peacock on the front, worn over jeans with a nice blazer. Baby's partygoer friends had left me little to choose from, and I hadn't had time to hunt down formal clothing options in a city full of people a third of my size. Baby descended the stairs in a little black dress that was so short it made me choke on my coffee, but I decided it wasn't the day to come down on her about her fashion choices.

She looked older. It had been only days since Ashton was shot dead right in front of her, a shock to her system that came only moments before she also witnessed the gruesome death of Martin Vegas. For a kid who had lost so much already, the week had stripped away her innocence and left her at times with a faraway look, the kind a person gets when they realize how easy it is to come face-to-face with death.

We hadn't talked much since the night at the water park, let alone about whether her future lay in Colorado or Manhattan Beach. She snapped her little handbag closed and checked herself in the hall mirror, eyeing the makeup she'd layered on over a deep gash carved high on her cheekbone.

I had passed her bedroom a couple of times a night and peeked in, saw her lying on her side scrolling the same news sites I was scrolling in my own bed. The world was just beginning to learn what Ashton and his friends had been up to in their spare time, and videos of their activities were surfacing on the dark web. The hunt for Vera was continuing without success, and a hidden room in Jacob Kanular's house, revealed during a search, was leading investigators down a long, dark path to discover just how many times the mysterious father had gone on the hunt before.

The doorbell rang.

"That'll be our ride," I said.

Short of any functioning vehicle, I had hired a pricey black limo to take us to the Hollywood Forever Cemetery, but I had the driver leave us just outside the wrought-iron entrance gates. When Baby stepped out of the limo beside me, she stopped dead at the sight before her. Six shiny black stallions stood harnessed to a gleaming black carriage, its top-hatted driver waving at us from the front bench seat. My father's coffin was visible in the back of the carriage through glass panels rimmed in gold filigree, surrounded by lush red roses. Baby and I climbed up into the front of the carriage to sit on either side of the driver.

"Where the *hell* did you get this?" Baby blurted.

"Warner Bros. is doing another Dracula reboot," I said.

As Baby and I stood by the grave, we looked around us. I'd invited a short list of people from my father's address book to the funeral, but somehow the word had spread. Among the neighbors and legitimate business associates were others with whom he'd clearly had more illegitimate dealings: tattooed bikers huddled under a tree, wraparound sunglasses glinting in the morning light, a small sub-gathering of chained pit bulls panting at their feet; sly-looking mafioso types in pin-striped suits; guys in sports jackets with suspicious bulges at their hips and ankles; and a smattering of what were clearly undercover cops there to eavesdrop on any criminal whisperings. A few women, maybe girlfriends or mistresses, cried loudly and elbowed each other for space close to the grave, throwing nasty looks at one another. And some other women, perhaps even more private than these, stood off in the distance, pretending to visit the graves of other people.

A few of these attendees—gangsters, hit men, loan sharks, or whatever the hell they were—gave Baby their condolences as the priest readied himself for the service, some pushing thick envelopes of cash into her hands, which she secreted into her handbag. I pretended not to notice. When the priest began speaking, I leaned in to Baby.

"I know about the kiss," I whispered.

"What?" She wheeled on me. "Are you kidding me?"

"No, I'm not."

"You're telling me this *now*?"

"When the hell was I supposed to tell you?" I said. "When Martin Vegas was shoving a gun in your face? When you were in your room crying about Ashton? Over cupcakes at the wake while we try to decide which one of these guys the undercover cops are after?"

"I don't know," Baby said. "How about three weeks from now, when I've had a chance to get over this." She gestured at our father's grave.

"I'm telling you now because I think it'll help you get over this," I said. I looked at the grave before us. "What happened between you and that teacher was just a silly mistake made by a confused kid."

"I can't believe this," Baby muttered, folding her arms.

"I'm trying to tell you that those times, when you're feeling confused and alone and you do stupid things, are going to keep coming. And while Dad's not here to help you through them anymore"—I pointed at our father's coffin—"I am."

Baby looked at the people around us. She sighed, but it was unreadable to me. It could have been exhaustion or solace—I didn't know.

"Look," I began, "I know I annoy the crap out of you—"

"You don't annoy me, Rhonda," she said. "You're cool."

"I'm cool?" I laughed. "Me? Of all people?"

"Sometimes." She smirked. "You're kind of exciting and weird. That's cool."

"Well, how's this for cool?" I said. "I quit my job this morning."

"You *what*?" Baby gasped. People turned to look at us. The priest kept speaking, oblivious.

"We're staying here," I said. "I'll take the bar exam and any other tests to get licensed in California. Try to get some local defense gigs, I guess. I don't know. I'll work it out. But the truth is, cleaning up after Dad is going to be hard. I've got to shut down his office. Make sure there are no more little criminal surprises hiding under the floorboards. We'll probably have to fend off legal action against the house. The police will want to know if it was acquired with drug money."

"Sounds hard," she said.

"Too hard to do from Colorado." I nodded.

She sighed again. This time I could hear the relief in it.

CHAPTER 122

THERE WERE INDEED MORE criminal secrets hidden in my father's office. Beneath the stacks of paperwork, boxes, and takeaway containers, I found what looked very much like a human thigh bone, a half-constructed ransom letter made from cut-out pieces of magazines, and a golf club spattered with blood. It took me three weeks to get the office tidy enough for a person to walk around in it without tripping over a crate of files, a concealed weapon, or the remains of a burrito rotting in aluminum foil. Baby spent most of this time lying on the couch playing with her phone or napping.

I was scrubbing ancient coffee stains and water marks from the surface of the bare desk when a man in a suit knocked on the half-open door. His hair was slicked back neatly, and he wore a leather shoulder bag across his chest. Baby looked up for long enough to calculate the types of things that interested her about men—whether the bag went with the suit, whether his stubble was deliberate, whether his eyes were the right shade of sapphire blue—and then she went back to her phone.

"Is this the office of Earl Bird?" the guy asked.

"It was," I said. "But he's no longer here. I haven't taken the lettering down from the door yet. Sorry about that."

"I'm actually here to see Rhonda Bird," he said, checking his phone screen.

I felt a little prickle of pain in my chest, the kind I'd had when I first walked into Ira Abelman's office. The same bodily warning bells that'd told me that my life was about to change, without any sense of whether it would be good or bad.

"That's me," I said.

"A guy named Summerly sent me." The man glanced around the room. "Said you might be able to help me with a private investigative matter."

I hadn't seen Dave Summerly in person since the night at the water park. But we had texted. A lot. I was keeping him in the wings of my life until I sorted out exactly what my new life in California would look like. I'd told Dave I needed time to get into step with Baby, to figure out just how much control and influence I could or should have on my new charge. He'd respected my wishes, and I liked that. But this new development was a bolt out of the blue.

"Dave said what?" I sputtered. "I . . . I'm not . . ."

"She'll meet you downstairs at the crab shack in ten minutes," Baby said, popping up from the couch. She was at my shoulder before I even saw her move. "Get a booth at the back."

Once the guy was gone, I shook my head at Baby.

"I'm not a private investigator," I said.

"Summerly seems to think you are." She shrugged. "Or at least that you could be. I do too."

"Well, that's just too bad," I said. "Because I don't know if that's the kind of job I want to take on."

"So let's go and find out." Baby smiled. I watched her for a moment, saw the excitement brimming in her eyes, and remembered that part of what came next for us would be working out a new life not only for Baby but for myself too. I needed to be open to experiments and mistakes.

"Okay," I said. "Let's give it a shot."

Baby clapped her hands in triumph and bumped my hip with hers, and for a moment I felt like a terrific mother.

Or sister.

Whatever.

Then Baby said, "Maybe we should start a detective agency."

I laughed. "That's the worst idea I've ever heard."

Alex Cross enters the final showdown
with the relentless killer who has
stalked him for years

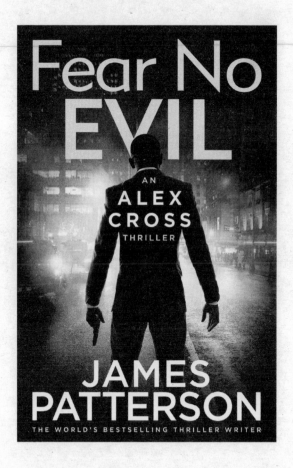

Turn the page for a preview of the
newest Alex Cross thriller

MATTHEW BUTLER COCKED HIS HEAD to one side, considering the big-boned blonde in front of him. She was handcuffed and shackled to a heavy oak chair bolted into the concrete floor beneath bright fluorescent lights.

If the woman was anxious about her predicament, she wasn't showing it in the least. She was as chill as the yoga outfit she wore. No sweat on her pale brow. Beneath her warm-up hoodie, her chest rose and fell calmly, each breath measured. Her shoulders were relaxed. Even her eyes looked soft.

Butler adjusted the strap of his shoulder holster.

"I know they've trained you for this sort of thing," he said in a voice with the slightest of Western twangs. "But your training won't work against me, Catherine. It never does."

A fit, balding man with a hawkish nose, Butler had workman's hands and wore black jeans, Nike running shoes, and a dark-blue polo shirt. He crossed his thick forearms when she smiled back at him with brilliant white teeth.

"Whoever you are, you are going to be destroyed for what you're doing," Catherine Hingham said. "When they find out—"

Butler cut her off. "You know, in my many years as a professional, Catherine, I have come to rather enjoy the delicate process of breaking into hearts and minds. They are very much interlinked, you know—hearts and minds— and I have found that one is almost always the key to the other."

"Langley will annihilate you," Hingham said, studying Butler as if she wanted to remember every line on his face.

"Your operators won't help you today," Butler said, gesturing at a pile of blank paper and a pen on the table before her. "Tell me the truth and we can all move on with our lives."

"I'll say it again: You have no jurisdiction over me."

Butler chuckled, gestured around the room. "Oh, but in here, I do."

"I want to see a lawyer, then."

"I'm sure," he said, sobering. "But we're talking about a serious threat to our national security, Catherine. A few rules of engagement can and will be broken in order to thwart that threat."

"I am not a national security threat," she said evenly. "I work for the Central Intelligence Agency, with the highest clearances, in support of my country's freedoms. Your freedoms as well."

"That's what makes your traitorous actions so hard to understand, Catherine."

4

Her face reddened and she shifted in her chair. "I am no traitor."

Butler took a step toward her. "The hell you're not. We know about the Maldives."

Hingham blinked, furrowed her brow. "The Maldives? Like, the islands in the Indian Ocean?"

"The same."

"I have no idea what you're talking about. I have never been to the Maldives. I've never even been to India."

"No?"

"Never. You can talk to my case officers about it."

"I plan to at some point," Butler said, taking another step toward her. He reached down to touch the back of her left hand before letting his finger trail across her wedding band and modest engagement ring. "Does he know? Your husband?"

"That I work for the CIA?" she said. "Yes. But he has zero idea what I actually do. Those are the rules. We play by them."

Butler sighed as he gently took hold of her left pinkie with his leathery hand, thumb on top.

"Do you know the surest way to sever the connection between the body and mind, and therefore the heart?"

"No," she said.

"Pain," Butler said. He gripped her little finger tight and levered his thumb sharply downward until he heard a bone snap.

CATHERINE HINGHAM SCREAMED in agony, fighting against her restraints, then yelled at him, "You cannot do this! This is the United States of America and I'm a sworn officer of the Central—"

Butler broke her ring finger, then waited for her to stop screaming and crying.

"You have eight fingers left, Catherine," Butler said calmly. "I will break them all and if you still do not tell me what I want to know, I will have your five-year-old daughter brought here and I will begin breaking *her* tiny fingers one by one until you confess."

The CIA officer stared at him in disgust and horror. "Emily has cerebral palsy."

"I know."

"You wouldn't. It's . . . monstrous."

"It is," he said and sighed again. "And yet, because there is so much at stake, Catherine, I will break your little girl's fingers. But only if you make it necessary."

The CIA officer continued to stare at him for several

moments. He gazed back at her evenly until her lower lip trembled and she hung her head.

"The costs," Hingham whispered hoarsely. "You have no idea what a child like Em…" She could not go on and broke down sobbing.

"The heart wins again," Butler said. He pushed the pile of blank pages in front of her. "Start writing. The Maldives. The numbered accounts. Their connections. All of it."

After a few moments, Catherine Hingham calmed enough to raise her head. "I need witness protection."

"I'll see what I can do," Butler said and held out the pen to her. "Now write."

The CIA officer reached out with both handcuffed hands shaking. She took the pen. "Please," she said. "My family doesn't deserve what will happen if—"

"Write," he said firmly. "And I'll see what I can do."

The CIA officer reluctantly began to scribble names, addresses, account numbers, and more. When she'd moved to a second page, Butler had seen enough to be satisfied.

He walked behind the CIA officer and nodded to a small camera mounted high in the corner of the room.

A gravelly male voice came through the tiny earbud Butler wore in his left ear. "Mmmm. Well done. When you have what we need, end the interview and file your report, please."

Butler nodded again before moving in front of Catherine Hingham. She set her pen down and pushed the pages across the table at him.

"That's it," she said in a hoarse voice. "Everything I know."

"Unlikely," Butler said, using the nail of his index finger to lift up the first sheet so he could scan the information she'd provided on page two. "But this looks useful enough for now. It will give us leverage. Was that so hard, Catherine?"

She relaxed a little and said, "Okay, then, I've given you what you wanted. Now I need a doctor to fix my hand. I need witness protection."

With his fingernail, Butler scooted the confession pages to the far right of the table. "You're a smart woman, Catherine. Well educated. Yale, if I remember. You should know your history better. We don't protect traitors in the United States of America. From Benedict Arnold on, they've all had to pay the price. And now, so will you."

The CIA officer looked confused and then terrified when Butler took a step back and drew a stubby pistol with a sound suppressor from his shoulder holster.

"No, please, my kids are—" she managed before he took aim and shot her between the eyes.

FROM THE TIME WE'D MET as ten-year-olds, John Sampson, my best friend and long-term DC Metro Police partner, had been stoic, quiet, observant. Since his wife, Billie, had died, he'd become even more reserved and was now given to long bouts of brooding silence. I knew he was still wrestling with grief.

But that late-June morning, Big John was acting as wound up as a kid about to hit the front gates of Disney World as he bopped around my front room, where we'd laid out all our gear for a trip we'd been talking about taking for years.

"You think we'll see a grizzly?" Sampson asked, grinning at me.

"I'm hoping not," I said. "At least, not up close."

"They're in there, big-time. And wolves."

"And deer, elk, and cutthroat trout," I said. "I've been studying the brochure too."

Nana Mama, my ninety-something grandmother, came in wringing her hands and asked with worry in her voice, "Did I hear you say grizzly bears?"

Sampson glowed with excitement. "Nana, the Bob Marshall Wilderness has one of the densest concentrations of grizzlies in the lower forty-eight states. But don't worry. We'll have bear spray and sidearms. And cameras."

"I don't know why you couldn't choose a safer place to go on your manly trip."

"If it was safer, it wouldn't be manly," I said. "There's got to be a challenge."

"Glad I'm an old lady, then. Breakfast in five minutes." Nana Mama turned and shuffled away, shaking her head.

"Checklist?" Sampson said.

"I'm ready if you are."

We started going through every item we'd thought necessary for the twenty-nine-mile horseback trip deep into one of the last great wildernesses on Earth and for the five-day raft ride we'd take out of the Bob Marshall on the South Fork of the Flathead River. An outfitter was providing the rafts, tents, food, and bear-proof storage equipment. Everything else had to fit into four rubberized dry bags we'd use on the river after he dropped us off.

We could have signed up for a fully guided affair, but Sampson wanted us to do a good part of the trip alone, and after some thought, I'd agreed. Six days deep in the backcountry of Montana would give Big John many chances to open up and talk, which is critical to the process of coping with tragic loss.

"How's Willow feeling about our little trip?" I asked.

Sampson smiled. "She doesn't like the idea of grizzly bears any more than Nana does, but she knows it will make me happy."

"Your little girl's always been wise beyond her years."

"Truth. Bree liking her job?"

Thinking of my smart, beautiful, and independent wife, I said, "She loves it. Got up early to be at the office. Something about a possible assignment in Paris."

"Paris! What a difference a career change makes."

"No kidding. It was like the gig was tailor-made for her."

"Maybe we should think about going into private-sector investigations too."

"Pay's better, for sure," I allowed.

Before he could reply, my seventeen-year-old daughter, Jannie, poked her head in and said, "Nana says your eggs are getting cold."

I put down my dry bag and went to the kitchen, where I found my youngest child, Ali, already finishing up his plate.

"Morning, sunshine," I said, giving him a hug. He ignored it, so I tickled him.

"C'mon, Dad!" He laughed, then groaned. "Why can't I go with you?"

"Because you're a kid and we don't know what we'll be facing."

"I can do it," he insisted.

Sampson said, "Ali, let your dad and me scope it out this year. If we think you're up to it, we'll bring you along on the next trip. Deal?"

Ali scrunched up his face and shrugged. "I guess. When do you leave?"

"First thing in the—"

My cell phone began to ring at the same time Sampson's chimed.

"No," John protested. "Don't answer that, Alex. We're supposed to be gone already!"

But when I saw the caller ID, I grimaced and knew I had to answer. "Commissioner Dennison," I said. "John Sampson and I were just heading out the door on vacation."

"Cancel it," said the commissioner of the Metro DC Police Department. "We've got a dead female, gunshot wound to the head, dumped in the garage under the International Spy Museum on L'Enfant Plaza. Her ID says she's—"

"Commissioner, with all due respect," I said, "we've been planning this trip for—"

"I don't care, Cross," he snapped. "Her ID says she's CIA. If you want to continue your contract with Metro, you'll get down there. And if Sampson wants to keep his job, he'll be with you."

I stared at the ceiling a second, looked at John, and shook my head.

"Okay, Commissioner. We're on our way."

Also by James Patterson

ALEX CROSS NOVELS

Along Came a Spider • Kiss the Girls • Jack and Jill • Cat and Mouse • Pop Goes the Weasel • Roses are Red • Violets are Blue • Four Blind Mice • The Big Bad Wolf • London Bridges • Mary, Mary • Cross • Double Cross • Cross Country • Alex Cross's Trial (*with Richard DiLallo*) • I, Alex Cross • Cross Fire • Kill Alex Cross • Merry Christmas, Alex Cross • Alex Cross, Run • Cross My Heart • Hope to Die • Cross Justice • Cross the Line • The People vs. Alex Cross • Target: Alex Cross • Criss Cross • Deadly Cross

THE WOMEN'S MURDER CLUB SERIES

1st to Die • 2nd Chance (*with Andrew Gross*) • 3rd Degree (*with Andrew Gross*) • 4th of July (*with Maxine Paetro*) • The 5th Horseman (*with Maxine Paetro*) • The 6th Target (*with Maxine Paetro*) • 7th Heaven (*with Maxine Paetro*) • 8th Confession (*with Maxine Paetro*) • 9th Judgement (*with Maxine Paetro*) • 10th Anniversary (*with Maxine Paetro*) • 11th Hour (*with Maxine Paetro*) • 12th of Never (*with Maxine Paetro*) • Unlucky 13 (*with Maxine Paetro*) • 14th Deadly Sin (*with Maxine Paetro*) • 15th Affair (*with Maxine Paetro*) • 16th Seduction (*with Maxine Paetro*) • 17th Suspect (*with Maxine Paetro*) • 18th Abduction (*with Maxine Paetro*) • 19th Christmas (*with Maxine Paetro*) • 20th Victim (*with Maxine Paetro*) • 21st Birthday (*with Maxine Paetro*)

DETECTIVE MICHAEL BENNETT SERIES

Step on a Crack (*with Michael Ledwidge*) • Run for Your Life (*with Michael Ledwidge*) • Worst Case (*with Michael Ledwidge*) • Tick Tock (*with Michael Ledwidge*) • I, Michael Bennett (*with Michael Ledwidge*) • Gone (*with Michael Ledwidge*) • Burn (*with Michael Ledwidge*) • Alert (*with Michael Ledwidge*) • Bullseye (*with Michael Ledwidge*) • Haunted (*with James O. Born*) • Ambush (*with James O. Born*) • Blindside (*with James O. Born*) • The Russian (*with James O. Born*)

PRIVATE NOVELS

Private (*with Maxine Paetro*) • Private London (*with Mark Pearson*) • Private Games (*with Mark Sullivan*) • Private: No. 1 Suspect (*with Maxine Paetro*) • Private Berlin (*with Mark Sullivan*) • Private Down Under (*with Michael White*) • Private L.A. (*with Mark Sullivan*) • Private India (*with Ashwin Sanghi*) • Private Vegas (*with Maxine Paetro*) • Private Sydney (*with Kathryn Fox*) • Private Paris (*with Mark Sullivan*) • The Games (*with Mark Sullivan*) • Private Delhi (*with Ashwin Sanghi*) • Private Princess (*with Rees Jones*) • Private Moscow (*with Adam Hamdy*) • Private Rogue (*with Adam Hamdy*)

NYPD RED SERIES

NYPD Red (*with Marshall Karp*) • NYPD Red 2 (*with Marshall Karp*) • NYPD Red 3 (*with Marshall Karp*) • NYPD Red 4 (*with Marshall Karp*) • NYPD Red 5 (*with Marshall Karp*) • NYPD Red 6 (*with Marshall Karp*)

DETECTIVE HARRIET BLUE SERIES

Never Never (*with Candice Fox*) • Fifty Fifty (*with Candice Fox*) • Liar Liar (*with Candice Fox*) • Hush Hush (*with Candice Fox*)

INSTINCT SERIES

Instinct (*with Howard Roughan, previously published as* Murder Games) • Killer Instinct (*with Howard Roughan*)

THE BLACK BOOK SERIES

The Black Book (*with David Ellis*) • The Red Book (*with David Ellis*)

For more information about James Patterson's novels, visit www.penguin.co.uk